FALLING
FOR
YOU

ANNAPOLIS
HARBOR SERIES

LEA COLL

FALLING FOR YOU

He's off-limits, continually underestimates me, and yet... I can't ignore the attraction between us.

Callie

When I landed my dream job, I didn't realize I'd be working with the one guy I've always avoided.

Jonah.

Caught off guard with a career-ending injury; he is the life and soul of every party, a likable, sociable guy on all accounts. His future relies on the success of the sports complex I've been hired to manage.

But...he doubts my capabilities from the get-go.

I'm tired of being underestimated, of having my capabilities judged by just my pretty face. This is my opportunity to prove everyone wrong, including Jonah.

I just never expected to fall for him, or to learn that Jonah isn't the man he pretends to be.

Now I'm not sure if I can handle the truth.

Jonah

It only takes one injury to ruin your career and I'm not even sure I still have one. Investing in a sports complex made sense, until I realized that Callie was hired to manage it.

She's young, beautiful and has an alluring innocence I have to remind myself to ignore. As my teammate's personal assistant, Callie is off limits in more ways than one. She's straight out of college, has no experience and now my future lies in her hands.

The closer we work together, the more I become captivated by her. She's nothing like I expected her to be, but then we all hide behind masks.

Especially me.

If Callie learns the truth, both my future and my heart could be shattered.

Download two free novellas, *Swept Away* and *Worth the Risk*, when you sign up for my newsletter.

Editing by Olivia Kalb Editing Service

Editing by The Ryter's Proof

Proofreading by My Brother's Editor

Cover Design by Okay Creations

Photography by Wander Aguiar

 Created with Vellum

BOOKS BY LEA COLL

All I Want Series

Choose Me

Be with Me

Burn for Me

Trust in Me

Stay with Me

Take a Chance on Me

Annapolis Harbor Series

Hooked on You (previously titled Easy Moves)

Only with You

Lost without You

Perfect for You

Crazy for You

Falling for You

Waiting for You

Mountain Haven Series

Infamous Love

Adventurous Love

Impulsive Love

Quick Snap Novellas

Lucky Catch

Trick Play

Download two free novellas, *Swept Away* and *Worth the Risk*, when you sign up for her newsletter.

To learn more about her books, please visit her website.

CHAPTER ONE

CALLIE

I PULLED OPEN THE WOODEN DOOR TO THE HORSE YOU CAME In On Saloon for Reid and Dylan's engagement party. They'd gotten engaged around Christmas but waited to hold the party for their friends until after the playoffs. I hadn't planned on attending, but Reid insisted.

Stepping inside, I let my eyes adjust to the dim lighting. A motorcycle hung over the lit fireplace. Sports highlights played on TVs mounted above the bar. The saddle-shaped barstools were empty because the saloon had been reserved for the party. Reid stood at the head of a long table where everyone was gathered, one arm around his fiancée, the other raised a champagne glass in a toast.

Not wanting to disturb the big moment, I slid into the only available empty chair next to Reid's teammate, Jonah Templeton.

I smiled at him before turning my attention to Reid. Dylan looked up at him, a large smile on her face, her eyes full of love.

"Thank you all for coming here tonight to celebrate our engagement. Not only do I love Dylan with all of my heart, but she pushed me to be a better person."

1

In the past, Reid avoided publicity outside of postgame press conferences. He'd hid a speech impediment for years before Dylan met him on a blind date and asked him to work with her law firm partner, Hadley's charity, Kids Speak. The organization brought speech therapists into schools to help kids. Over the years, I'd encouraged Reid to be up front about his speech issues, but it was Dylan who convinced him.

"Tonight wouldn't have been possible without Callie's help." He tipped his head toward me.

I flushed, not wanting to be the center of attention in front of his teammates and friends.

"Thank you for coming out tonight." Reid drank his champagne.

Silverware clinked on glasses around the room.

Dylan's cheeks flushed pink as Reid kissed her.

Cheers erupted around the room. Several of Reid's friends clapped him on his back while Dylan hugged her friends. I was so happy for them.

Jonah leaned over, his jaw sporting days-old scruff. "You're late."

Dark circles ringed his eyes. I wondered if he was sleeping okay. He wore a Baltimore team polo shirt and khaki shorts. He'd taken a hard tackle in the last playoff game, tearing his ACL and MCL. His return was questionable.

"I didn't want to come. Reid insisted." As Reid's personal assistant, I didn't think it was necessary for me to attend. I felt out of place among his teammates, their girlfriends, and their wives.

"You're his friend." Jonah's voice was low.

I could barely hear him over the conversation carrying on around us.

"I'm his employee." I helped him when he needed me. He was a conscientious boss, willing to work around my class schedule.

"He doesn't see you as just an employee." Jonah's gaze was locked on mine.

His focus was unnerving. He was always the life of the locker room, cracking jokes and quick to help a teammate, but he'd never singled me out before.

Conversation carried on around the table, but it was like we were alone—in our own bubble. I took a drink of the water the waitress poured for me. "What do you mean?"

"He said you were off-limits."

I choked on the water, coughing, and clearing my throat until I could breathe again. Was he saying Reid told his team-mates not to date me? I'd never considered the possibility.

"Are you okay?" Jonah leaned over, his large hand spread across my back. His touch was solid, comforting.

I wiped my mouth with a napkin. "I'm okay now. What did you say?"

Removing his hand, he settled back into his chair. "He said you were off-limits."

"Why would he say that to you?"

"You know." Jonah tipped his bottle back, taking a long swig. He wiped off the moisture on his mouth with the back of his hand.

I wondered if he was drunk.

"No. I don't know." I wanted to ask if he should be drinking if he was on pain medication, but I was more curious about what he was going to say next.

"You're gorgeous." He flipped a hand at me in a way that made me think he'd had more than a few drinks. "You know you are."

Glancing at the table, there were several empty shot glasses. Were they his? "Thanks."

I glanced at Reid, but he was laughing with some of his teammates.

"He warned us off you," he repeated as if that explained everything.

I shifted in my chair. "I didn't know anyone was interested."

I'd kept my distance from the players because I liked my job. It paid well, and Reid was a great boss.

Dylan stopped by our table. "Callie. You made it."

I stood, thankful for the disruption, allowing Dylan to pull me into a hug. Reid stood next to her.

"Congratulations," I said to them when I pulled back.

Dylan smiled wide. "Thank you for organizing everything! I'm so glad we were finally able to get everyone together."

It wasn't the fancy party Dylan usually planned for Kids Speak's nonprofit galas, but it was the low-key event Reid requested.

"You deserved a celebration."

Dylan smiled at me before her gaze landed on Jonah, turning concerned.

"Do you have a minute to talk?" Reid asked me.

"Hey, Jonah, how are you feeling?" Dylan asked him, slipping into the seat I'd vacated.

I followed Reid away from the table. "Of course. What do you need?"

"I have a proposition for you."

"Oh?" I wondered if Reid would let me go after I graduated. He'd hired me to deal with Baltimore's PR team, the fans, and anyone who wanted to talk to him. Now that he was dating Dylan, he didn't need me anymore. The problem was I didn't have anything lined up in my field.

"I don't know what you have planned now that you've graduated, but I need a manager at Rebel Sports."

Rebel Sports was the athletic complex Reid and his teammates, Jonah and Chase, built to accommodate more youth sports programs in the community.

"Absolutely. I can draft an ad, help you interview possible candidates, and narrow down your choices." I reached into my purse to start a to-do list on my phone.

"Callie." Something in Reid's voice made me pause my search, looking up at him.

"I want you." His tone was serious.

"I'm sorry?" I shifted the strap of my purse on my shoulder.

"I want *you* to be the manager."

My heart sped up. "But—I don't—" I don't have any experience. That probably wasn't the best thing to tell your employer who was offering you an amazing promotion. "I don't know what to say."

I looked over at Jonah who was watching our exchange with interest over Dylan's shoulder.

"Say yes," Reid pleaded. "I need you."

I couldn't pass it up. "It's an amazing opportunity. I'd be crazy to say no."

"That's what I was hoping you'd say." Reid grinned.

"That's it? I'm hired. Just like that?" It wasn't on a probationary basis or until he could find someone more qualified?

He lowered his voice. "I need someone I can trust. In season, I'm not going to have time to field questions or deal with employees."

"Thanks. I'm flattered you're trusting me with such a huge responsibility." I'd only ever been his personal assistant. It wasn't exactly on the same career path as a manager.

Reid's hand closed over my shoulder. "You can handle it."

"Do Jonah and Chase have any say in the matter?" I wondered if they agreed.

"They're silent investors. They won't be involved in the day-to-day operations."

"Okay." I couldn't believe this was happening. Majoring in sports management, this was my dream job. I hadn't expected to be offered a management position straight out of college. When I saw Reid's advertisement in the university's student center my sophomore year for a part-time personal assistant, I thought it was a way to make money and be near the sport I loved—football.

A smile spread over his face as he shook my hand. "Welcome on board."

I smiled to cover my uncertainty. Could I handle such an important job straight out of school?

Reid walked away, grabbing Dylan's hand to continue mingling with the guests.

I returned to my seat, still a little stunned by the job offer.

Jonah's legs were spread wide. He looked rougher, more rugged than usual. Even with his injured leg propped on a chair, he was sexy.

He cocked his head. "You take the job?"

I sat, surprised by his question. "You knew he was going to offer me the manager position?"

"I did." His words were clipped.

I studied his face. "You don't approve."

"You just graduated. You don't have any experience running a business."

Even though I'd had the same thoughts, irritation shot through me. I was already planning lists in my head, plans for the sports complex, things to do, things that needed to be done. My stomach sank as I realized I'd need to move or commute all the way from Baltimore.

"What are you worried about?" Jonah shifted his elbows to his thighs.

"Rebel Sports is forty-five minutes south from here. My grandfather lives thirty minutes north of the city. I'm not sure it makes sense to move, but I'll have a commute." My mind was whirring with the possibilities. I'd applied for the MBA program at the University of Baltimore for the fall. Could I handle all of it?

Jonah's face softened. "Your grandfather, is that Frank? The man Reid visits in the nursing home."

I relaxed thinking of my grandfather, the one who took

me in after my parents died in a car crash. "Yeah. They're close."

"You're close to Reid." His muscles tensed as if the answer mattered to him on some level.

Was he trying to figure out whether we'd ever dated? It had to be the alcohol talking because he'd never expressed any interest in me before. "He's a great boss."

Jonah fell silent, taking another sip of his beer, his Adam's apple working up and down. I moved my gaze away from the sexy image.

Determined to get his focus off of me, I changed the subject, "How are you doing with everything?"

His face tightened. "In pain from PT. Tired of the restrictions."

"It'll get better." I leaned over, patting his good leg; the warmth seeped through his shorts, sending tingles through my arm. My gaze lifted to his wondering if he'd felt it too.

"I hope so."

I moved my hand away. I'd never touched Reid like that. Why was I touching Jonah? Why was my heart racing?

"No one asks how I'm doing. They ask me *if* I'll play again, not when."

"I'm sorry. What about your family?"

"They were here for the surgery, but I sent them home. They were driving me crazy."

"Your parents came?" I couldn't remember what his family situation was but having a hovering one sounded pretty good.

"My mom and my sister. My dad stayed in West Virginia to work."

"That's nice they were able to come." I got that familiar pang in my heart whenever anyone talked about their parents.

"What about you? You have family in the area?" His expression was thoughtful as if he was sifting through his memories trying to remember if he'd heard something before.

"It's just my grandfather and me."

"That's why you're so worried about living close to him." The deep, steady drawl of Jonah's words soothed me.

"Yeah. I visit as often as I can and pick up whatever he needs. I'm all he has." The words I'd left unsaid ran on repeat through my head. He was all *I* had.

I waited for the inevitable question, what happened to your parents? But it didn't come. Either he remembered someone else talking about it, or he had the good grace not to pry. Either way, I appreciated it.

As the evening wore on, Jonah ordered more beer and appetizers, offering them to me.

I drank one beer, refusing any more. I went a little wild when my parents died, but after my grandfather helped me pull myself together, I was careful not to drink too much. Even if I was walking home or could get a car, I didn't like that out-of-control feeling it gave me.

Jonah had no such issues. With each glass, he loosened up even more, eventually throwing an arm around the back of my chair.

"Don't judge. It helps with all of this." He gestured down at his injured leg.

"I get that." I bit my lip, wanting to say more like it wouldn't help him get better or heal any faster.

Reid stood in front of us, holding Dylan's hand. "We're going to head out."

I looked around, realizing only a few people were still around, and they'd moved to the bar area. "Do you need me to do anything?"

I rose, but Reid held up a hand to stop me. "The bar staff will handle it."

Dylan hugged me. "Thanks for organizing everything."

"Of course."

Reid's gaze shifted from Jonah to me. "Do you need a ride?"

"I'm good to drive. Thanks though."

Reid nodded at Jonah, opening his mouth as if he was going to say something when Dylan tugged on his hand. "Come on."

An uncomfortable silence fell between us. I should have said it was time for me to leave too. With Reid and Dylan gone, there was no need for me to stay. Instead, I felt rooted to my chair, my gaze on the sports highlights on the TV. I felt some obligation to Reid, the team, or maybe it was to Jonah to make sure he was okay.

"You like hockey?" Jonah nodded toward the ice hockey game on TV.

"No. Just football. It was something my grandfather and I did together. We watched games on Sundays, and he'd teach me everything about the sport—the plays, the positions, the players." It was time I cherished with him. Looking back, I probably latched on to any way for me to bond with him. Yet the memories were good ones.

"That's rare for a girl." His tone was appreciative.

I smiled to cover the melancholy that thinking about life after my parents brought. "Lena said there's a ton of die-hard female fans."

Lena was the head of PR for the team.

"That's true, but I haven't dated many women who knew anything about football. Sure, they say they like it, but it's pretty obvious when they don't know anything about it." His expression was bitter.

I knew the kind of women the younger players attracted. They weren't interested in much besides bragging rights and money.

"They want to pretend they have something in common with you."

His nose crinkled. "It would be nice to be wanted for me, not my job. Especially since I might not have it much longer."

My heart clenched at his vulnerable admission. I knew he

wouldn't want me to acknowledge his slip, so I leaned over to slap his stomach playfully but lost my balance, falling heavily against his chest. His arm banded around my back. His breath whispered over the strands of my hair, sending shivers down my spine. "Easy, tiger. These abs are hard as steel. You might hurt yourself."

Laughing at the return of the old teasing Jonah, I placed a palm on his hard chest, pushing myself up. The heat of his body singed my skin. "Oh yeah?"

Was I flirting? Why was my voice so high-pitched? Why did I sound so out of breath? I shifted back to my seat; my skin prickled from the chill of the air now that I wasn't touching him.

"I can't do leg work, so I do extra upper body and ab exercises." His grin was lazy and slow, one I'd seen him use on women at bars before. Even though I knew it was an act he put on to pick up women and not a glimpse into him, it still made me feel warm and tingly all over. I'd known he was handsome and charming, but I'd placed him in the playboy category, never taking him seriously.

"It's not like you were slacking before." My voice was slightly breathy, and I couldn't blame it on the alcohol. Other than my warm cheeks, I didn't feel out of control. Just slightly buzzed from having Jonah's focus on me.

There was no mistaking his broad shoulders and bulging biceps. The guys kept themselves in top shape, and it showed.

With one hand on the bottle of beer, the other one slid lower, resting over his stomach. I wanted to squeeze my eyes against the vision of him unzipping his jeans to fist his cock.

There were beads of sweat on my forehead and my neck prickled with awareness. I wanted to ask him if he was warm, but I was sure it was just me. I swallowed some water, hoping it would cool me off.

A slow smile spread over his face, bordering on cocky.

I was falling under Jonah's spell, and it didn't feel manufactured, not when I remembered the vulnerability on his face when he talked about his injury and his fears for the future.

This thing between us felt different, heightened because I knew he wouldn't act this way if he were sober. Reid had warned him away from me. Jonah probably wouldn't jeopardize his relationship with his teammate and co-captain. Spending time together when it was forbidden felt a little naughty.

"Why are you still here?" Jonah asked.

"I don't know." I could have said I was worried about him, but he wouldn't like that. I could have said I liked spending time with him, but that would be admitting too much. I didn't want to be another one of those women desperate for his attention.

He shifted his arm from the back of my chair to my shoulders, leaning in close. All I could hear was a roaring in my ears, the blood pumping through my veins. His scent, leather and soap, surrounded me. He was so big everywhere. I felt protected, safe with him.

Any mention of me being off-limits dissipated. I couldn't remember why being with Jonah was bad when it felt so good. His lips brushed my neck and ear, my skin tingled with awareness. His hand tangled in my hair, tugging so my face turned to his. There was a second I could have said no, but refusing him never entered my mind. When he turned his attention on me rather than football, he was potent. His lips touched mine lightly, pleading for entry. My lips parted. He shifted closer, tightening his arm around me as his tongue moved with more confidence.

Tingles ran down my spine. My skin heated with every pass of his tongue and the tightening of his fingers in my hair. I wanted more. More of Jonah, his heat, his strength. What would it be like to be with him? It would be so much better than the guys I'd wasted my time on in high school and college. He was all man.

Yet I couldn't help but wonder if I was merely a distraction for him or a way to sabotage his friendship with Reid.

When his fingers tightened in my hair, I couldn't care less about the whys. *I wanted him.* I wanted to straddle his thighs and grind on his cock. I wanted to ask if he wanted to get out of here. I hadn't felt this wild or out of control since my parents died.

With a groan, he pulled back, running a hand through his hair; his expression was filled with regret. "You're my teammate's assistant. You're like his little sister. I can't go there."

I cringed at his reference to me as a little sister. I'd never been that. It made me feel small.

The sense of loss was acute. He'd unraveled himself from me so easily. Like what just happened meant nothing. He was used to bar hookups. How could I have fallen into his arms and under his charm so easily?

I couldn't believe I'd acted so carelessly. Getting involved with a player would jeopardize my job, but, in the moment, I hadn't cared. I was reckless.

He got up so quickly his chair rocked back once before settling. "I'm sorry."

He walked out. A couple of his teammates sat at the bar talking to the bartender. No one noticed my world had just shifted.

I'd touched my fingers to my lips, wondering if I'd ever feel the same again. Kissing Jonah felt different than the guys I'd experimented with after my parents died.

I stopped being reckless years ago. No matter how soft Jonah's lips felt, how scratchy his scruff, or how good his arms felt around me, I didn't need him in my life. He'd destroy what I'd worked so hard for—my relationship with Reid, my job, and my reputation.

The things he took for granted—money, safety, security—were precarious for me. I wasn't willing to risk it for him.

CHAPTER TWO

JONAH

I RESTED MY ACHING HEAD IN MY HAND, WINCING AT THE bright light shining through the window. "What are you doing here?"

Last night was coming back to me in bits and pieces. Was I doing shots and drinking beer—with Callie? The feel of her hair under my fingers, her mouth opening sweetly for me, the soft whimpers as she moved closer. Was it real? Why were Reid and Chase here?

Chase leaned back on the couch, crossing his arms over his chest. He kicked a leg out under the coffee table. "You look like shit."

I shot him a rueful look. "Thanks."

"We need to talk." Among the captains on the team, Reid was the most serious one.

Had I crossed a line with Callie last night? I'd noticed her before. Everyone had. She was young and beautiful. She had that girl next door innocence that pulled you in. It was the same reason Reid warned us away from her. She was nothing like the women who hung around the locker room looking to score a football player.

Even cuter was the fact that she knew football. She'd held

her own several times while talking about the game with the other players. But I'd never thought of her as a woman I was attracted to until last night.

She wore a peach-colored ruffled top that bared her belly with soft, weathered-looking jeans that cupped her butt and thighs. I couldn't remember how we crossed the line. Did she come on to me, or had I made the first move? Bits and pieces of the evening floated around in my brain, her smell, the feel of her hair, but not what we talked about. Had she straddled my lap, or had I imagined that after I fell asleep?

"We're worried about you." Reid leaned his elbows on his thighs.

Reid's voice startled me from the feel of Callie's lips on mine.

"You're worried about me?" Anxiety that he was here to confront me about Callie dissipated as I realized they were here about my downward spiral. My *who gives a shit* attitude.

The sidelining injury made me remember I was no better than that kid I left behind in my hometown. I was still a screwup. I'd let the team down by dropping the ball, then getting injured. I wasn't worth their worry or concern.

"Yeah, you're not yourself." Chase's expression was grim.

After high school, I'd fled my hometown for college. The football scholarship was my escape from the soul-sucking guilt that burrowed deep in my chest. My high school coach told me it was my chance to start over.

I was your go-to guy to pick up a six-pack at the store or to help you move, but not the one you relied on for advice. I was the good-time guy. Always quick with a joke. When I let that facade go, people asked too many questions.

I needed to divert their attention. "I let loose last night. Had a few too many. I won't let it happen again."

I tensed, hoping they'd let it go.

Chase scrutinized me. "If something's going on, we want to help."

"You're not hanging out. You're not responding to anyone's texts."

The room filled with an awkward silence. I wasn't sure what to say. I wasn't screwed up in the head. That wasn't the case, but what could I tell them to get them to back off?

"We don't blame you for the season ending." As the quarterback, Chase's opinion held a lot of weight.

"It was a hard hit," Reid added.

I shrugged as if there wasn't a weight on my chest. "I'm just worried about my career."

Reid raised a brow.

"I'm nothing without football." That familiar worthless feeling wrapped around my chest, tightening more with each breath I took.

Reid gave me a pointed look. "There's more to life than football. I learned that when I met Dylan."

I laughed without any humor. There was no girlfriend in my future. "Seriously?"

Chase shook his head. "You're the one who's moody as fuck all of a sudden."

Reid shook his head. "You're not going to recover if you're screwing around drinking too much."

"I need my knee to cooperate." I needed a miracle. Tearing the ACL and MCL was a difficult injury for anyone to come back from, much less a professional football player.

"If anyone can do this, it's you," Reid said.

"I'll get it together." I waved a hand at them. "This morning visit wasn't necessary."

"We're here for you. Whatever you need—some company at PT, your personal coach… Whatever," Chase said.

"I'll return your texts. Hang out more often. Are we good?" It seemed like the only way to get them to back off was to go along with whatever they wanted.

I didn't want them showing up unannounced again.

I started to rise, thinking they were done when Reid and

Chase exchanged a look.

"What?"

Reid gave me an uneasy look. "We have a solution. We want you to work at Rebel Sports."

"What? Why?" When Chase mentioned us partnering together on the sports complex, I was all for it. I had plenty of money to invest, and his proposal was a good one. I never planned on being involved in the day-to-day operations.

"We need someone to help out this summer," Reid said.

"I thought you hired Callie."

"You're the one who said she's young and inexperienced. You can help her." Reid was appealing to my practical side, my concerns about leaving the new business in her hands.

I shook my head. "I don't know anything about business."

"Maybe not. But you need something to focus on besides your knee."

I could practically feel his unsaid words. *This will be good for you.*

I rubbed the irritation prickling my neck. I didn't want their interference.

Sports highlights played on the large flat screen mounted on the wall. My headshot from the prior season flashed on the screen. Reid picked up the remote, raising the volume.

"I don't know if he can come back from an ACL/MCL tear, Bob. Very few players are healthy enough to come back in six months, and the ones that do are plagued with issues the rest of their careers. Why would JT be any different?"

I liked the JT moniker when my teammates gave it to me in college, but the reference to it now only heightened my irritation. It was a reference to who I used to be—could I be that guy again? I was young. I was healthy. I'd come back from this, wouldn't I?

The second commentator went through the list of players with a similar injury, spouting their fates like a grocery list.

Ever since high school, when my college coach sat me

down and told me I could go all the way if I were disciplined, I'd made it my mission to prove myself, to be better than my competition. I did everything the team wanted me to do on and off the field. But Reid and Chase were right, I was letting everyone down, not just myself, by drinking too much and not taking my recovery seriously.

For the first time since my injury, I felt a stirring of hope. Maybe they were right. It would be good to have something else to focus on besides the sports reporters' commentary on whether my knee would ever be the same again. If I didn't have football, the past came back. The guilt weighed heavier than my mom begging me to visit.

"You need to start thinking about what you're going to do if you can't play again. Are you staying here, or will you go back home?" Chase asked carefully.

The air whooshed out of my lungs as if he'd punched me in the gut. "I'm not moving back to my hometown."

I wouldn't be the football star returning home, I was the cautionary tale.

"Then overseeing the opening of Rebel Sports shouldn't be an issue," Chase said, his tone firm.

I did need to focus on the future and the very real possibility I wouldn't play another season. Initially, I'd agreed to invest in Rebel Sports so that I'd have a reason to stay in the area when I retired. I hadn't thought I'd need it so soon.

If he was suggesting I work at Rebel, it meant he didn't know about what happened with Callie last night. Relief surged through me.

"Fine." I'd have to ask Callie not to tell Reid about what happened. It was a one-time slip.

"You'll do it." Reid clapped his hands, standing as if to leave.

"Is Callie okay with it?" The conversation about Reid offering her the job came back to me.

She'd bristled when we discussed my concern about her

ability to do the job even though it wasn't personal. I'd invested a lot of money into the project. I believed in Reid and Dylan's vision to help the community. This way, I'd keep an eye on Callie to make sure the business was running smoothly. I'm sure that kiss wasn't as hot as I'd imagined.

"I haven't talked to her about it yet, but I'm sure it won't be a problem."

I wanted to disagree with him, but that would be admitting we'd talked last night.

Reid glanced at his phone. "I have to head out. I'm taking Dylan to brunch with her parents."

Dylan's parents lived closer to Annapolis where the sports complex was built.

"I have to get going too," Chase said.

I followed them to the door.

"You stink. Why don't you take a shower?" Chase teased before he walked out.

Looking down at the worn T-shirt and threadbare sweatpants, I smelled stale beer. "I'll do that."

I didn't need Coach Ackerman at my door, telling me to get my shit together. I needed him confident I was doing everything in my power to get better and to make a comeback.

Reid touched my shoulder briefly. "We want you on the field."

"I know you do." I barely kept the emotion from my voice. There was no shame in admitting I was scared to these guys. Career-ending injuries were every player's worst nightmare.

Reid nodded before leaving. I closed the door, determined to get my life together. When I got hurt, everything from my past came roaring back. I wasn't the perfect football player with a bright future in front of him. I was the fuckup in high school. The one everyone pitied and blamed for what happened. I couldn't get out of that town fast enough, and I had no desire to go back there. No matter how many times my mom begged me. I'd come too far to go back now.

CHAPTER THREE

CALLIE

"ARE YOU READY FOR THIS?" REID SAT IN ONE OF THE PLUSH leather seats at the head of the conference table.

I still wasn't sure I was the best candidate for the job, but I was determined to prove myself. "Absolutely."

We'd talked more about the job and expectations over the weekend, planning to meet at the complex first thing on Monday morning.

"I know we talked about Jonah and Chase being silent partners, but with Jonah's injury, things have changed."

My heart rate picked up. "What do you mean things have changed?"

My stomach did a slow slide as Jonah Templeton walked into the room with an easy smile, only faltering slightly when his gaze touched on me.

Was he remembering that kiss? Did he think about it when he was lying in bed at night, or did he think it was a mistake?

He wore a white button-down shirt tucked into suit pants, so different from the athletic gear I was used to seeing him in. The stark white of his shirt emphasized his tan skin and blue eyes.

"You started without me?" His tone was gently chiding as

if he belonged here, as if he *owned* the place, which technically he did.

He pulled out a chair, sitting across from me.

Why was he here? I looked to Reid for an explanation.

"I was explaining the situation to Callie," Reid said easily as if my pulse wasn't racing.

"The situation?" I asked, looking from Reid to Jonah. Was I being pushed out? Did Reid not need me anymore because Jonah was the new manager?

No. Reid wouldn't do that to me, not when I needed this job to support my grandfather, who still sat in a nursing home north of Baltimore.

Jonah clasped his hands in front of him on the table. "I'm going to be overseeing Rebel Sports."

My brain scrambled to keep up. "I thought…"

I couldn't voice it out loud. The disappointment was like a knife in my chest. I wanted to pull it out, but I couldn't. I needed to feel the pain, remember why things never worked out for me.

Images flew through my head, graduating without my parents in the audience, staying home and attending evening classes rather than moving away to college, and living in the dorms like my friends had. When my parents died, my hopes and dreams did too. This was the first thing that felt close to the life I'd imagined before.

Reid's jaw tightened. "Not exactly. You'll be working together."

I shifted through the papers on the table in front of me, the words blurring as I tried to take a deep breath. I wanted to sink into the floor beneath my feet and disappear, but I wasn't that weak child anymore, I was strong. I could stand up for myself. "I thought Jonah and Chase wouldn't be involved."

When he'd offered me the job, Reid assured me I'd have autonomy.

"I know that's what we talked about, but Jonah wants to be more involved." Reid's eyes were pleading.

All the guys were worried about Jonah since his injury. I'd do anything for Reid, but I didn't think I could handle working with Jonah, especially after that kiss. There was something in Jonah's eyes Saturday night that drew me in—a vulnerability—it was so different than his usual confidence. Would he act like nothing happened between us? Did I want him to?

Jonah was the fun guy in the locker room. The one everyone gravitated to for a good time, a laugh, or a pick-me-up. After his injury, he was different—grumpy, quicker to snap. Everyone understood why—his career was on the line. Even if he could play again, sportscasters and coaches would always speculate if he was one hundred percent. An injury like that would follow him for the rest of his career.

"I'm focusing on the complex since I can't—"

"Since you might not be able to play anymore." The words shot out before I could retract them.

Jonah looked away but not before I saw the pained expression on his face.

"I'm sorry. I shouldn't have said that." I should have softened my words. I shouldn't have brought up his injury. I knew it was devastating for him and his career, but the complex was supposed to be my chance, not only to prove myself but to support myself and pay back my student loans. I didn't have parents to fall back on. I had a grandfather in a nursing home to support.

Reid shot me a reproachful look.

The guys never talked about Jonah's injuries in terms of not playing again. It was always, *when he's healthy enough,* or *when he comes back.*"

"My focus is on the sports complex." Jonah swallowed hard, as if saying those words was difficult. "I want to make sure the grand opening is a success."

"It will be." Was he insinuating I couldn't handle it, or was he distracting himself from his injury? The resolve I'd shored up when he walked into the room slowly dissolved.

I was devastated when he'd sustained that hard tackle in the end zone of the last playoff game, ending Baltimore's playoff bid and potentially his career. If I'd learned anything being Reid's assistant over the last three years, it was that football was life for these guys. Most of them lived and breathed the game. It was all they talked about, all they did. To have that potentially taken away before he was ready had to be scary. I sympathized with him.

Jonah tipped his head. "I'll make sure of it. We're on the same page."

"Actually, we're not. I'm the manager." My heart thumped wildly in my chest as I waited for Reid to agree.

Reid held a hand up as if that act alone would ease the tensions in the room. "Jonah wants to step in. He's an investor. He has every right to be involved in the day-to-day decisions."

I could see what Reid was trying to tell me, Jonah needed this distraction. *What if he never played again?* The words rested in the air between us.

I swallowed over the lump in my throat. Ultimately, it was Reid's decision. He'd come up with the idea of a private sports complex not run by the county recreation department, catering to kids who needed an outlet. He and Dylan wanted to offer used and new equipment to any athlete who needed it, even scholarships for kids who couldn't afford to join a team. I loved his vision. I was lucky enough to work with him, someone who had enough money to make those visions a reality.

Reid gave each of us a pointed look. "I need to know that you two can work together."

A flush crept up my neck remembering how I'd wanted to straddle Jonah at the bar, kissing him. The feel of his hands in my hair and on my body was burned into my memory. I licked my suddenly dry lips, trying to remember why we were here. If it came down to it, Jonah was part owner, I was the expendable one.

"I can do that." My voice wavered slightly.

My curiosity about him hadn't been quelled by kissing him that night in the bar, it had only burned hotter. There was more to him than the easygoing persona he showed to everyone. This was an opportunity to figure him out.

"It won't be a problem." Jonah's jaw was tight.

The high I'd been riding since securing this job dimmed. I'd no longer be responsible for the decisions. I'd be working with Jonah. I had a feeling he wouldn't make it easy.

"Good." Reid shifted through the papers I'd placed on the table before the meeting. "We need to discuss the next few weeks."

I sat across from Jonah, trying to ignore his larger-than-life presence as he settled his elbows on the table, focusing on Reid.

"We have the grand opening in three weeks. We need to outline the programs we'll offer, set up the used and new equipment program, and finalize the website."

This was where I felt most confident. Organization was my strong suit. I'd already contacted the website developer, Ava Breslin, after Reid outlined my duties on Sunday. "Ava will have the final revisions for the website completed today for you to review."

Nolan, one of the contractors for the sports complex, referred his fiancée's sister, Ava Breslin, to Reid.

"Good. We'll need the team sign-up page ready to go before the grand opening."

"She assured me it will be."

Reid hired Morrison Brothers' Construction, owned by his friend Cade, to build the complex. Cade had taken it on with the promise it would be completed before preseason started in July.

"The grand opening will be this weekend, so three weeks from now." I pointed at the calendar Reid had placed on the table between us. "I thought we'd have games and programs to entice parents with children to come and have fun, see the facility, maybe sign up for a sport. It would have a festival feel."

"Why not invite the rest of the team, make it a meet and greet? I know they'd want to support us. That would attract media attention." Jonah mentioned publicity like it was a good thing, but Reid generally avoided that type of attention even though he'd recently come clean about his speech impediment.

"I want the focus on the community, not the players." Reid rubbed a hand over his chin as he considered it.

"The fact that the owners are football players is bound to come up. I think we need to go with that angle," Jonah insisted.

This was a common bone of contention between them. As Reid's personal assistant, I'd been front and center when Jonah or Chase, the other captains of the team, wanted to do something that required publicity, and Reid wanted to avoid it.

"You know Lena would like it," Jonah said, referencing the team's head of public relations.

Reid made a face. "I don't do things based on what Lena would do."

I took that moment to study Jonah. He was more put together than Saturday night. His shoulders were broad under his white shirt, his hands large and calloused from throwing the football and weight training, but there were still dark circles under his eyes. Was he in a lot of pain or was he losing sleep worried about the future?

Jonah's gaze settled on me, startling me from my reverie. "What do you think?"

My cheeks heated. I hoped he hadn't realized I'd been staring at him. I took it as a good sign he'd asked for my opinion. Working together wouldn't be too bad if he treated me as an equal. "Maybe we could do both. We can still have the festival but sell tickets to meet the players or spend more time with them. We could use that as a fundraiser for the scholarship and equipment fund."

"Spend time with a player, kind of like that blind date Dylan won to meet me?" Reid asked.

The idea of people bidding on a date with Jonah didn't sit well. Any time there was a meet and greet, Jonah was the most sought-after player because of his play on the field as well as his personality. "Kind of. It wouldn't be a date though. Fans could get an autograph and ask any questions they have of the player."

Jonah nodded in approval. "I like it."

"I figured you would," Reid said wryly.

Jonah was warm and welcoming, always taking the time to sign an autograph. Whereas Reid had shied away from meet and greets over the years due to his speech impediment.

"It's part of the job." There was an edge to Jonah's tone.

"Maybe it's not a good idea for you to do it now. They'll be asking about your injury, your physical therapy."

"Yeah, you're right. I'll let Chase and the other guys offer up their time." Jonah's jaw tightened.

I needed to change the subject from his injury and his current limitations. I wanted Jonah to feel good, maybe even excited about something.

"What do you think about a mentorship program?" It was something I'd been mulling over ever since Reid brought up his plans. I'd been waiting for the right time to suggest it.

They both looked at me expectantly.

My heart rate picked up with their attention on me. I wasn't helping their vision come true, I was pitching my own. I cleared my throat, pushing out any doubt. "It has nothing to do with the grand opening, of course. But we could pair players with kids, kind of like a big brother thing, but you'd offer advice on their play, form, and training."

My nerves made my words rushed. I held my breath, hoping they'd at least consider the idea. I knew a lot about football from my grandfather but also watching the guys the last few years.

Their opinion mattered. I'd gotten this job because I was good at organizing Reid's life, but this was a way to prove that I had other things to contribute.

Finally, Jonah said, "I like it." Then he looked at Reid. "What do you think?"

"I like it too. You'd be perfect to head it up. You'd only be dealing with the kids, not the parents, so you shouldn't get too many difficult questions about your injuries."

"I can handle kids." Jonah's tone was gruff.

"I agree. This is great. You two can work on that." Reid's phone buzzed. "I have to take this."

I was happy they'd both loved my idea even if I couldn't believe I'd offered up another project I'd need to work on with Jonah.

Reid walked out, leaving us alone. The clock ticked in the background.

I wanted to address what Jonah said at the bar. "I know you think I don't deserve this job or this opportunity, but I'm going to prove you wrong."

"Did I say that?" Jonah asked, his expression genuinely confused.

"At the bar after Reid offered me the job," I said the words slowly, waiting for any recognition he remembered. If he'd had too much to drink, did he even remember the kiss?

"Do you remember anything from that night?"

His gaze dropped to my lips. "I remember some things."

I shifted in the chair, my skin heating.

"I don't remember everything we talked about." He stood, coming over to my side of the table.

I stood to even the playing field, even in heels, he still towered over me. I channeled the same take-charge attitude I'd used with Reid over the years.

"Reid trusts you." The way Jonah said it made me think he didn't. "But you're right, I don't think you're qualified for the job."

I couldn't disagree with him. I was a college graduate with no business or management experience. "I'm going to prove you wrong."

He leaned closer, his eyes darkening.

I sucked in a breath. Was he going to kiss me again?

"I look forward to it." He turned and walked away.

I stood rooted to the spot.

When he got to the door, he paused, turning back to me. "Please don't mention what happened at the bar to Reid."

I crossed my arms over my chest. "Are you embarrassed, or is this about that ridiculous promise to stay away from me?"

"It doesn't matter why. It's not going to happen again." He slapped his hand on the doorframe before he walked away.

He was cocky, so sure of himself and his ability to resist me. I wanted to knock him down a peg, show him I wasn't one of those women who hung around the locker room waiting to score a player. Nothing that happened Saturday night was fake even if he was drinking and didn't remember everything. I saw the desire in his eyes this morning. It was a bad idea to get involved with him but getting under his skin wasn't against the rules.

CHAPTER FOUR

JONAH

I SHOULD HAVE ASKED HER NICELY NOT TO SAY ANYTHING TO Reid about our kiss, then stuck around until she agreed. Instead, I ordered her around like a cocky asshole, the type of player she probably thought I was. Then I walked out without getting any assurance she'd keep it a secret.

That flash in her eyes when she told me she was going to prove me wrong set every nerve ending in my body on edge. Blood hummed faster in my veins. I wanted more than one kiss I could barely remember. I wanted to know what it would be like to be with her.

I couldn't deny I was attracted to her. It was too late to place her back in the category of Reid's personal assistant or quasi sister.

What had changed Saturday night? Was it the alcohol that lowered the barriers between us? If so, what was her excuse? I don't remember her drinking that much.

Was she as attracted to me as I was to her? Today she seemed irritated by my presence. It was almost as if she saw me as a threat.

None of it should matter. Reid warned us away from her because she was too good for us. I certainly wasn't good enough for her. I might not have football to fall back on anymore. I had almost nothing going for me unless you counted the money I'd made, which she probably could care less about. She'd been around the team for years, and I never saw her flirt with any of the guys.

I headed to Reid's office. He was pacing the office talking on the phone. When he saw me, he held up his finger, indicating I should wait for him.

"Okay. Thanks, man." He hung up. "Sorry, that was Cade giving me the rundown on what needs to be completed."

"Not a problem. It gave me a chance to talk to Callie."

"You talked to her about what you'll be working on together?"

"Yeah." I choked the word out because we hadn't talked about Rebel Sports. I didn't accomplish anything when Reid walked out of the room except making myself look like more of an idiot than I had on Saturday night.

He tilted his head, considering me. "You think this is a good idea?"

"Opening Rebel Sports? Of course. I wouldn't have put my money behind something that wasn't."

"Not that. Callie."

"Callie? What are you getting at?" Did he not want me working with her because he knew I was attracted to her? Was the chemistry between us that obvious?

"She gets along with everyone. Yet she doesn't seem to like you."

"I questioned whether she's the right person for the job."

Reid steepled his fingers. "The mentor program was a great idea. She's organized and hardworking. She might not have any experience, but she has a lot of potential."

"It was." I wanted to ask more questions. Why did Reid seem so protective of her? Why was he so close to her grandfather? Where were her parents? I vaguely remembered some talk when she first started working for him, but I couldn't remember any details. I couldn't ask without sounding more interested in her than I should have been.

"I trust you'll keep an eye on her, help her out. You're just as invested in this place as I am."

"More so if you think about it. If I can't play football anymore, this is all I have."

"You ever thought about what you'd do after?" Reid's question rang in the room. It was the question no one dared ask anyone for fear of jinxing them.

"No." I was only twenty-six. I was supposed to have at least five more years. As a wide receiver, I could play well into my thirties if I took care of myself, which I did.

"It's why I came up with the idea of this place. I won't sign with another team if Baltimore lets me go. Dylan's family's here."

"I didn't know you'd thought about leaving."

"Yeah, when you meet someone, you start to think long term about the future. Things that sounded doable before become less than ideal. Like being traded and traveling around the country. We'll want to have kids one day. I don't want to be the guy who's playing football while my wife is giving birth."

"Yeah, no one wants that." It's just I hadn't ever thought about dating anyone seriously, much less marriage. After the accident, I'd decided I wouldn't get seriously involved with anyone.

"What do you want?"

"You mean if I can't play football?"

He nodded.

Football was my escape from reality. If I didn't have that, the darkness seeped back in, reminding me that I wasn't worthy of more than I already had. "I have this."

"Take this time to figure out what you want."

When I focused on something besides football, I felt empty. Nothing excited me.

"You can work around your physical therapy."

"Yeah, I can go there in the morning, then head here."

"Good. When camp starts in July, you're in charge."

"I know." I wouldn't know if I could play until the end of August. The recovery time was six months post-surgery, but it could take as long as two years. I focused on the six months.

It would be good to have something else to focus on besides the fact I wouldn't be at camp in July or that I might not play again. At the same time, it was tough to see past August. Did I want to run a sports complex? Not wanting to go back home was the only clear desire besides playing football. I'd been singularly focused for so long it was hard to switch gears.

"Good."

We spent the rest of the afternoon going over the construction, plans for opening, and the day-to-day operations of the complex. I wasn't used to working in an office, but by the end of the day, I felt useful. Sometimes I felt like a fraud getting paid so much money to catch a football and run down the field.

"Keep an eye on Callie. She tends to take on too much."

"You seem close." Had they dated at one point, then decided they were better off as friends? Reid was relatively private. If anyone could pull off a secret relationship, it was him.

"She reminds me of my sisters, except she lost her parents. All she has is her grandfather who asked me to watch out for her."

"I get that." It was more of a reason to keep my hands off of her because he did see her as a sister. He wouldn't want a teammate sleeping with her and walking away, which was all I was capable of.

Callie didn't seem like a one-night stand kind of girl. She was a keeper. The one you made yourself worthy of, then if you were lucky, took her home to meet your parents.

A chill ran down my spine at the thought of taking her home, of her finding out. This was why I never got involved with anyone. "How'd her parents die?"

"Car accident. The lady was high as a kite and T-boned their car. Callie was asleep in the back seat."

I couldn't imagine losing my parents that way. She had no siblings to share in her grief. "She ever talk to you about it?"

"Only to say the doctors told her she was lucky." A haunted look crossed over his face. "I'm not so sure she was."

I wondered if she'd experienced survivor's guilt. I certainly had. Even if I was interested in her, her parents were killed in a car accident. If she found out about my past, there's no way she'd be interested in me. I wasn't driving the car, but I might as well have been.

"She's a sweet girl. That's why I keep her away from assholes like you." His tone had an edge to it.

"Yeah, no shit. I don't deserve someone like her." She seemed like the girl next door. Someone I could easily dirty up and not in a good way. I'd tarnish her light with my dark. She didn't deserve that.

"Is that why you don't date anyone seriously? You don't think you deserve it after what happened?"

Chase and Jonah knew what happened, but it wasn't something I talked about. "What guy my age is looking to settle down?"

When Reid just cocked his head at me, I appealed to his good sense. "How can you trust that a woman isn't interested in your bank account?"

"Not all women are like that. Dylan was never after my money."

Dylan was the ideal girlfriend. She came from money. She wasn't interested in the football hype. She was an attorney and involved in charity work. "I don't think I'm going to find a woman like Dylan hanging outside the locker room or at the bars."

I didn't mention that women like Dylan and Callie were so far out of my league it was ridiculous.

"Maybe it's time to start thinking about something more serious. Then when things like this happen," he gestured at my knee, "you're not alone. You have someone to ease some of your burden."

That did sound nice.

"Your injury eliminates the cleat chasers anyway," Reid teased.

"Thanks for that, man. Appreciate it." The few times I went out after my injury, women weren't approaching me. At first, I thought it was because I was surly, but it was probably the fact that everyone locally knew my future was tenuous.

"The right woman won't care if you're a football player."

I destroyed my ex-girlfriend's life. I still felt the weight of her family's blame. I wouldn't do the same thing to Callie.

CHAPTER FIVE

CALLIE

"There's over one hundred and sixty thousand square feet, eight basketball courts, and four turf fields that can be used for soccer or football. State-of-the-art fitness center, locker rooms, and even arcade games." Reid led us through the complex, stopping in the lounge area to show us the framed blueprints of outdoor football, soccer, and baseball fields that were to be completed by next spring.

"This is impressive." Jonah rubbed his chin as he considered the plans.

What started as an indoor sports complex quickly morphed into plans for outdoor facilities when local leaders approached Reid about the necessity for more fields. It was an easy decision for Reid, since he had the space and the financial backing for it.

"The sheer size and offerings rival the best complex in the Northeast," I said.

Reid shifted to face me. "You've done some research?"

"I have. I looked into Premier Sports Complex for comparisons and ideas. I'm not saying we have to do everything they are, but I think we should consider some of the things. At a minimum, we're offering soccer, basketball, and football leagues and providing equipment. Lacrosse is a big sport in Maryland. I think we should add it as well."

"That won't take away from football?" Jonah's forehead wrinkled.

"I don't think so. It will only add to our appeal." I held my breath waiting for their opinion.

"I'm open to considering it. You have anything prepared for it?" Reid asked me.

I pulled the graph out of my folder. "I ran the numbers so you'd have them."

I'd planned out each sport for the season, predicting how many fields would be needed.

Reid took the paper from me while Jonah raised his brow as if surprised by my preparation. What I lacked in experience, I'd make up for in sheer determination.

"Lacrosse camps are big in the area. Take a look." Reid handed the paper to Jonah.

I'd attached numbers to the percentage of kids in the area who attended sports camps, highlighting the most popular.

Jonah studied it before handing the paper back to me. "I'm not opposed to the idea. I just don't want to take on too much."

"I'm not saying we do everything at once. Just that we discuss the options, then implement them when it makes the most sense." I didn't want to overwhelm Reid.

Reid nodded, heading to the window that overlooked one of the massive soccer fields. He'd invited a local soccer team to practice today and provide feedback on the facilities and the field. The yells of the players were muffled through the glass. Large TV screens were mounted on the wall, showing each field and court. Jonah sat on the plush leather couch against the wall, his arm outstretched on the back. I tried not to pay too close attention to the way his strong legs were splayed out on the couch. He was deceptively relaxed, but his wary gaze was trained on me.

"What else do you have in mind?" Reid asked, leaning one shoulder against the window frame.

It was important to appeal to the financial advantage of some of my suggestions, but also Reid's strong desire for community involvement.

"I know it's important to you and Dylan that we partner with the local community to see what other kinds of programs we can offer. I contacted the mayor, the heads of the park and recreation programs, and a few sports teams. The teams need a place to play that isn't tied to public schools and county facilities. They love the idea of a private complex. They feel like it provides more opportunities for growth. The basketball program in particular has been limited with access to one elementary school. I toured the gym, and there isn't even room for spectators to sit. The parents are waiting in the hall-way, jockeying for position to see their kids play."

Reid nodded in approval. "I like that we're providing something they're looking for. Let's make sure the basketball programs are contacted. Offer them a fair price to rent the facilities in the winter. I want them to have more room."

"The director of the program mentioned they'd be able to sign up more kids for the program. They have a long waiting list of kids who want to play but there just isn't room."

"Thanks for checking into that, Callie. This is the exact issue I'd like to remedy." Reid exchanged a look with Jonah.

They were impressed with my research and initiative. I let that feeling seep into my skin before launching into the next thing on my agenda.

"We'd already discussed offering summer camps and birthday parties since we have the arcade and the Ninja Warrior Course."

Reid nodded, his gaze shifting to the team on the field below us.

I hoped I hadn't lost him. I decided to discuss the last thing on my list, the one I was least sure about. After my

FALLING FOR YOU

research on similar facilities, this was the one thing that set the best ones apart. It wasn't just about sheer numbers, it was the quality of the programming. "What about offering specialized training from well-respected players and coaches, maybe even to the level that people might travel here for it?"

Jonah raised a brow. "That's an interesting idea."

He shifted, leaning his elbows on his knees. I tried not to think about how sexy that move was.

I had my typed notes in front of me, but I put my file down on the large conference room table. "From what I read, this is the single biggest thing that sets the best sports complexes apart. It will be expected from you guys. Three football players running the sports complex. You have the connections and the draw; you're respected. We can focus on football at first, enticing recently retired players to impart their wisdom."

Reid and Jonah were silent, gazes on me, not the soccer team, so I continued, "I took the liberty of reaching out to several local players and coaches."

I took a deep breath, handing the list to Reid.

"You're thorough."

"I know you're busy with training camp, and you didn't want to be involved in the day-to-day operations, I wanted to show you that I can do this."

Reid's forehead wrinkled. "Still, we're going to need to hire more people to assist you. This is a lot."

"I can handle it."

"I want to focus on getting the basketball teams in here in the winter, keep the baseball teams updated on the completion of the outdoor fields, and work on the program to identify kids who'd like to participate but can't afford to."

I took notes as he talked, marking the most important with asterisks. "We need a name for the program. Have you and Dylan thought of something?"

"No. We haven't."

37

"Do you mind if I work with Ava on that and a logo? If I'm talking to former athletes and coaches, it would be something to mention. We're not just offering elite programs, we care about the community."

"That's fine. Run the final design by me." Reid started to pace. "Lacrosse, football, and baseball require the most equipment and will be the most cost prohibitive."

"I ran numbers on that too. I reached out to a local sports store for a discount."

"You've thought of everything."

"I tried to anticipate what you'd want to do based on the vision you discussed with me." It was a skill I'd learned being a personal assistant, assessing what Reid needed before he did.

"I'm impressed. I want you to hit the ground running on the training programs. I'll give you a list of athletes and coaches I want to work with. Reach out to them, set up a meeting."

"Will do."

I wrote notes frantically as Reid talked, murmuring or nodding when he touched on a particular idea I loved.

I felt Jonah's questioning gaze on the side of my face, but I kept mine on my notebook.

"You want to finish the tour, Jonah? I'm meeting with Cade and Nolan to go through the facility to make sure everything's completed."

"I can do that."

Reid touched my shoulder as he passed. "Good job. I know I made the right decision hiring you."

His approval was everything. I wasn't just a lackey anymore, bringing Reid whatever food or drinks he wanted, running interference with fans, or answering fan mail.

I finished scribbling out the last few notes. I sat next to Jonah, entering some of the dates Reid mentioned into our shared calendar. Organizing Reid's schedule was one duty I retained.

"That was impressive."

I flushed, looking over at him. "Thank you. *Some* people were skeptical about whether I was right for the job, so I wanted to make sure I'd done my homework."

"You definitely did." He stood. "You ready for the rest of the tour?"

"Absolutely." He took me through the locker rooms, telling me what was important to have in terms of being an athlete. Where the equipment should be stored. It was invaluable information I wouldn't have known otherwise.

"This is the fitness center, and next to it is the Ninja Warrior Course."

The fitness area was huge. I assumed it had everything an athlete could want since Reid designed it. "We're offering limited gym memberships to the community during certain hours, allowing the sports athletes priority access. It will be a good source of additional revenue."

"You're welcome to use it if you want."

"Me? Oh no. I don't work out. I don't have time."

His hands were tucked in the pocket of his dress pants as he rocked back on his heels. He must not have had physical therapy today because he was in business attire. I detected a hint of aftershave or cologne.

He tilted his head. "I thought you were a football fan?"

"I am. That doesn't mean I'm athletic."

"You never played a sport?"

"Nope." I wasn't sure why this was so important to him.

Jonah fell silent, leading the way to the Ninja Warrior Course. The obstacles looked intimidating.

"We should do the course."

"I'm not exactly dressed for it." I laughed, gesturing at my blouse tucked into my pants, and heels.

"Bring a change of clothes tomorrow so we can work out together. Then I'll show you the course."

"I don't know. That doesn't sound—" Particularly pleasant.

"I think it would be fun to do the course. Plus, you need to experience everything in the facility so you know how things work."

"I don't know about fun. Scary, intimidating—"

"The word you're looking for is challenging."

Even with an injured knee, he was more in shape than me. "I'm a little disappointed."

"Why?" My stomach sunk. Did he still not think I was suited for the job?

"I thought you were up for the challenge. I've seen you argue with seasoned athletes about their plays."

I cringed. I tended to feel strongly about football. It was my grandfather's fault. "I'm more of a behind-the-desk kind of gal, what do you call it? Monday quarterbacking? Something like that." Why couldn't I think of the right words now that Jonah was focused on me?

His lips twitched. "Monday morning quarterbacking."

I pointed at him. "That's it. I'm not what you call a participator. I'm happiest cheering from the stands."

He crossed his arms over his chest. "Now you work with three football players. We'll turn you into an athlete, whip you into shape."

I started backing away. "I don't think I need to be whipped into shape."

He cocked his head. "Are you saying you're not up for it?"

I licked my suddenly dry lips, my voice coming out squeaky, not as confident as I wanted. "I am."

I never backed down from one before, but I'd never been asked to do this.

"Bring your workout clothes tomorrow."

I cringed.

"You do have workout clothes?"

"Um, it's more like loungewear." Comfy sweats and

40

stained tees. Nothing I'd wear to work out with Jonah Templeton.

"If you're going to work here, we're going to have to turn you into a sporty girl."

"And are you the one to do it?" I crossed my arms over my chest, surprised to find myself flirting with him.

"Someone has to." He gave his signature wink.

It was the same one I'd rolled my eyes to over the years, but now that it was aimed at me, it was potent. My heart sped up, my stomach was all fluttery, and my fingertips tingled. It was easy to disregard him when he walked around the locker room and football field as JT, this larger-than-life presence who attracted women to him like moths to a flame. Now that I'd seen a more vulnerable side to him because of his injury, I felt like I was seeing the real Jonah, not the one he presented to everyone else. That guy was harder to resist.

He leaned in closer. "You think you're immune to my charms, but you're not."

I bit my lip watching as his gaze was drawn to the motion. "I'm not immune. I'm just smarter than those other girls. I wouldn't get involved with my boss."

His jaw tightened. "Reid's your boss. He's the one who hired you."

"That sounds a little like semantics, doesn't it? What happened to you saying I was like Reid's little sister and you wouldn't go there?"

"I love a good challenge."

I crossed my arms over my chest. "Is that what I am to you? A challenge? I'm nothing like the women who chase you, so I'm suddenly appealing?"

He shook his head in disbelief. "It has nothing to do with the chase."

His tone was low and gravelly, the words intended only for my ears. A tingle ran down my neck, making my hair stand on end.

I wasn't sure what to say to that. His words sparked something in my chest, all my nerves were firing. He was talking about more than my athletic abilities or prowess on a ninja course.

I was the challenge. The idea thrilled me. When a man like Jonah sets his sights on you, you grab on with both hands and go for the ride. Screw the consequences or the inevitable heartache.

He turned to walk away. "Don't forget your ninja gear tomorrow."

Could I handle him? I hadn't been with anyone who felt this risky in a long time. It wasn't that he was a bad boy. He was trouble in a different way. He was going to get under my skin and shred me from the inside.

He wasn't the kind of guy that committed to anything outside of football. I had a feeling he'd discard me as soon as someone else caught his interest. I was expendable in more ways than one.

I was positive he'd be amazing in bed. He'd probably even show me glimpses of that secret side of himself, but would I get all of him?

He stopped at the doorway, looking back. "You can't walk away from a challenge any more than I can."

Then he was gone.

He had a knack for exits. When had anyone ever viewed me as something more than the girl whose parents died in high school or the pretty girl next door?

My pulse pounded in my throat. Jonah made me feel desired. He thought I was beautiful when he could have anyone he wanted. Was I a distraction from his everyday life, or was he genuinely interested in me?

CHAPTER SIX

JONAH

WHAT WAS I DOING? THE MORE TIME I SPENT WITH CALLIE, the more I wanted to know her. She'd been prepared for the tour, coming out with one well-researched suggestion after another with the numbers to back them up. Reid was right to hire her. She was intelligent, hardworking, and passionate about the sports complex.

I wanted to ruffle her cool exterior, her perfectly made-up face, and her pressed clothes. I wanted to know if she burned hot when the right guy touched her. I wanted to know if that guy was me. Instead of telling her all of that, I'd challenged her to a ninja course. It was the playground equivalent of tugging on her pigtails, and it made no sense at all.

I should have asked her out, using one of my well-practiced modes of seduction, lowering my voice to that gravelly tone most women seemed to enjoy, standing closer than necessary, maybe even brush a strand of hair out of her face. Then I'd watch her eyes dilate and the involuntary shiver down her back. I was usually confident with women, but Callie was different.

She was studious, hardworking, intelligent, confident, yet vulnerable and soft underneath. There was something about her admission that she wasn't athletic that touched me. Most women lied or said whatever I wanted to hear, but not Callie. She was so genuine, so real, so unlike me. I craved her presence. I wanted to be in her sphere, revolving around her, soaking up her goodness. I didn't deserve any of it. I didn't deserve her, but I sure as hell wanted her.

I popped my head into her office. Her gaze was on the computer, her spine ramrod straight, her forehead wrinkled as she read whatever was on the screen. She was probably preparing more graphs and spreadsheets. It was time to have some fun. "You ready for the ninja course?"

She sighed before looking at me. Her lips turned down slightly. "You were serious about that?"

From her crestfallen expression, I could only assume she either thought or hoped I wasn't. "Of course. Someone has to test out the course and make sure it's a good one."

"I don't think Reid would have installed a boring ninja course. If there even is such a thing." She shook her head, but a smile played on her lips.

Hopefully, she wasn't just tolerating me because I was one of her bosses but enjoyed my company as much as I did hers. Even if I didn't have much to offer besides my fun persona. "You bring something to change into?"

She stood, walking slowly around her desk, leaning a hip against it.

The narrow red skirt emphasized her small waist, curving over her hips. Her tan legs were bare, the neutral heels emphasizing the curve of her calf. Clearing my throat, I said, "I don't mind watching you on the course in that skirt, but you might be uncomfortable."

"You wish. I brought clothes." She crossed her arms over her chest, raising a brow. "If you leave, I'll get dressed."

"You don't want to try out the locker room? As the manager, I think you should partake in all areas of the complex so you get a better idea of how everything works."

She pursed her lips as if she were amused by my suggestion. "I'll change in my office and meet you at the course."

"Suit yourself." I shrugged, enjoying pushing her buttons.

When I turned to go, she asked, "Will it just be us?"

I turned back to see the worried expression on her face.
"Just me."

I wanted her all to myself. The course was an excuse to get
closer to her, under the spreadsheets and her carefully
prepared speeches. You could tell a lot about a person when
they did something hard for them or out of their comfort
zone.

I was already dressed in a T-shirt and shorts, so I grabbed
a water from the fridge that Reid kept stocked and headed to
the ninja area. I walked through the course, figuring out what
I could do without injuring my knee. Monkey bars and
climbing shouldn't be an issue if I relied primarily on my
upper body.

"Getting the lay of the land?" Callie asked.

I turned to find her standing in the entranceway in a tight
tank top and black leggings. The outfit left nothing to my
imagination, every curve and every dip and valley was on
display. It was very possible the obstacle course was a bad
idea. There was no way I could stop thinking of her as sexy, or
go back to her being Reid's personal assistant and my
employee.

"Something like that." I wanted to get the lay of her body.
I wanted to trace her curves with my hands. I moved toward
her without consciously thinking, my fingers itching to grip
her hips and pull her flush against me. Suddenly the room was
warm. Instead of reaching for her, I stopped in front of her,
twisting off the bottlecap and taking a long pull of the cold
water.

"How does this work?" Her gaze shifted nervously to the
contraptions and mats behind me.

I needed to focus on the obstacle course and not how she

looked. How I felt about her was going to be obvious. I couldn't hide my body's reaction under mesh shorts.

I walked her through the course, detailing how she'd get through each section. She listened carefully.

I got the impression she was making notes in her head, trying to remember every suggestion I'd made for hand position.

Standing at the beginning of the course, she drew in a shaky breath. "I'm not sure about this. I'm not exactly coordinated."

"You'll do better than you think you can."

She offered a small smile. "We'll see."

"Let's go through it slowly." I'd challenged her to get to know her better, but I didn't want her to be nervous or scared. I wanted to reassure her, to help her through the other side. She'd feel accomplished when she was done.

I stood next to her as she grabbed onto the ropes, climbing to the rings, then swinging her way across, biting her lower lip in concentration. I encouraged her every step of the way. She placed her foot on the mat on the other side, a triumphant smile on her face.

"We're just getting started."

"Let's keep going." She turned, assessing the next challenge, then jogged toward the climbing wall, making it partway up, then slid back down. She groaned in frustration, her hands on her hips as she gauged the obstacle. Then she backed up, running harder, trying again. Her fingers grasped for purchase on the ledge as she climbed almost to the top before slipping again.

"Any suggestions?" Her brow was furrowed, her shoulders rising with her heavy breaths.

My respect for her grew exponentially. I couldn't help but think if she'd been one of the women I spent time with in the past, she'd be giggling and asking for my help. She'd listened to my suggestions, but she wasn't flirting. Her entire focus was on what she was doing.

I stepped closer to her. "You might need to strength train. Do you do any exercise, even walking?"

She was willowy as if she was built to be a dancer or runner.

"I don't."

"You might need more upper body strength. Want a boost?"

Her cheeks flushed, she nodded.

I moved onto the mat until her back was to my front. I leaned over her, showing her where to put her hands. "Put your hand here, foot there."

She gripped the climbing apparatus, her butt stuck out, brushing against my groin. I pulled back, knowing the contact was merely an accident. She wasn't coming on to me. She probably hadn't noticed the near miss while my blood was now pooled below my waist.

"What's next?" she asked over her shoulder.

I cleared my throat. "I'm sorry, what?"

"You said you were going to give me a boost." She refocused on the wall.

What was I thinking when I offered? I clearly hadn't thought it through.

I'd need to boost her up by her ass. I could hold her foot, but it wouldn't be enough. If she were a guy, I'd be standing back trash-talking her through the course. It would be safer than standing a hairsbreadth from her, debating what her ass felt like through her leggings. When I realized she was probably wearing a thong or nothing underneath, I tipped my head back, staring at the ceiling. I took a deep breath.

"Jonah?"

"Let's go." I said it with more confidence than I felt.

I waited until she adjusted her grip, placing my hands on her ass, boosting her up. I tried not to think about the warmth of her body seeping through her leggings, the flex of her muscles, or the way my hands molded to the curve of her ass. She scrambled up and over, cheering when she reached the other side. I took a few deep breaths before joining her.

"I did it!" she exclaimed when I met her on the other side.

"I told you that you could." I shifted on my feet, feeling like a bastard for taking advantage of the situation by touching her.

She flexed her arms. "Maybe I should work on my upper body strength. It feels good to do something with my body. My head feels clearer, like I can do anything."

My gaze fell to the top of her tank top where her hot pink sports bra was now visible. I forced my gaze up to her eyes.

"I love working out too." I'd discovered the thrill of what my body could accomplish at a young age. I easily gained muscle mass when I lifted, improving my speed and strength. I loved the high I got when I worked out hard.

Looking ahead, she had to run over a long, moving cylinder.

"Are you ready to keep going?"

She nodded. "Definitely."

Pride soared through me that she felt more confident. She took off at a run, immediately falling off to the side. She laid on her back as if she was stunned.

I rushed to see if she was okay.

She held up a hand to ward me off. "I'm okay." She stood, brushing off her ass. "Well, that was embarrassingly quick."

Chuckling, I said, "The faster you run on this, the faster you'll fall."

"Good to know," she mumbled to herself right before she took off.

This time, she made it halfway before her arms went out for balance, she flailed on one foot, then went down, landing hard on her side.

"Are you okay?" I held my hand out to her.

"I'm going to make it across." Her hand wrapped around mine.

Easily pulling her up, I said, "You are."

She didn't need me trash-talking to her or shouting encouragement, she could do it on her own. Not only was she intelligent, she was mentally strong. As an athlete, mental strength was more important than physical. If she could do this course and keep getting up after falling over and over again, I could apply the same attitude with my injury and physical therapy. I'd keep trying to get better and stronger. I'd stop thinking about what would happen if I didn't get better. If I thought I'd return no matter what, maybe I would. Maybe believing in my body's ability to overcome, to heal from the injury, would be the difference.

"You're pretty amazing."

Callie laughed. "Because I keep falling?"

"No, because you get back up more determined to scale the wall or make it across that." I gestured at the slowly moving cylinder. It moved deceptively slow, easing the participant into thinking it was easy, but it was the hardest obstacle on the course.

"I know I can do this." Her eyes were determined.

"You can." I'd never been prouder of anyone. She wasn't a seasoned athlete who was used to training mentally and physically for challenges. It had nothing to do with coordination or physical strength. It was all her. She believed she could handle this job, so she could. She believed she'd make it through the obstacle course, and she would. Maybe not today or the next day, but eventually.

How could I have ever doubted she was the right choice to run Rebel Sports? It was because I didn't know the strength of her character. Now that I did, I admired her even more.

She stood so close I could reach out and tuck the strand of hair that fell out of her ponytail behind her ear.

Her breath hitched as she looked up at me. "Are you trying to distract me?"

"Is it working?" My voice was low.

She licked her lips. "Maybe."

She took a step back from me. "I'm not going to let you though."

She turned away from me, focusing on the cylinder, taking in a breath before running. She made it halfway across before she stumbled, straddling it.

I winced, holding my breath that she'd be okay.

Straddling the moving cylinder, she gripped it with both hands, yelling as she lifted herself up, and finished the run across. She stumbled a few times, almost losing her balance, but she made it. "I did it!" She turned to face me, to get my reaction.

"That was amazing." It was a great example for me. I might have gotten knocked down due to the tackle and my injury, but it wouldn't keep me down. Even if I never returned to my original abilities, I'd compensate in other ways, lifting heavier, getting stronger and faster, and come up with new ways to dodge linemen. I should mention the course as a team-building exercise for our employees, maybe even suggest renting out to other groups.

"You're an inspiration."

Her hands settled on her hips. "Me? How am I an inspiration?"

"You kept getting up and doing it again. You didn't give up." Somehow, I knew even if she hadn't made it across, she'd come back another day and keep trying. It was her personality to keep going. Even after losing her parents, she'd clearly brushed herself off, refocused, and got back to living. When I doubted her ability to do this job, she researched and worked harder. Nothing got her down.

"I guess."

I moved closer to her, not wanting to fight this attraction

to her anymore. Her chest was heaving from exertion, her cheeks flushed. Her eyes widened as I moved closer to her, stepping onto the mat next to her. I did what I'd been thinking about earlier, I gripped her hips, pulling her against me, groaning when I felt her heat.

My lips crashed down on hers. My heart was beating erratically in my chest. I kissed her like she'd pull back at any second and this would be the only chance I'd ever have to taste her. I kissed her like someone was going to walk in at any second and interrupt us.

I moved her back against the wall of mats, angling her chin, taking the kiss deeper. I wanted to pull her tank top over her head, to feel her nipples through her bra. My hand curved over her ass, tipping her against me as she moaned into my mouth.

Her hands traveled over my chest then down, slipping under my shirt. My muscles spasmed in response to her touch, wanting her to go lower, wanting her to push my shorts down and pull out my cock.

Fuck. She was my employee. I shouldn't be here. I sure as fuck shouldn't be kissing the hell out of her, feeling her up. I had no business doing this, but I couldn't stop myself. I couldn't—I didn't *want* to be the voice of reason in this situation. I'd take and take until someone put a stop to it.

Her hand pressed flat against my stomach. I chanted in my head, *move your hand lower* while I devoured her mouth. I was frantic to get as much of her as I could, whatever she was willing to give me. Pressing her back against the mats, my hands dipped under her shirt. She pulled in a sharp breath when I touched her flat stomach, flirting with the edge of her sports bra. Ripping her lips from mine, she nipped my chin, kissing down my neck, then placing the lightest kiss on my collarbone. I took the opportunity to palm her breasts, my thumb passing over her nipples that were hard as pebbles poking through the thin material.

"Jonah." Her hand tugged on my hair, the sharp bite welcome as she pulled my mouth back down to hers.

I wanted to feel everything, her lips on mine, the touch of her fingers on my skin. My blood pounded in my ears. *I wanted her.*

"We need to—we have to stop." She'd pulled back, her eyes wide, her chest heaving.

It was like she'd dropped ice down the back of my shirt.

"Of course, we do." Was she ashamed she'd kissed me? Was I not good enough for her? The old insecurities bounced around in my head, even though she didn't know anything about my past.

"The reality is that you're my boss." She gestured between us, her eyes filled with anguish. "This would be bad for me if Reid finds out. If things got messy, I'd be the one who'd be let go."

"I'm just a silent investor." I kept my tone light, trying to lighten the mood.

Her lip quirked. "It turns out you're not so silent."

I hung my head, taking a step back. "I'm sorry. I didn't mean to put you in a bad position."

She leaned against the mat, her hands splayed across her stomach, watching me warily. Was she restraining herself from taking a step toward me to continue what we'd started or worried I'd kiss her again?

I wanted her to want me as badly as I wanted her. When I was with her, things felt so light, so easy. I felt like I deserved her goodness. It was a dangerous feeling. One I'd be an idiot to entertain. Even if she was interested in me, she didn't know who I was or what she was getting into. I didn't want to tarnish her.

"You're right. I'm sorry. I don't know what I was thinking." I wasn't thinking at all. I felt the draw of her, the pull, the exquisite sense of rightness when our lips met. Now I had a kiss to remember, not one in a bar when I was drunk. I'd have something to hold on to when I was by myself at night with nothing but the silence of my condo.

"It's okay. I was just as much to blame."

Blame. Fault. Guilt. All words I was intimately aware of. I wore those words as a blanket, a shroud for the last few years. "You're not."

"If you want me to talk to Reid, to take a step back from the complex, I will."

Her forehead wrinkled. "I don't want that."

Her voice was small, almost regretful.

"Yeah, okay. I'll see you around then." I took a few more steps back before spinning on my heel to get out of there. Walking fast, I realized I was still trying to escape my past by pretending it didn't happen, that I could have someone like Callie. When would I accept I didn't deserve an easy out? What happened, *what I caused* was part of me, who I was, and forever would be.

If I got involved with Callie, I'd mark her soul, snuff out her light. She didn't deserve that. She was sweet, innocent. She'd never hurt anyone. She deserved a man without secrets. One who could give her all of him. I wasn't that guy.

CHAPTER SEVEN

CALLIE

I DREW IN A LONG SHAKY BREATH, MY MUSCLES STILL quivering from Jonah's frontal assault. He was a force when he focused his attention on one person.

I didn't delude myself into thinking I was anything more than a stop along the way to his recovery, a nice diversion to forget about his troubles. Once he was back on the field, the ball and his teammates would have his undivided attention. I was someone he could pass the time with while he was injured.

I touched my fingers to my swollen lips. Why did it feel like he was reveling in my touch, soaking up my essence? It felt like he was holding on tight because he was afraid I'd pull away at any second. I'd never felt like that with any guy before. He didn't treat me like Reid's personal assistant, his employee, or the help. He treated me like I was made of cold glass he wanted to warm all over with his lips and hands. I was delicate, something to be treasured. It was an addicting feeling, one I wanted to hold on to.

I understood why he'd walked away. Technically he was my boss, and we worked together. We couldn't be kissing in the office, even on the ninja course. If things went badly, I had the most to lose—this job and Reid. He was the only one I could rely on since my parents died. I had Grandpa, but I was the one taking care of him. Without Reid, I'd be alone.

I lowered my head against the mat behind me, fisting my hands, trying to remember the feel of Jonah's skin under mine, the softness of his hair, the scruff on his chin. I wanted him even more than I had at the bar. I was slowly getting to see him, the real Jonah. He was deeper than he'd let on. I wanted to know everything about him, why he was outgoing, what he was hiding, what he'd be like in bed.

I'd been so careful over the years, not to let go, not to do anything risky. Life was precarious, we weren't guaranteed tomorrow. Couldn't I have one indulgence? One night with Jonah Templeton to find out if our chemistry translated to the bedroom. I squeezed my thighs together to ease the ache he'd caused in my core.

I climbed down off the mats. I'd felt the high from making it across the ninja course, then the intensity of being in Jonah's arms, but my overheated skin had cooled, leaving goose bumps in its wake.

Should I have stopped him, or should I have suggested one night together? Could I handle it with grace when he walked away, or would I get too attached? Would I want more when he seemed like he had nothing to give? I'd never seen him with a serious girlfriend. I'd seen him flirt with fans and women at the bar, but he never flaunted anything in front of his teammates. If he was seeing anyone, he was discreet.

"Callie?" Reid asked, his eyes widened, taking in my outfit.

"Sorry, I was on the ninja course." I should have said fitness center. That wouldn't have raised any brows.

"By yourself?"

"Oh, no. Jonah was there." Please don't ask any questions. "He wanted to test it out."

Reid crossed his arms over his chest. "Jonah wanted to test out the ninja course with you."

"He said I should partake in everything the complex has to offer so I'm aware of how things work and what our customers will experience when they're here." The explanation was perfectly reasonable. The kiss on the mats wasn't. It was wild, reckless. The experience was a high I wanted to repeat.

He bobbed his head as if I was making sense. "What did you think?"

"Apparently, I need to work on my upper body strength," I joked.

"If you need any help with a fitness program, I can help you or one of our trainers can."

I wanted to ask if Jonah was available for that job. If all of his sessions ended the way today's had, that was a workout I'd sign up for. "Sure."

"I'm on my way to my office." He gestured for me to follow him.

My mind was still frozen on that moment in the gym. The one where Jonah winced when I said we should stop. A shroud came over his face. He looked ashamed of himself. It could have been because he viewed me as his employee, or it could have been something else. I wanted to find out why he walked away.

I took a seat in one of the guest chairs, wondering what he wanted to talk about.

Reid leaned against the desk, crossing one leg over the other. "You're doing a great job. I'm really happy you agreed to come on."

I clasped my hands together in my lap. "I'm really enjoying it. Thanks for giving me the opportunity."

The conversation felt stilted.

He took a deep breath. "Sometimes I worry about you."

I smiled. "You mean, my grandfather worries about me, and tells you to watch out for me."

Reid's shoulders relaxed as he nodded. "Yeah, pretty

much. Are you happy here? Or did you see yourself going in another direction?"

"This is my dream job. I just didn't think I'd get it so soon. I applied for the MBA program at UB because I hadn't found a job yet."

"I don't want to interfere with your school plans."

"I haven't gotten in yet, but I'm hoping I can go to class around my work schedule. UB is known for working with students who have jobs." Most of the undergrads and the MBA students worked while attending class.

"I want you here, but school comes first. Whatever you need to do, a flex schedule, whatever, we'll work it out."

"Thanks. You're so good to me."

Reid pushed off the desk, walking around to sit. "You have good business sense. You would have gotten a job like this eventually. I'm glad I found you first."

The sincerity of his words wound around my chest. "I'll do a good job."

"I know you will."

Jonah rushed in, pausing when he saw me. "Did you—"

I thought he was going to ask me if I'd told Reid about the kiss. I shook my head no.

His shoulders lowered in relief. "Oh good. I can come back later."

I stood. "No need. I was just leaving."

I wasn't sure why but it bothered me he kept asking me to keep our relationship a secret. I didn't want Reid to know, but it still rankled.

"Oh, Jonah. Callie wants to work out. Can you help her get started? Show her around the gym, give her a program to start on."

I tensed, waiting for Jonah to push me off on one of the trainers we'd just hired.

"Of course." He touched my arm as I brushed past him to

leave. Lowering his head to whisper in my ear, he said, "I'm not going to go easy on you."

I smirked. "I wouldn't expect anything less."

My body hummed from his proximity and the challenge in his voice. I looked forward to spending more time with him. If being physical led to other activities, I was all for it. In a few weeks, Reid would be returning to training camp. As long as I remembered he wasn't serious about anything, much less me, I wouldn't get hurt.

~

THAT NIGHT, DYLAN INVITED ME OUT WITH HER COWORKERS and friends, Avery and Hadley. They were partners at a law firm.

I met Dylan when she won the blind date with Reid. She'd tried to include me in girls' nights before but living in Baltimore made that difficult. Now that I worked closer to Annapolis, it made after-work get-togethers possible.

I pulled open the heavy wooden door to the restaurant, heading toward the bar where I knew they'd be seated. Screens over the bar played a basketball game. The girls sat at a high-top table by the windows.

"Callie!" Dylan exclaimed, giving me a quick hug before settling back in her seat.

"I needed to get out." Working, then making time to visit my grandfather, and the commute was a lot. Even though I wasn't in school, I wasn't used to the long hours of an office job.

"I hope it's okay we ordered some appetizers to share. Beer?"

I nodded.

Dylan poured me a glass, sliding it across the table.

"How's Rebel Sports?"

I was very conscious that Dylan was Reid's fiancée, so I

thought carefully about my answer. Finally, I settled on the truth. "I was a little worried about working with Jonah, but he's been fine."

Dylan cocked her head. "He's such an easygoing guy. Why did you think he'd be a problem?"

Immediately, I realized my mistake. Jonah got along with most people. Sighing, I said, "He didn't want Reid to offer me the manager position."

"He said that?" Avery's forehead wrinkled.

My cheeks heated at the memory of the first time we'd talked at the bar. "He'd been drinking the first time, but he repeated it the next time we talked."

I felt a little bad about talking about this with them because I enjoyed him in other ways. The feel of him pressing me into the mats popped into my head. My face heated, and I squirmed in my seat.

"He's been testy lately because of his knee," Dylan said.

I shrugged. "I get it. I just graduated and I'm inexperienced, but I'll prove him wrong."

"Reid's impressed with your initiative," Dylan said.

I flushed from the praise.

"He trusts you," Dylan said as the waitress placed the dishes of food in front of us.

"That means a lot." Not only was he my sole support system the last few years, he was a friend.

The waitress passed out plates, and we took a few minutes to pass around the food, digging in.

"Reid said Jonah's helping you get in shape?" Dylan asked in a casual way, but I could tell she was interested in my answer.

Did she know that there was an attraction between us?

"He wants me to experience the club so I can be a better manager." I hoped it was his way of spending more time with me.

Avery tilted her head.

"What?" I knew exactly what she was insinuating with the cock of her head. These women all had significant others. They were engaged. They wanted that for everyone, but they were a few years older than me. We were at different places in our careers.

"Is it possible he's attracted to you?" Avery asked.

I wanted to take a bite of the chicken wing in front of me to buy more time, but that would have been too obvious. Should I tell them the truth? Anything I said to Dylan, could and would make it back to Reid.

"You're making her uncomfortable. Reid's her boss," Dylan chided.

I wanted to confide in someone though. I wanted to get their take on it. I didn't have close friends or a parent to talk to. I certainly couldn't talk to my grandfather about my love life. He'd wanted me to date Reid. He'd probably be thrilled a football player was interested in me. "Don't say anything—" The girls leaned in closer. "But he kissed me."

"What?" Dylan lowered her fork to her plate.

Telling them the truth made me feel light-headed. Talking about it out loud made it real. I couldn't push it off as a random event that didn't mean anything. "He was drunk the first time. You know, at your engagement party."

Dylan's mouth dropped open. "You were sitting together when we left."

Avery pointed at me. Her eyes were bright. "Wait a minute—you said the first time—that means there was a second."

I couldn't believe I was telling them everything. "We were on the ninja course. I'd just completed this difficult obstacle, and he was excited for me." The memories rushed back, one after the other, the pride in his eyes, the way he crossed the mats toward me, the grip of his hands on my hips. The feel of his hardening erection against my stomach. *I wanted him.* "There was this crazy buildup. Lots of tension."

My heart was racing, the blood pounding in my ears.

"Oh, do tell." Hadley rested her elbows on the table, giving up all pretense of eating.

It was like he couldn't stop himself from moving closer to me, claiming me. I shivered just thinking about the possessive way he'd plunged his hand in my hair, pressing me against the mats.

"It was intense." The most amazing, mind-blowing kiss I'd ever experienced. That alone made me want to see what else he'd be good at.

"What happened after?" Avery asked.

"I told him nothing could happen between us. He's my boss." The explanation sounded flimsy to me. That wasn't the real reason since there were no rules against it. It was more this bone-deep fear that I was endangering the stability I'd worked so hard for—my friendship with Reid, my dream job.

"You didn't really want him to stop, did you?" Hadley asked.

Avery giggled. "Of course not."

I relaxed slightly that they were judging me. "If he asked me out, I wouldn't say no. Is it so wrong to take something you want?"

I couldn't get Jonah's words out of my head. He'd said he was used to taking what he wanted, asking questions later. Could I do the same? Be impulsive, reckless even.

"There's no rule against dating," Dylan said.

"I just worry that I'm a distraction for him. A way to pass the time before he goes back to playing football." My chest tightened at admitting my real worry.

"Reid said he's never dated anyone seriously. Not since he signed on with the team." She tapped her chin deep in thought. "I think he mentioned something about a high school sweetheart. Someone he never got over."

I didn't like the sound of that. Who hasn't gotten over their high school relationship? You either married them or moved on.

"Or maybe he hasn't met anyone he's ready to take that step with," Avery said, excitement filling her voice. She clearly hoped I was the woman to change him.

Even I knew that was unlikely. He was a professional football player used to getting anything and anyone he wanted. I was probably a conquest to him.

"I think he's hiding something." I looked at Dylan to see if she had the same impression.

"Reid hasn't said anything."

"It's not just his injury. He gets this look in his eyes like he's known sadness. I don't know if it's because I've been through something or if it's something else." I picked at my food, not as hungry as I'd been when I arrived.

"You might be more in tune with that kind of thing. You recognize the pain you've experienced in someone else. When I met Cade, he was a widower, and I'd lost my mother at a young age—we had that in common. The difference was that I'd moved on from it a bit. I'd always miss those moments with my mother, like graduation and buying a wedding dress, but Cade lost his wife, his hopes for the future. It was different. He was stuck in the past, unable to move on," Hadley said.

"Jonah's always been this put-together guy. He's great at football, meeting with fans, he's quick to work with whatever charity the team's working with. He doesn't seem like a guy who's hiding anything. It's hard to believe he's been through something we all missed," Dylan said.

"You said yourself that no one knew about Reid's speech issues. He kept that locked up tight. Who knows what other people are hiding in their pasts? Not everyone talks about it," Hadley said.

"Sometimes it takes the right person for them to open up, like Cade with Hadley and me with Reid."

Dylan's words brought a glimmer of hope that I'd be that person for Jonah. But I didn't delude myself into thinking this thing with Jonah would last longer than his injury did. The

second he was cleared to play football, I had a feeling whatever attraction he had for me would be forgotten. Even
knowing that, I didn't want to put a stop to whatever was
brewing between us.

"You know, it doesn't have to be anything serious. It could
be a fun fling for the summer," Avery said.

I pointed at her. "That has a nice ring to it."

I liked the idea of removing any expectations and
exploring the chemistry between us. I just had to remember
what it was.

Talk turned to the news that an old friend and law school
classmate of Avery and Dylan's, Taylor, and her fiancé, Gabe,
were moving from New Orleans to Annapolis. She'd be
working at the firm until she had her baby, then might move
to part time. Not knowing Taylor, I listened with one ear, just
enjoying being out with women. Going to class and working
odd hours for Reid kept me busy the last few years. I hadn't
formed lasting friendships.

CHAPTER EIGHT

JONAH

I'D ASKED CALLIE TO MEET ME IN THE FITNESS CENTER FOR A workout. I'd done some research on training for an obstacle course.

"You summoned?" Callie strode toward me in another skintight outfit.

It was late, so only a few employees were working out on the machines, and a couple of guys lifted dumbbells in front of the mirror.

"Are you ready for this?"

She flexed her bicep. "If you can make this bigger, that would be nice."

I couldn't help reaching out to squeeze the small muscle that formed. Her smile faded as her eyes heated from my touch.

"I'll work you over." Fuck that was not what I meant to say.

She pulled her arm from my grip with a saucy grin and a wink. "Let's get started then."

I was so used to Callie being serious, this flirty version threw me for a loop.

We went through a quick warm-up before walking

around the track which ran on the second floor. It was a great way to see the whole facility. We went past the soccer fields and basketball courts before taking the steps back to the fitness center to one of the rooms where classes would be held.

"I thought we'd be doing weights." Callie cocked her head.

The floor was padded, and the walls were mirrors. A bar ran the length of one wall. "We'll do both."

She raised a brow. "This is a little more serious than I thought."

"I don't do anything halfway." I started my timer. "We'll go through a series of HIIT exercises, Tabata style, then finish with total body lifting."

She waved a hand at me. "That sounded like gibberish to me."

I smiled. "HIIT stands for high-intensity interval training, and Tabata just means you'll do the exercises for a total of four minutes, but it's really twenty-second intervals. It sounds short but—"

"In reality, it's brutal?" She laughed.

"It's not too bad. Just follow my movements. I'm not cleared to do the jumps yet, so when I do a calf raise, you'll jump. You'll be fine."

"Okay." She eyed me warily.

I took her through squat jumps, burpees with tuck jumps, and jumping lunges. We started each move slowly, then picked up the pace as she caught on to the movement.

Breathing heavily, she said, "You know burpees are bad enough without adding on push-ups and tuck thingies with them."

"So, you have heard of burpees before?" I took a long pull of water, wishing I had the go-ahead to work out full bore.

"My friends have dragged me to a boot camp once or twice before." Sweat beaded on her chest.

"If you want to scale the wall in the ninja course on your own, this helps."

"Why not just do the treadmill or elliptical?" She lifted her shirt, wiping the sweat from her forehead.

My gaze caught on the wide expanse of skin she'd exposed. A flat belly, lightly defined muscles, and her belly button.

I got the impression she was asking questions not just out of curiosity but because she was stalling. She wanted a longer break before we started on the next exercise.

"Those are static exercises, good for a warm-up, but they don't provide much functional strength."

"Don't tell that to all of the people who slave on those machines five days a week. What is functional strength?"

I crossed my arms over my chest, feeling satisfaction when her eyes were drawn to my biceps. "It's what helps you pick up boxes or scale a wall. It helps you with everyday real movement. Overall, it's a better workout than doing repetitive movements like you would on the elliptical."

"That makes sense. Although the elliptical would have been easier," she teased.

"Nothing is easy when it comes to athletics or sports. You have to work hard to get where you want to be."

She bit her lip, looking away from me. "You always knew you wanted to play professionally?"

"I knew I was good at sports early on. I picked it up easily, pitching to my little league baseball team, tackling kids in flag football. Instinctively I knew when to pivot, when and how to move my body for the best impact. I easily built muscle mass. It came easier for me than other kids, but when I got older, I had to work harder. Eventually, everyone's on the same level. You have to constantly improve to stay relevant."

"That's a lot of pressure. When did you know you wanted to do it for real?"

"My high school coach thought I had what it took. College

scouts were recruiting me. It seemed like the best option. My ticket out of my town." A chill ran over my body. I worried I'd revealed too much.

"You didn't like your hometown?" There was nothing but genuine curiosity in her tone, but it set me on edge. I didn't like to talk about where I was from. It was hard for all of those feelings not to come back to me, flavoring my tone and mood, tipping someone off that things weren't good when I left.

I shrugged like she hadn't just asked the hard-hitting question. "Like any kid, I wanted to experience something different. I was in a hurry to grow up."

She nodded. "That makes sense. I had plans to move away too, but when my parents died, I stayed closer to home. I lived with my grandfather instead of moving into the dorms. I changed to a cheaper school."

"You did what you had to do." I was relieved she'd changed the subject to her, taking the heat off me.

"After he was diagnosed with early-onset Alzheimer's, he went into a personal care home earlier than he needed to so I wouldn't feel responsible for him. He wanted me to go to college and enjoy life. He didn't want me to be burdened with taking care of him.

"I'm sorry."

She gave me a sad smile. She'd resigned herself to losing the people she loved, her parents, and she'd eventually lose her grandfather over time.

I couldn't help but see the parallels in our histories. As much as I hoped it would draw us together if I told her the truth, I knew it wouldn't. Her parents were taken from her in a horrible accident, one that was someone else's fault. It was no different than what I'd done.

To cover my thoughts, I picked up my water, leading the way back to the weight room. "We'll finish with some total body strength moves."

I showed her the movements, helping her adjust her

weights. "You're doing compound movements, so you'll want to start light. You can squat more weight than you can with an overhead press."

"Got it."

I stood close by so I could spot her or step in if she needed my help. She was a trooper, doing everything I asked.

Going through the cooldown, I told her, "Make sure you eat a healthy snack or meal with protein."

"Got it, coach."

"Are you being cute with me?"

"I feel like your little project."

Except I wanted to do more than shape her body, I wanted to explore it. "It's something else to focus on besides my training."

"You want to be doing all of this, don't you?" She gestured around at the weights.

I couldn't do the compound movements or the jumping exercises. "I'd like to be back to myself."

"Will you miss this place when you're cleared to play?" Her gaze was on me.

It felt like a weighted question.

"Yeah, but I'll be back in the off-season." What I should have said was that I'd miss seeing her every day. Now we had an excuse to talk during work, to work out. Reid wouldn't understand if I kept our friendship, or whatever was happening between us, during the season. But if I wasn't cleared to play, I'd still be working here. That thought buoyed me more than I thought it would. For the first time, I realized I had other things in my life I enjoyed and looked forward to seeing.

"I have you lined up to coach some camps in the spring and summer."

"Perfect. I love working with kids." When I ignored that voice in my head telling me I wasn't a good influence.

"You are really good with the fans. I've always admired that about you."

Her praise felt good. *She admired me.* I let that sink down deep because I rarely allowed the good to penetrate. I focused on the fans and mentoring kids to make up for my past—to turn a negative into a positive. I might seem like a hero on Sundays, but deep down, I wasn't.

"Reid struggled with meetings with fans. Mainly because of his speech issues, but you're a natural."

I didn't tell her it was an act I put on. It wasn't the real me, or maybe it was the me from before. The one that let go of inhibitions, he said exactly what he thought, was quick to laugh.

"It means a lot that you think that of me. I think a lot of people dismiss me as a typical jock."

She studied me for a second before continuing, "I think I did the same. I feel like I'm getting to know you better though. There's a lot more to you than you let on."

"Not really." I wanted to know her better without her delving too deeply into who I was. I wished I could be with her without letting her all the way in. It was possible, but she deserved more. Just like that kiss on the ninja course, I'd take whatever I could before she realized I wasn't worth her time.

"You know, we haven't talked much about the mentor program."

"You're right. We should. Maybe over dinner?" I arched a brow, challenging her to refuse.

"We could talk about it easily in the office. Or now." She arched her brow. She was challenging me to make it official, to say what I meant, not to couch my request in terms of work.

"That wouldn't be much fun, now would it? Maybe I want to take you out." The thought sent a sweet feeling through my body. I did want to spend time with her outside the complex. Every minute I spent with her had me craving more.

"You could have just asked me out. Not couched it as a business dinner."

My chest felt like a balloon filling with air, pressing on my skin, threatening to burst. "Callie, can I take you out to dinner?"

A smile played on her lips. "I'd like that."

Happiness filled my body before a twinge of regret took over. This could only go so far. I could enjoy her for now, but then I'd have to set her aside, push her away because Reid wouldn't like it. Working together made things complicated, and ultimately, I had nothing to give her. She deserved so much more, but I was going to push those worries aside to live in the moment.

"How fancy will it be?" Her voice was teasing.

"What's your ideal date?" Women I went out with expected the yacht clubs, the hardest to get reservations at the most sought-after restaurants, VIP access to clubs, but my instincts were telling me Callie was the opposite.

"Listening to music, walking around Annapolis in the evening."

"Yeah?" Was it that simple with her? Was I the one making it complicated?

"Annapolis is one of my favorite places." Her smile was shy.

I loosely demonstrated the next stretch, unable to place my legs in the proper butterfly position.

She mimicked my movement.

"Pull your feet in a little more. I don't have enough range of motion yet."

"I like you because you're different. You don't say or do anything I expect."

I held up a hand when she opened her mouth. "I know you say it's because a certain kind of woman places herself in my path, but it's not just that. Everything that comes out of your mouth is fascinatingly, refreshingly unexpected."

I could easily fall for this woman. Asking her out, even if we talked about business, was a slippery slope, the beginning of a never-ending slide. My pulse pounded in my ears. I was done avoiding her. I was going to barrel toward temptation, taking what I wanted, ignoring the ramifications.

She leaned forward, deepening the stretch, looking up at me from under her lashes. "Just don't treat me like something that's disposable."

My heart twisted painfully. "I won't."

My voice cracked on the words. The promise was empty, even if I didn't want to treat her like that.

CHAPTER NINE

CALLIE

"What's Callie short for?"

I looked up from the spreadsheet on my computer. Jonah stood in the doorway in a T-shirt that read Rebel Sports and athletic shorts. Jonah had a habit of interrupting my work to joke around. Instead of being annoying, it was a nice distraction.

"Calliope." My face heated. "Not exactly the easiest name to pronounce growing up."

"Kids made fun of it?" Jonah smiled; his eyes sparkled with humor.

I rested my elbows on my desk, smiling. "They did. In a sea of Emmas and Maddies, I was different, but it was easier to go by Callie."

"Why don't you change it now that you're an adult?" His expression was sincere.

It felt like he was pursuing me, flirting, getting to know me. It was nice.

"I've gone by Callie for so long, I can't imagine changing it."

"It's a beautiful name either way." His blue eyes were intent on mine.

"Thank you." Jonah saying my name was beautiful heated me from the inside out.

I hadn't felt good, really good since before the accident. My parents' death left a hollow cavern in my chest that would never be filled.

His eyes brightened. "You want to get out of here? Grab dinner. Blow off some steam?"

"As attractive as that sounds, I was going to work a little longer, then go to bed early."

"Calliope Goodwin." His tone was chiding.

"Yes?" I raised a brow at him, wondering what charm he was going to use to convince me otherwise. Anticipation heated my veins.

He held his hand out. "I asked you out. You said yes. I'm cashing in my chips. Let's go have some fun."

"Is that all it takes to get women to go out with you? A boyish grin, a twinkle in your eye, and some smooth words?"

He winked. "Is it working?"

I wanted to get up and go with him more than anything. I laid my hand in his larger one. "I like to think I'm stronger than that."

Jonah curled his fingers around mine, laying his free hand on his chest. "No one is immune to my charms."

I snorted as tingles sprang from our joined fingers traveling up my arm. The warmth of his calloused hands surrounding mine felt so good. I'd never wanted a guy to hold my hand before. We walked down the hallway to the parking lot. Reid was gone for the day, and no one else was working this late, so I didn't have to worry about what anyone else would think. I could let go and be myself with him.

I glanced at his profile. His expression was lighter today. Sometimes, he was quiet and had this brooding look on his face. It was more than worry, it was like this darkness that took over sometimes. I wondered if anyone else even noticed it. Noticed him.

I was probably just hypersensitive to his moods.

We stopped by his large black SUV. "Where are we going?"

"You want to go to Annapolis?" Jonah stood in front of me, our joined hands between us. He was dressed casually, but this felt like a date.

"It is my favorite place."

He opened the door for me.

The cabin of the truck was clean, an athletic bag in the back seat, and a bag of footballs on the floor. "You're always prepared."

"Yeah, you never know when you're going to want to throw a football around."

"You carry balls around so you can play pickup games?"

"Yeah." He shrugged like it was no big deal which, I suppose, it wasn't. It was just me who thought that was adorable. Here was a guy who played football professionally, but he must love the game to always carry balls around wanting to play more.

"It's cute."

"Cute?" His tone was testy like he didn't like to be called that.

I smiled, looking out the window. "Yeah, it's cute."

He leaned over, lightly pinching my thigh.

I shot him a shocked look. "Hey."

His lips twitched. "Don't call me cute."

I crossed my arms over my chest. "Geez, you're sensitive."

"Only around you."

I shifted, facing him. "What do you mean?"

His expression was open, more vulnerable than I'd ever seen him.

"I care what you think."

"You don't normally care what people think?"

"No. I do. Probably too much, but not what women think of me. I'm not explaining myself very well. I'm a football player. That's all most people care about. They want to talk about the game last Sunday, the calls, the plays. Women want to know what kind of car I drive, want to be taken out to fancy restaurants. No one looks past that."

Maybe it wasn't so much a mask he put on but giving people what they expected. "Huh."

"You didn't think football players had feelings?"

"I worked with Reid for years. He was sensitive to what people thought of him, of anyone finding out about his speech impediment. So, I don't think that."

"I like you, Calliope. You're a cool girl."

I felt giddy like I had when I dated my first boyfriend in high school, when the possibilities were endless, and the future was an unchartered map.

"Let's go to the harbor and walk around. We'll go wherever looks good."

I closed my eyes, relaxing into the seat. I couldn't remember the last time my day wasn't scheduled into my calendar on my phone. The idea of doing whatever we felt like, having fun, rolled through my body.

"I'm going to get you to loosen up."

"I look forward to it." We exchanged a smile.

The thought of letting go sounded amazing.

He parked by the harbor. Music played from the city dock. "Want to walk around first?"

"Sure."

His hand touched my elbow; my breath caught in my throat. Then his fingers oh so slowly slid down my forearm, touching my wrist before intertwining with mine. Sighing, I touched his arm with my other hand and looked up at him. A girl could get used to this.

We sidestepped the evening crowd of tourists until he finally tugged me down a side street. "These are my favorite streets of Annapolis."

Away from the tourists, it was quiet, almost intimate.

"Main Street's always packed." It was lined with tourist shops selling Navy T-shirts and hats, fudge, and ice cream.

Here, I could admire the architecture of the historical homes, the window planters, and the little details you didn't see in a modern town, like the plaques designating certain homes as historic landmarks, or the iron door markers.

"Doesn't Dylan live somewhere around here?"

"She does. I'm not sure which street though." The hollowness of my chest gave way to an ache, a longing for something more. A home, the white-picket-fence, someone to share my space and day with.

I should ask Jonah what he was doing holding my hand when he had no intention of taking things between us further.

Before I could open my mouth, he opened a door to a pub, indicating I should go in first. The Irish pub and restaurant was darker inside, cool, with only a few tables filled with families, and a couple of people at the bar drinking.

"Not many people venture this far off the main drag."

"I see that." Did he want to be alone with me? Sitting at a small wooden table, it felt like an extension of the first night we spent time together at the bar. Except this time, both of us were sober.

We gave our orders to the waiter.

"Should we discuss the mentor program?"

He shrugged. "We don't have to. I just wanted to get out of the office."

I smiled. "I haven't exactly worked in an office the last few years either. Once we're officially open, I suppose I'll be moving around the complex, making sure things run smoothly."

Something passed over Jonah's face. Was he thinking about how he should be getting ready for football camp soon but not this year?

"How's physical therapy going?"

He leaned back in his chair. "I'm working hard. I'm

itching to get back out there, but they're telling me to go slow, pace myself. They don't want to test the knee out before it's ready."

"When do they think you'll be ready?"

"Hopefully, by the end of August." Jonah tensed. He was probably thinking about the young rookies out there working hard on the field, vying for his position.

"Just in time for the end of preseason."

"That's right."

"It must be tough not being out there."

"It's the first training camp I've missed."

"The coaches know what you're capable of. They won't want you rushing out there either. They want you back when you're healthy."

"You mean *if* I'm healthy."

"The unknown must be so difficult."

He shook his head. "It drives me crazy. I never thought I'd be in this position so early in my career."

It was bad luck for the guys to think about it, much less voice any concerns out loud. "No one expects it. Life just happens sometimes."

Jonah's gaze caught on mine. "You know something about that."

"Yeah, what happened to my parents was unexpected— devastating." The familiar pain I felt when I talked about it filled the crevices of my heart, throbbing in its intensity.

"I can't even imagine. I'm sorry." Yet his eyes were filled with the pain of someone who knew heartache, loss, and utter devastation.

He mentioned his family, a dad, mom, and siblings. Had he lost a grandparent? I wanted to ask him more questions, but the waiter positioned our plates in front of us.

"Need anything else?"

Jonah lifted his glass. "More water please."

The waiter took the glass as he left.

"Not drinking tonight?"

"I'm treating this summer like any other before training camp. Eating as healthy as I can—dinners out with beautiful women notwithstanding—so that I'm giving myself the best chance possible."

I unwrapped my silverware, laying the napkin on my lap. "What changed since the engagement party?"

"Reid and Chase sat me down, gave me a come to Jesus talk."

"Ah. I'm glad to hear it worked." I took a bite of my shepherd's pie.

"It did. That's when they mentioned me working at the sports complex."

"Do you like it?"

"I suspect I'll like it more when people are coming and going."

"An extrovert, huh?"

"I'm energized around other people. That's why this injury feels so isolating. I can't work out with the guys, or at least that's how I felt. Chase and Reid reminded me to come down to the team gym to do upper body. It helped me feel a part of things again."

"I can see that." We fell into an easy silence while we ate, the bar filling up around us.

When I finished, I pushed my plate away from me, seeing a man approaching us from the bar. His eyes were on Jonah, a question in his eyes. "Excuse me, are you JT—Jonah Templeton?"

Jonah placed his fork on the table in front of us, moving his napkin from his lap to the table. "I am."

"Can I get an autograph?" A boy, about nine or ten asked.

"Of course." The friendly mask Jonah reserved for fans slipped over his expression. He signed the boy's napkin, handing it back to him.

"Can I get a picture with you?"

When Jonah nodded, the boy's dad handed me the phone. Jonah stood in the middle of the father and son. The smile I thought was so friendly before I knew him, now seemed forced.

I handed the phone back, sitting down while the boy flipped through the images.

"Are you going to play this year?" the father asked.

Impatience flashed across Jonah's face before he quickly smoothed it out. "I sure hope so. I want to be out there with my team, you know?"

"I do." He held up the signed napkin. "Thank you."

Jonah nodded.

I wanted to acknowledge what just happened. At the same time, I didn't want to bring it up. Jonah waved at the waiter when he walked by, asking for the check.

"Are you okay?"

Jonah looked at me like he was surprised I'd asked.

"It has to be tough to have your meal interrupted only to be reminded of your injury." And his tenuous position with the team and sport he loved.

"It is. I don't mind fans. They're the reason I'm here, but—"

"It's okay to want to keep certain things to yourself. I watched Reid struggle with that."

His gaze was knowing. "You knew about his speech impediment before he admitted to it, didn't you?"

"I guessed. It wasn't something he was able to hide from me. He avoided R*s* in conversation as much as possible, but when he was tired or had been drinking, they slipped out."

"That's not one of those secrets you can bury down deep."

That made me pause. Examining his face, it was carefully blank. Was he referring to himself, or was it a throwaway comment? "Those closest to him knew. I think he said Coach Ackerman suspected."

"I don't think I paid close enough attention to figure it out."

"Reid was good at hiding it. I encouraged him to come out with it. I suspected fans wouldn't care as much as he thought."

"I don't know. There's always someone who has something negative to say."

"True, but overall, the response has been encouraging. It's brought more attention to Kids Speak." The organization was Hadley's nonprofit. Dylan partnered with Baltimore's football team to bring it to the city. A team captain in a professional sport suffering from a speech impediment brought more awareness than any other charity function could.

"Not every secret is so innocuous."

"I guess. He was just embarrassed by it. His father wasn't exactly nice about it when he was younger."

Something was bothering Jonah, something bigger than a fan asking about his injury. He seemed on edge. When he signed the receipt with a flourish, he asked, "Ready to get out of here?"

"Yeah."

He didn't grab my hand again, making me think his earlier gesture had been friendly. I breathed easier when we passed his truck in the lot, continuing to the city dock where the music still played. We sat at an open bench, his arm stretched out behind me. The wind off the water lifted my hair, cooling my cheeks.

He leaned in closer, speaking by my ear. "How often do you let go? Go clubbing with friends, grab a drink with coworkers."

"Not often. I went a little too crazy in high school, partying and hanging out with the wrong crowd."

Jonah shifted so he could see my face, a smile playing on his lips. "You—Calliope Goodwin—got into trouble?"

"The police brought me home once or twice," I admitted, not proud of that time in my life.

He cocked his head. "Were you charged?"

"No."

"No police officer wanted to tarnish your impeccable record. You look like the girl next door. They probably figured you weren't going to grow into a hardened criminal."

"They knew about my parents, so they gave me the benefit of the doubt. My grandfather talked some sense into me. Reminded me I still had a life to live. I'd want my parents to be proud of me."

"It obviously worked. You graduated college. Got this job."

I waited for him to tease me about how lucky I was but instead, his eyes filled with regret before he looked out over the water. A muscle ticked in his jaw.

I wanted to cup his cheek, turning him to face me, and ask why the sudden change in his demeanor. Instead, I watched his profile as he looked out over the water. There was something weighing on him, and it wasn't his injury. Had I never taken the time to notice it, or had he buried it down deep, keeping it a secret from everyone like Reid had his speech impediment? Had he lost someone too?

I wanted to ask him but I sensed it would be better to wait for him to open up to me. The truth would come out eventually. The only question was, could I handle it when it did?

CHAPTER TEN

JONAH

LAST NIGHT, I'D SAID I NEEDED TO GET HOME BECAUSE I HAD an early physical therapy appointment. Callie was quiet on the ride back to Rebel Sports. I appreciated that she didn't try to fill the silence with inane chatter. She seemed to sense that I didn't want to talk.

I parked then waited for her to get out of my truck. She'd placed her hand on my knee, telling me she was there for me if I needed it because my teammates wouldn't be as good of a listener as she would be. Our eyes met, and I saw so much understanding in her eyes, I wanted to erase the distance between us and pull her into my arms. I wanted to take solace in her. I wanted to confide in her, but at the same time, I didn't want to see the judgment in her eyes. Instead, I nodded tightly, trying to stay in control.

Watching her walk to her car, her head bowed, her keys in her hands, I let myself imagine that we were dating. That I had someone to talk to, to accept me for who I was. I felt light, almost hopeful. I hadn't felt that outside of football in a long time. Excitement filtered through me. The possibilities seemed endless. Too quickly, the darkness crept back in. The idea of allowing that sweet girl in, only to hurt her, was unforgivable.

Football allowed me to be someone else. A hero to a kid, a fan, for those four quarters on Sunday. But I knew the truth, I was no one's hero, and I'd certainly never be hers.

I worked harder than ever in physical therapy, determined to get better. If I didn't have football, I didn't know what I had.

After the grueling physical therapy session, I walked into Rebel Sports, almost running into Callie. Instead, I stepped to the side, steadying her with my hand on her shoulders.

"Sorry." She didn't look up. She looked preoccupied with something.

I squeezed one shoulder lightly to get her attention.

She looked up at me in surprise, recognition filtered over her face. "Oh, Jonah."

"Where are you going?"

Callie's gaze darted from me to the parking lot. "A nurse called from my grandfather's personal care home. She said he's forgetting things. He's easily agitated. I wanted to check in."

"Oh." Should I offer to go with her?

She pulled her arm away from me. "Reid said it was okay."

"Of course. Want me to drive you?" From what I remembered, her grandfather was in a home north of the city. A far drive for someone who was as upset as she seemed to be.

"Oh, that's not necessary." She licked her lips.

She was worried.

The decision to help settled my gut. "I'll drive you."

I walked to my SUV, hoping she'd follow.

"You don't have to," she said when I opened the passenger side door for her.

"I want to." I infused confidence into my words so she'd go along with it.

She climbed in, her gaze on the windshield.

Emotion filled the cracks and crevices of my heart. I was

worried about her, but it was something more. I wanted to help her if I could. I wanted to be there for her.

Sliding into the driver's seat, I turned on the SUV, glancing over at her before backing out. Her posture was stiff. Her arms wrapped around herself as if she was holding herself together.

"You're not alone in this. You have Reid, Dylan, and me." I'm sure it felt that way not having other relatives to help.

"I know." Her voice was soft as she looked out the window.

"Is he okay?"

She looked at me cautiously. "Yeah, I mean, he has early-onset Alzheimer's, so it's a matter of time before things progress. The medicine had been working."

I assumed it wasn't anymore. I leaned over, squeezing her knee. "You're worried."

"He's all I have."

"I know." That one admission, even though I already knew that was the case, splintered my heart. It cracked wide open for her.

He was the only family she had. I might have lost someone important to me, but I still had my parents, my sisters, my friends, and my teammates.

I handed her my phone. "Can you put his address in the GPS?"

I hoped focusing on something else would take her mind off what she'd lost, and her grandfather.

She typed quickly on the phone, handing it back to me. "Thank you."

"That's what friends are for." Was I her friend? I was her boss she'd kissed a couple of times. We'd crossed that line already. I studied her carefully before turning my attention to the road. Her brow was furrowed, her spine rigid.

She didn't acknowledge my statement which made me worry about her even more.

"He'll be okay."

Her gaze shifted from the road to me. "I thought I'd have more time."

"What's been going on?" I wanted to keep her talking.

"It wasn't often, but here and there he'd forget what we'd talked about, asking me the same questions all over again. Why are you here? Shouldn't you be in school when he knows I graduated. He'll forget what he was doing a second ago. It was disturbing but not bad as far as symptoms go."

"What's different now?"

"The nurses are saying he's more forgetful, more agitated. Eventually, he'll need to be placed in a specialized facility for Alzheimer's patients. He's supposed to be caring for himself where he is now."

I couldn't imagine losing someone slowly over time. Knowing it was coming, but not able to stop it. My chest ached for her. I wanted to say I'm sorry, but the words seemed trite for what I was feeling. "You're worried that it's coming soon."

Pain slid over her face. "Yeah."

I couldn't do anything to ease her pain. I felt so helpless to do anything. At the same time, I felt out of place. Reid should be here. He was friends with Frank. He's the one who's always been there for Callie.

It cost me to mention him when I wanted to be her go-to guy even if I couldn't explain why. I had no claim to her. "Do you want me to call Reid? Would he want to know?"

"I'll tell him." She leaned back, closing her eyes.

She was quiet the rest of the way to the facility. I turned right, pulling down a long drive to the sprawling home. There was lush green grass, a pavilion to visit with loved ones, and paths surrounding it. It seemed nice. Was money something she was worried about?

I parked, unhooking my seat belt.

Her eyes opened immediately. Stress lined her face.

"You ready to go in?"

She pulled the handle to get out. I wanted to reach out to take her hand like I had last night on the way to dinner, but we weren't on a date. We walked inside, I waited while she signed in and then lead the way back to his room. She paused at a door, turning to me. "Thanks for driving me. I can take an Uber home."

"No."

She crossed her arms, raising a brow. "No?"

"I'll stick around in case you need me."

She considered me for a moment before her shoulders relaxed. "Do you want to come in? If he's in a good mood, he loves talking football. If you don't mind?"

Her expression was vulnerable. She'd felt bad when that fan had interrupted our dinner, so I knew it cost her to ask me to play the part of a player for her grandfather.

"Sure." I wanted to say I'll do whatever you need, but it was too soon for that.

I followed her in, not sure what to expect. The man sat in a chair by the window. Callie moved closer, kissing his cheek before sitting next to him.

"How're you doing?" Callie's shoulders were still tense.

"They keep bringing me breakfast. I already ate."

Frank turned, seeing me in the doorway. "Come sit down. Don't just stand there."

His words were clipped.

"Jonah, this is my grandfather, Frank. Grandpa, this is Jonah, he plays football with Reid."

Frank turned in his chair, a spark of recognition in his eyes. "JT?"

"Yes, sir." I was JT with my fans, most people in fact, but I liked being Jonah to Callie. I moved farther into the room, stuffing my hands in my pockets. I wasn't sure what to do with my hands or where to sit. Frank and Callie were seated in two of the chairs. The bed was neatly made.

"You're friends with the players now?" he asked Callie.

"I work with him at the sports complex."

At his blank look, she continued, "Remember, Reid opened a sports complex. He asked me to manage it. Jonah is one of the investors."

From his blank expression, it was clear he didn't remember.

Callie chewed her lip.

I moved things off a chair in the corner so I could sit.

We watched TV quietly for a few minutes. It was sports highlights.

"How's your knee?" Frank tipped his head toward my injured leg.

If it had been anyone else asking, I would have been annoyed, but this was Callie's grandfather. She shot me a pleading look, one that begged me to humor him.

"It's been better." I went for light.

"I bet. You going to be ready to play soon?" The sharpness in his eyes and his question told me he was fully present.

"I hope so."

He nodded. "We sure could use you out there."

"I want to be on the field." There was something about his words that warmed my chest, easing the pressure inside. Other fans were less nice about it. They accused me of losing the last game and ruining their shot at the playoffs.

"You gotta keep up with your therapy." He nodded reasonably as if we knew each other well enough to give advice.

Callie shot him a look. "Don't you need to as well? The nurse said you refused to go this morning."

His expression turned blank. "No one came to take me for therapy this morning."

Callie sighed, patting his hand. "Okay."

I wished I'd had some time to look up his disease, do some research on the best way to talk to someone whose memory came and went. I took my cue from Callie, she seemed to go with it, not arguing with him.

A few minutes later, Frank said, "You took a hard hit. It woulda knocked anyone for a loop."

Fans said all kinds of things to me. I usually nodded, signed my name on whatever they held up to me, and took a picture with them. Something about him saying it was okay was nice.

"That's football though, right?"

Frank nodded. "You take the hard hits and keep getting up."

"That's right." It's what my coaches had always said. It didn't matter what the fans said, you keep getting up and working hard.

"You'll be fine."

Something about his confidence made me want to believe him. I wanted to ask him if he meant I'd play again or if I'd be okay in general. He was so sure of himself, so confident, yet he had memory issues. Who knows if he even knew what he was saying?

"I hope so, sir."

The nurse paused in the doorway. "Oh good. You're here. Do you have a minute to talk?"

"Of course," Callie said to her. She paused, placing a hand on my shoulder, "You'll be okay with him for a minute?"

"We'll talk football. Go," Frank said.

"I'll be right back," Callie said, following the nurse out of the room.

"You take care of her?"

I braced my elbows on my knees, searching for the right thing to say. "I don't think she needs anyone to do that."

"She's never brought you by before." Frank wanted to know why I was here.

"She seemed upset. I didn't think she should drive here

alone." I went for a partial truth. It wasn't completely altruistic.

Frank nodded, seemingly pleased with my answer. "This is your first big injury."

He knew enough about me to know my history. "It is."

"How you deal with it will be a test of your character." I could see why Callie was so upset about Frank losing his memory. He was wise.

"I haven't dealt with it the best." Only a few weeks ago, I'd been drinking too much, I'd kissed my employee twice, and now I was here, somewhere I had no business being.

"How are you doing now?" Frank considered me.

"Better. My teammates sat me down. My head's on straight now."

"You're not always going to make the right decisions. It's how you evaluate where you're going, changing course when necessary, that defines you."

Talking to Frank, I felt like a man who was worthy of a spot on a professional team. I didn't feel like the guy hiding his past, putting on a facade, pretending to be someone— anyone—else.

He settled back into his chair, crossing his arms over his chest. "Who are you to Callie?"

"I'm her boss." I shifted, not liking his focus on my personal life. Football I could handle.

"I thought Reid was her boss."

"He is. I'm only a silent investor in the sports complex. I'm helping out while I'm out of commission."

"Callie asked you to come here?"

I wasn't sure if he'd forgotten our earlier conversation or not. "She looked like she could use some company."

"Are you dating her?" He gave me a pointed look.

"No." Kissing wasn't dating, yet I felt dishonest with Frank's intense gaze on me.

Frank nodded. "You like her."

I cleared my throat, wanting nothing more than to get out of this conversation. I wasn't ready for it.

Frank chuckled. "No need to answer. Would a man drive all that way to meet with an old man if he isn't interested?"

"I care about her." That admission cost me because the last time I'd cared about someone, it hadn't ended well. Caring about someone meant taking an important role in their happiness, *their safety*. I wasn't sure I was ready for that.

I tensed, waiting for him to call me on my uncertainty but instead, he nodded, seemingly accepting my words at face value.

The conversation changed to Frank's life, what so and so was doing down the hall, the activities, the nurses, but my mind was split between the conversation with him and what the nurse was saying to Callie in the hall. She'd been gone a long time. I wanted to know what was going on.

When Callie finally returned to the room, her face was tight before she carefully relaxed it, greeting Frank before she sat down. I wanted to ask her what the nurse said, but I didn't think she'd want to discuss it in front of Frank.

"What do you think about the rookie?" Frank nodded toward the screen where they were discussing training camp. A picture of the recently acquired rookie wide receiver came on the screen.

My heart stopped then raced forward. "He's gunning for my position."

It's what I would do if I was him. Go for the weak link. Being on injured reserve was a tenuous position I didn't like.

"He has a similar style of play."

I'd noticed. I didn't like it. Of course, a coach would prefer to replace me with someone younger and faster.

"Youth isn't everything, Grandpa. Jonah has the experience of a veteran. That can't be discounted, especially in high-pressured situations like playoff games. He's a leader."

Frank didn't acknowledge Callie's words but they flowed through me, making me feel like I could do anything.

~

ON THE WAY HOME, I SAID, "THANKS FOR LETTING ME MEET Frank. He's one of a kind."

He loved football. He was a good man. One who wanted the best for Callie. I was glad she had someone in her corner. My heart ached that he wouldn't always be there for her. How was she handling that knowledge?

"Thank you for answering his questions. He's obsessed with football."

"I didn't mind." I was more than a statistic to him. He cared about how I was doing, not just when I'd be catching balls again for his team or boosting his fantasy football stats.

"I know how irritating it can be—fans wanting a piece of you all the time."

"It wasn't like that." Even if he was, Frank was important to Callie, so he was important to me. Even if I never acted on my attraction to her in the future, she was someone I wanted in my life.

"Sometimes it feels like I'm an avatar running around on a screen to people. Like they don't realize I'm a real person with feelings, hopes, and ambitions. It's all about how I lost the game for them, or how my statistics made their fantasy football team lose."

"Give the fans a glimpse into who you really are. You're not just a football player, you're a real person. Then they'll identify with you."

Every muscle in my body coiled tight. Being me meant being honest about my past. I'd never be okay with that.

"It's almost like you're a different guy with the fans."

"I don't think there's any requirement I have to let them

in." I rubbed my neck, wanting to change the subject, move the focus off me.

"There isn't, but you were the one complaining how they don't see you as a person. You're the only one who can change that."

No one wanted to know who I was before. I didn't even want to know that guy, much less be him.

"What did the nurse say about Frank?" I desperately wanted to shift the focus to anywhere else but me.

She sighed, long and hard. "He's getting worse. They can keep him for a bit longer, but I need to start thinking about moving him to a facility that's equipped to deal with an Alzheimer's patient. He's in personal care, so he's supposed to be taking care of himself. I can't be there every day because of where I work."

"You can take any time you need to be with him. I know Reid won't care."

"I'm not equipped to handle his disease either. When he was diagnosed, he said he didn't want to be a burden to me. He wouldn't want me quitting my job to care for him."

"I can see that." Frank seemed like a proud man. It was commendable he looked out for Callie and wanted what was best for her.

The fear and stress emanated from her.

"It'll be okay."

"It's just so overwhelming. They gave me a list of possible facilities. Looking at them makes it real."

"I'd like to help any way I can." There wasn't much I could do. Other than being there for her.

"There's a new medication that just came out, but it's not approved for general use yet, so it's not covered by insurance."

I wondered if she'd born this stress by herself ever since Frank was diagnosed. "Do you have anyone helping you? Friends? Family?"

She sighed. "No. It's just me."

I knew Reid visited with Frank, but they were friends. I didn't know if he was a support system for Callie.

"Are you close with Dylan?" I knew her mother suffered from some health issues. She might be able to give her advice.

"We're becoming friends."

"She might be able to help." I didn't want to betray her confidence if she hadn't discussed her mother's situation, but I wanted to point Callie in the right direction. I wanted to do something to help.

"I'll talk to her."

I usually shied away from people needing me. I'd proven that I wasn't reliable, but maybe with Callie, I could be different. The hope wasn't that strong. It was more like a flicker of a candle that would blow out at the slightest gust of wind, but it was there.

CHAPTER ELEVEN

CALLIE

ON THE RIDE BACK TO WORK, MY HEAD ACHED. I KNEW THIS day was coming, but I hoped I'd have more time before I had to make this decision. I needed to do some research before I talked to my grandfather. The nurse was understanding but adamant they weren't equipped to handle Alzheimer's patients, especially not in the personal care unit where he was expected to do more for himself.

If his mind kept going, he would need specialized care, more than they could provide. The difference in cost between personal care, a nursing home, and an Alzheimer's facility was huge. I hoped I'd have more time to prepare, a longer work history, a higher salary to draw from.

I wanted to be able to afford that new medication, especially if it made a difference.

Instead, I was in a new job where my position wasn't guaranteed. Reid was helping me out, doing me a favor, but we all knew I wasn't the most qualified candidate for the job. If I couldn't deliver, Reid would have to replace me or move me to a lower-paying position. He wouldn't want to do it, but he'd have no choice. It was a good reminder to be careful with

Jonah. He might be looking for a way to pass the time, but I had a lot to lose.

After talking to the nurse, I'd gone to the bathroom, pulling up the costs of some of the homes on her recommended list. The monthly costs were staggering. Insurance only covered a percentage.

Jonah wanting to help in any way he could was nice, but realistically, there wasn't anything he could do. Taking care of my grandfather was my responsibility.

"Are you sure you're okay?" Jonah asked.

His concern was sweet.

I forced myself to relax, to smile. "Yeah, I will be. I was expecting this—"

Jonah glanced over at me, his concerned gaze drifting over me before he turned back to the road. "Just not so soon."

"I'll figure it out." I'd make a list of the pros and cons of each facility. I'd make a spreadsheet of accommodations, prices, and locations.

Parking in front of Rebel Sports, I tried to pull myself together. Jonah was my boss. I needed to show him personal stuff wouldn't affect my job performance.

With my hand on the door, I said, "Thanks for driving me."

"No problem." He made no move to get out. "Keep me updated on Frank. I'd like to know how he's doing."

His words were sincere.

"I will."

"I meant what I said. I want to be there for you, whatever you need."

I sighed. "There's not much you can do."

He nodded. "I can listen. I can go with you to visit Frank."

"Why would you though?" I looked at him, studying the sincerity of his expression.

That question seemed to make him pause. "I care about you."

His declaration felt different than Reid's friendship with Frank. Jonah cared about Frank because of me. A warmth spread through my body, making my breathing shallow, my head light.

In a lot of ways, I'd been on my own since my parents died. It would be nice to have a sounding board, someone to lean on.

"I have an idea for the grand opening," Jonah said as we walked into the complex toward our offices.

I was happy to shift from worrying about my grandfather to something more within my control—the grand opening. "I'd love to hear it."

"I thought it would be cool to have a football competition like what they do before the big game each year. Separated by age group of course, but how far can you throw, how fast can you run, how accurate are your passes…"

"I love that idea." I knew exactly what he was talking about. It was always televised before the game. It would be the perfect activity to highlight the fact that football was a big part of the complex's focus.

"Yeah?"

We paused outside of his office.

"It sounds fun. Hopefully, it will attract a lot of local kids who'd want to participate in the leagues and camps."

He leaned against the doorframe as if he wasn't ready to end the conversation. "I thought so too."

"We talked about you heading up the mentor program, are you still interested?"

He pushed off the doorway, heading into his office.

Had I said something wrong?

He sat in his chair, gesturing for me to do the same. "Are you sure I'm the right guy for the job?"

Where was this doubt coming from? "You have to know you're amazing with fans, especially kids."

His expression was uncertain. "I don't know. Wouldn't Chase or Reid be the better option?"

I was genuinely confused by his hesitance. It was something I'd expect from Reid, not him. "You've never backed away from a PR opportunity before, why now?"

"First of all, Lena doesn't pose it as a question." Jonah's mouth turned into an easy smile almost making me forget his show of nerves.

"True, but I didn't expect you to say no."

"I'm not saying no, I just wanted to make sure."

There was something about his hesitance, the uncertainty, and almost pain I saw in his gaze, then his swift switch back to the cool, nonchalant acceptance that had my instincts tingling.

His face was that facade I knew so well. The one he wore with fans. He'd been more real in our last few interactions. It hurt that when I asked for something deeper, he'd reverted back to his old self.

He tilted his head. "Was there anything else?"

"I guess not." I chewed my lip, wondering if I should dig deeper. "Is there more to you questioning your ability to be a mentor?"

"I said I'd do it." His shoulders were stiff.

"You went with me to see Grandpa today. I can be there for you too."

But his expression was closed off. I wasn't going to reach him right now. His walls were up.

Then I did what I'd done the other night in his SUV when he'd been so quiet, I stood, touching his forearm, the muscle under my fingers flexing.

His expression softened as his gaze moved to my hand on his arm. It was technically inappropriate to touch a coworker, especially one that was technically my supervisor, but with a guy like him, words weren't enough. He seemed to respond to my touch. Whether my touch was different than anyone else's, I wasn't sure.

"Anytime you want to talk, I'm here. No judgment." I squeezed his arm before walking away. The warmth of his skin sent tingles through my body.

I didn't expect him to open up, not today, but maybe he will eventually. There was more to Jonah than this happy guy he appeared to be with everyone else. It was almost as if underneath, he wasn't as confident. Did he not think he was good enough to be a mentor?

It was hard to imagine a professional football player not being cocky and sure of himself, but Reid hadn't been confident. Maybe Jonah was like that too.

One thing was certain, I liked hanging out with him when his control slipped, when he was the real Jonah. The one who was vulnerable, who offered to drive me to the nursing home because I was upset, who sat and talked to my grandfather because *he cared about me.* That was the guy I wanted to know.

It had nothing to do with the fact I still thought about that kiss in the gym or that my skin heated each time it came to mind. If I stopped thinking of him as this cocky player, then I'd start thinking of the vulnerable side he'd showed me. That side was addicting. That side had me craving more of him, and it wasn't just his kiss and touch I wanted. I wanted to know who he was on a fundamental level—what he did in his spare time, did he have friends outside the team, and did he have dreams and aspirations outside football?

Talking to him, kissing him, did nothing to quell my curiosity, it only made it burn hotter.

CHAPTER TWELVE

JONAH

THE LAST FEW DAYS, CALLIE LEFT THE OFFICE TO VISIT FRANK before I came in. I wanted to help, but she hadn't invited me. I had no reason to show up. Not knowing what was going on was driving me crazy. My fingers hovered over her name on my contact list. As her friend, it was okay to ask for an update.

Jonah: How is Frank?

I waited a bit for her to answer, going through the changes to the website, making notes on things that weren't working or could use a design tweak. Finally, my phone buzzed.

Callie: He's okay.

He might be but she probably wasn't. I hated to use work as an excuse to see her, but we did need to go over the schedule for the grand opening, and I wanted to make sure she was okay.

Jonah: We need to go over the grand opening. Want to meet in the city?

I held my breath, waiting for her to see through me, to know I was using work to see her. My phone buzzed.

"Callie?"

"Hey, sorry. I'm driving. Can't text."

"Gotcha. What do you say? Want to meet in the city for

dinner." I checked the time on my computer. "If I leave now, I can get there in forty-five minutes, assuming there's no traffic on a Friday night."

"I really don't mind coming to the office. I've been taking off all week."

"Don't worry about it. Frank's more important." I knew Reid would agree.

I could see Callie was doing her work. She emailed spreadsheets and updates each morning. I figured she was working late at night to keep up.

She sighed. The sound coming through the phone making my chest tighten with worry.

I had to see her, to make sure she was okay with whatever was happening with Frank. I wanted to help. I just wasn't sure what I could do other than be there for her.

"Look. I don't want you driving while you're tired. I can meet you at your apartment."

"Mine? Oh, that's okay. I can come to yours."

I liked the idea of having her in my space, but I wanted to do what was easiest for her. "You'll be in the city before me. Go home and rest. I'll pick up dinner."

"Thanks, Jonah. That does sound kind of great."

"Drive safe." I got off the phone, packing up my stuff. What would it be like if she was my girlfriend and we met up for dinner after work? I let myself sink deeper into that delusion as I drove to the city. The warmth settling in my chest felt good. I wanted to hold on to this feeling.

I sent her a picture of the subs when I picked them up. She texted me back her address. She lived near the university. Made sense since she went there for so many years.

I parked, ringing the buzzer for her apartment. I wondered if she lived alone, or whether she had roommates.

Walking up the dim stairs of her old building, anticipation built to see her. I knocked on her door, wondering what I was doing. When had I ever used an excuse to get closer to a girl?

She opened the door, her hair pulled back into a low ponytail, wearing a tank and shorts. She stepped back, gesturing for me to come in. "Sorry, I wanted to get comfortable."

"Don't worry about it. This is a casual work thing." A casual work thing? Where was the charm I was known for?

The lines on her face smoothed out as she relaxed.

I closed the door behind me, following her into the kitchen, placing the subs on the small island in the kitchen. It was open to her living room, which consisted of a small couch and a TV on a chest. It reminded me of how I lived in college —with the bare minimum—back when we were waiting on our chance at the big time. A way out of whatever situation we were in.

"Let's eat on the couch." Callie opened a cupboard, pulling out two glasses, the hem of her shirt drifting up so that a sliver of her toned stomach showed.

I swallowed hard. I wanted to touch her there, to see if her skin was as soft as it looked. I wanted to come up behind her, touching her stomach, pulling her against me so she could feel how she affected me. The desire was so potent, I ripped my gaze from her, looking at the chipped counter between us.

Taking a deep breath, I asked, "Where are your plates?"

She filled the glasses with water, slicing lemons to flavor it.

"Right there." She pointed at the cabinet next to the sink.

I didn't want to watch her move around the kitchen, relaxed and comfortable with her skin on display. It was an entrancing mix of too much yet not enough. I was here for business, not to get in her pants.

Satisfied with my pep talk, I sat next to her on the small couch since there was no other seating. She slowly unwrapped her sub. "Thanks for coming and bringing dinner."

"You're tired." Up close, I saw the dark smudges under her eyes as if she hadn't been sleeping.

"This week has been tough. I knew this was coming, but

it's so hard to see the man I loved, the one who was always sharp, forget things. It's just little things here and there. But I know—" She looked at me, her expression pained. "At some point, I'm going to walk into his room and he's not going to know who I am. And then—" She broke off, dropping her head.

You'll have no one. I couldn't voice her fears out loud. I couldn't say what we were both thinking. It would break the small amount of control she seemed to use to hold herself together.

"I can't imagine how hard that is." My words weren't enough. I'd never experienced a slow, drawn-out loss of someone I loved.

She drew in a shaky breath, her gaze on the TV. "We talked about his diagnosis when he got it. What to do when he moved to the next stage when things got worse. This morning, the nurse gave me a list of facilities he had researched. He'd taken detailed notes of each one. Things he wanted to ask or know. What he wanted."

"That's helpful." I choked out the words. My throat was tight. My hands itched to draw her close.

"I want to do what he wants. It's the only thing I can control in this situation.

"He wanted to make it easier for you." Having met Frank, it didn't surprise me. He wanted to protect her. It was the same feeling she'd evoked in Reid, and now me. The only difference was my feelings for her went beyond being support-ive. I wanted to comfort her physically as well as emotionally. I wanted to be the one she talked to about this stuff at the end of the day.

The fact that Frank made decisions that made things easier for Callie, moving to the personal care home so she wouldn't feel responsible for him in college, researching Alzheimer's facilities before she'd need to move him to one. It made me respect him even more. "He's looking out for you."

"I can look after myself. He doesn't want to be a burden, but he'd never be one. He's been my rock since——"

I moved our subs to the coffee table. I wanted to put my arm around her, but I wasn't sure that would be okay. Instead, I touched her knee. I meant it to be an innocent touch, but her shorts were threadbare and soft underneath my skin. Her heat singed the palm of my hand.

Did she lean closer to me? I placed my other arm over her shoulders. When she sagged into my touch, I relaxed.

I snuggled closer, my chin in her hair, breathing in her scent. "It'll be okay. You're doing everything right. You're there for him. You're making the tough decisions."

"It's so hard." She spoke softly into my chest, but I heard the pain in her words.

I couldn't imagine losing someone slowly over time. Knowing it was coming yet dreading it at the same time. I tried to imagine how it would feel if my mother didn't remember something I'd said. If suddenly she didn't remember me. The pain was hot and searing, stealing my breath.

I pulled her tighter to me. Her hand pressed solidly against my chest.

Could she feel how fast my heart was beating?

She pulled away abruptly. "You didn't come here for this. I'm so sorry."

I kind of did though. "I wanted to make sure you were okay."

The admission felt rusty on my lips. I usually steered clear of emotional entanglements. This girl was testing my boundaries without even trying.

She turned her head away from me, swiping under her eyes. "I'll be okay."

She picked up her sub, resting it on her lap.

Being here eased an ache in my chest. Even if I couldn't do much to ease her stress, being present was something.

I didn't eat until she took a bite, chewing slowly before taking another. I could make sure she ate, that she took care of herself. It was something, even if it wasn't enough.

Eating in silence, she didn't bother to turn on the TV or even music for background noise. I was content to be in her presence, being that rock she'd described.

She was the most genuine person I'd spent time with lately. When she was upset, you knew it. Her emotions weren't orchestrated for attention. She didn't want or need anything from me. In fact, she repeatedly told me she didn't want to be a burden to anyone.

Standing, she wrapped what was left of her sub, placing it in the fridge. Turning back to me she asked, "Are you ready to work?"

That was my excuse for being here, even if I didn't want to think about the sports complex. Nothing mattered more than how she was feeling. "Sure."

She sat next to me, pulling her laptop closer. "This is what I have so far."

She pulled up the itinerary she'd emailed to Reid and me this morning. "You're in charge of the football competition since it was your idea."

"That works." I took the last bite of my sub then stood to throw out the trash.

"Do you think you could get your teammates to show up and help with it? The kids will love it. We won't advertise it. It could be a nice surprise, and having the support of your team would be nice."

"Sure."

"I'll walk around, making sure things are running smoothly and no one feels left out. Reid will talk to potential donors, answer questions, and deal with the media."

I relaxed into the cushions. "He's come a long way. I remember when he'd avoid cameras at all costs."

"True." A smile played on her lips. "Dylan's good for him."

That made me pause. Was that what a relationship was? Being there for someone, supporting them, encouraging them to do things they wouldn't otherwise. Be good for them? It sounded great.

"I haven't had many relationships since high school." None really, but I couldn't tell her that. She'd think I was a player, a freak, or something.

"No?" she paused, waiting for me to expound on my answer.

Why had I said anything at all? I opened myself up to more questions. I went with part of the truth. "It's tough to find someone who isn't looking to be with a player."

"Ah. Yeah. I remember Reid talking about that, but he was more closed off than you. I don't think women chased him as much."

The irony was I was closed off. No one knew the guy I was underneath. I didn't even know him anymore. He was buried under the quintessential football player, fun teammate, and hardworking athlete.

"I never thought I'd say this, but it must be hard to date as a professional athlete. Never knowing who wants you for you."

Did I want someone to want me for me? To do that, I'd have to open up to them. "It is."

She studied me.

I cleared my throat then drank a large sip of water. Had I said something wrong? Was it my expression? Could I be with her but not open up, at least not entirely? Would she be okay with that? We had chemistry. I cared about her. Was that enough to see where this went, knowing it could only go so far?

"I guess I'm as much at fault. I figure you have these women surrounding you. It's so easy for you, but it's not."

"You must have the same issue, hanging around the team.

The guys must hit on you," I teased, wanting to take the focus from me.

She smiled. "You know Reid took care of that. No one has dared."

The words left unspoken were *except for me.* I had already. I'd kissed her twice.

"What about the other teams?"

She blushed. "I always say I have a boyfriend. When I was in school, I was focused on graduating, now I'm taking care of my grandfather, worried about making enough to afford his care. I don't have time for a boyfriend, especially not an athlete."

My brain tripped on the word *afford,* but I let it go for now. "You love football."

"I do. It doesn't mean I want to date a player."

This was interesting. I don't think I'd ever had anyone tell me that. "But why not? What do you have against us?"

"Players can be cocky. What's going on with them might come first. I want to be equal in the relationship. If the guy plays for a team in another city, it's unlikely he'd want to date. He's just looking for some fun."

"That's smart."

I'd been contemplating kissing her again, taking whatever this was to the next level. I hadn't considered that she might not be interested. That was a rookie mistake. I should have considered all angles.

Usually, when I went for something, I got it. At least when it came to sports and my career. Would it be the same if I wanted to make her mine? Or would she think of me as a cocky player, one that was only looking for a good time?

I rubbed my sweaty palms on my jeans, wondering why I was stressing over a woman. I couldn't remember the last time the woman hadn't been interested in me first. It was a different feeling, sitting next to this beautiful woman, wondering what she was thinking, whether I was good enough for her. Would she think I was smart or a dumb jock? My biggest asset wasn't in my favor. She didn't care that I was a football player.

I rested my elbows on my knees. "You've never been tempted, not even once?"

I spoke slowly, emphasizing each word. I held my breath, her answer mattered.

Her breath caught. Her face flushed. "Maybe."

She wasn't being coy, not like I was used to. She was flustered. Her eyes cast down, she was embarrassed. God, she was sweet. Too sweet for me. I had no business going after her, but I couldn't stop.

I wanted to ask if I was the exception, but I wanted to make the right play. Something told me that this moment would define our relationship going forward. Were we coworkers, friends, or something more? The kiss we'd shared told me the potential upside was huge.

She licked her lips, and the words I wanted to say disappeared. Inching closer, the blood pounded in my ears. She looked up in surprise, when her eyes met mine, they heated.

She wanted me. There was no question.

I had to kiss her one more time. I wanted to eliminate the space between us. I ached to touch her. I cupped her cheek, tipping her to the right angle. She was so soft, and for this moment, she was mine.

Our lips touched, the touch was light, then I kissed her again, deepening the kiss, moving closer to her. Her smell surrounded me; my blood hummed in my veins. When her lips parted, I'd never experienced anything sweeter. Her fingers knotted in my shirt, pulling me closer.

Pulling back slightly, I whispered, "Callie."

I wasn't sure what I wanted, maybe some indication she wanted this too. Her eyes were bright with desire, her fingers still held me tight.

"Yes," she hissed.

My lips crashed down on hers, harder, more insistent than before. I'd never experienced anything like this. I'd never felt anything for another woman except for my high school sweetheart, but we were young. We didn't know how life could smack you down or lift you up. I didn't know it could be this good.

Being near Callie, touching her was a rush, one I never wanted to end.

She whimpered, the sound doing something to my insides, squeezing them, making it hard to catch my breath. Leaning back on the couch, I was overcome with emotion. Something I'd never felt from merely kissing a woman before.

"Jonah, what's wrong?" A hint of insecurity shot through her expression.

I reached for her, encouraging her to straddle my lap. "There's nothing wrong."

For a second, I wondered if I was merely an escape for her, a way to forget about her troubles with her grandfather. As soon as the idea entered my mind, I pushed it away. Her reasons shouldn't matter.

I brushed her hair back from her face, my fingers trembling with my desire to slow down. "I don't want to rush this. I want to savor you."

She lifted a leg, straddling my hips.

I ignored my aching dick that wanted more contact, ignoring the impulse to lift my hips.

She was too good for me. As much as I wanted her, I'd let her make the next move.

CHAPTER THIRTEEN
CALLIE

My heart pounded under my ribs. I wanted to feel the bite of his grip, the softness of his lips, the scruff of his chin against my skin.

His blue eyes were fixed on my face, his tight grip on my hip anchoring me in place. The expression on his face was one of awe as if he couldn't believe I was here with him. He'd said I was different than the other women he'd dated, but I wasn't looking for anything serious. I wanted to forget about what the nurses were saying, what my grandfather was going through.

I leaned forward, kissing him.

He groaned, bucking his hips so I felt every inch of his hardening erection. The friction from the movement sent tendrils of desire curling through me.

His free hand drifted up my shirt, my abs spasming at the light touch on my stomach. When his hand inched upward, my nipples hardened; heat spread like wildfire through my body.

I wasn't going to worry about what this meant for our working relationship. We'd kissed a couple of times, and it hadn't changed anything. This wouldn't either. I needed this too much to back out, to make excuses, to worry about the future. There was only the here and now, the sensations, his touch, his scent, and the emotions rolling through me, one after another.

His large hand settled over one lace-covered breast. I paused, my mouth hovering over his. This was the moment to back away, to say this was a mistake, to beg him not to hold this against me at work. But I didn't want to stop.

He gently squeezed, his thumb strumming my pebbled nipple. I moved over him, chasing contact, something to ease this ache inside. The emptiness inside of me could only be filled by him.

"Jonah." *I need you. Inside me. Over me. Pressing me into the mattress.*

The images flowed through my mind, one after the other. I wanted nothing between us, just the feel of slick skin.

He stood abruptly, his arm banded around my lower back, my legs wrapping around his waist. It was a rush to be picked up this way. Even with his injured knee, he didn't miss a beat, striding down the hall to my bedroom, slowly lowering me onto the mattress.

I would have expected him to let me bounce a little, a cocky smirk on his lips. Instead, he'd followed me onto the mattress, hovering over me, his forearm braced next to my shoulder. His expression was serious, his eyes dark with desire for me.

I licked my lips, wanting to urge him on, yet wanting to see what he'd do next. Jonah was nothing like I expected.

He cupped my cheek, and a dam burst inside me, sending heat soaring through my body. My skin heated, my face flushed. I tugged his shirt up, my fingers spread over the taut skin of his back. His muscles flexed at the contact.

When had I ever reveled in each moment, the feel of someone's skin under mine, the softness, the heat? The weight of his lower body pressing me down. I wanted to hold on to each sensation.

If I thought he would go hard and fast, I was wrong. He seemed in no rush as he pushed my shirt up, lowering his head to kiss my stomach. My muscles jerked in response. My fingers tangled in his sandy blond hair.

He was destroying me with his touch and the slow glide of his tongue over my skin. I wanted the friction of his cock between my legs, but he held himself away from me. He reached around my back to unsnap my bra.

My breasts were swollen, aching for his touch. The anticipation was killing me. Impatient, I lifted myself, pulling off my shirt and bra. Leaning on my hands, the air cooled my overheated skin.

"Gorgeous." Jonah leaned forward, taking one nipple into his mouth; the slight scrape of his teeth zinged like lightning to my core.

That one word pierced my heart, causing my eyes to sting with unexpected tears. I closed my eyes, dropping down to my back on the cool sheets, my shaky arms unable to hold my weight any longer. I'd never felt so much with a guy before. Sensation after sensation flowed through my body, making me hyperaware of every move and shift of his body.

He turned his attention to my other nipple. He lowered his hips between my legs, slowly dragging his jean-clad cock over my pussy.

My breath caught, need building inside me. He licked my nipple, then scraped it with his teeth, soothing it with his tongue at the same time, setting a rhythm with his hips that drove me wild with desire.

"Jonah, please." I'd been reduced to whimpers and pleas.

I was hot. I tugged hard at his shirt until he settled back on his knees, pulling it over his head with one hand.

"I want to feel you." I wanted him naked, skin against skin, the prickle of his hair against my smooth legs. I didn't want to miss any part of this.

He stood at the bottom of the bed, shucking his pants,

pulling a condom from his wallet. I hooked my fingers at the waistband of my shorts.

"Wait." That one word, spoken softly, made me pause.

He kneeled between my legs, his cock jutting out. "I want to do it."

I wanted him in my mouth, but he kissed my stomach. Moving lower, he slowly slid my shorts over my hips and off my legs. Grabbing my ankles, he pulled me to the end of the bed. The air did nothing to cool my pussy.

I usually couldn't relax enough to enjoy oral. I was too worried about what I tasted like and what noises I made. If anyone could make me lose any sense of control, it was Jonah. I wanted his mouth on me.

I lifted my hips in silent invitation. I felt wanton.

Jonah blew air over my throbbing clit.

My thighs trembled. I lifted onto my elbows, the sight of Jonah on his knees caused my heart to stutter. "Please, Jonah."

With his eyes on mine, he licked my opening, circling my clit. It was light, too light to satisfy the burning need inside me.

His fingers gripped the skin of my inner thighs; his shoulders held my legs apart. His hair was mussed from my fingers. His eyes held a challenge as if there was nothing more important than giving me pleasure.

The feeling was heady. I was determined to enjoy each moment, to remember it for later.

When his tongue slipped inside, he increased his rhythm, my hips moving on their own accord. I needed more. I needed his cock inside me. Falling onto the mattress, his finger entered me, his mouth closing over my clit. Moans ripped from my throat as the orgasm built to a feverish pitch. My body bowed off the bed when I went over the cliff. I gasped as white light burst under my eyelids.

"Jonah, Jonah, Jonah." His name fell from my lips. I needed more. I needed him filling me up.

With an arm banded around my back, he gently moved me farther up the bed, his cock teasing my entrance.

"Yes," I hissed, encouraging him to go deeper.

His muscles tensed, holding himself back. He lifted away to rip open the condom wrapper, sliding it down his cock.

When he positioned himself between my legs, I gripped his biceps. "I want you, Jonah."

My words unleashed something inside him because his hips snapped forward, his cock surged inside, filling me to the hilt.

He felt so good. I felt every ridge of his cock even through the condom. Everything with him was so much bigger and brighter.

"You're so beautiful."

For a flash, I wondered if he said something similar to other women he'd been with, but his expression was so raw. He was sincere.

When had sex ever felt like this? I felt special, cherished even.

It was only one night, yet there was this weight in the air between us. Tingles erupted over my skin.

Then he moved, my thoughts drifting away with each thrust until I was mindless, the need building quicker and bigger than last time.

He leaned down, kissing my neck, my chin, my lips. "So good."

Sweat glistened on his chest, his muscles flexing with each push and pull. My hips lifted to meet him. His pelvis grinding against my clit with each thrust until the orgasm rushed through me.

I was vaguely aware of him saying, "Fuck, yes."

His movements were jerky as he thrust one last time, emptying himself into the condom. He lowered himself over my body. His weight grounded me, keeping me in this moment with him.

I closed my eyes, breathing in his scent, savoring the feel of skin against mine. I tried not to think about what came next, enjoying the aftermath.

Finally, he lifted up slightly, kissing me. "I need to clean up."

He moved off the bed, closing the door to the bathroom.

Boneless, I stayed where I was. The slowly rotating ceiling fan cooled my skin.

I closed my eyes, listening to the water run.

Jonah opened the door, crossing the room. I braced myself for cool indifference, for him to lean down to pull on his jeans, to walk out of my apartment. Instead, he placed a knee on the bed, moving a strand of hair off my temple.

"You're so beautiful." His eyes were dazed as if he couldn't believe I was here. That he was with me.

I nestled my face into his hand, then turned to kiss his palm.

Something like awe flashed in his eyes. "I don't deserve you. I don't deserve this."

"Why—" my voice cracked. My throat was dry. "Why do you think that?"

He was the professional athlete, the superstar. I was the nobody in this scenario.

"You're so sweet. Too sweet for me." There was a haunted expression on his face.

I licked my lips, wondering what his past was like that he thought this way. I didn't want anything from him, but it had to be more than that. Something had happened to him, making him think he didn't deserve good things or good people in his life. "That's not true."

He laid down beside me, propped up on his elbow. "It is."

I shifted, tucking my hand beneath my cheek, facing him. "Why do you think that?"

Indecision warred with longing on his face.

He wanted to confide in me.

I just wasn't sure he would.

"I've done things. Things that I'm ashamed of."

My forehead wrinkled in confusion. "What would you have to be ashamed of?"

Was he talking about treating women callously? Maybe having one-night stands? It was almost expected with athletes, but I'd never seen him treat anyone with anything other than respect.

He plopped onto his back, his forearm shielding his eyes. He was shutting down, blocking me out.

It was too soon to push. I'd be there for him like he was for me. I curled into his side, resting my head on his bicep. I kissed his chest. "You don't have to tell me."

I only wanted one night. Confessions weren't required no matter how much his vulnerability tugged on my heartstrings.

His arm moved from his eyes to wrap around me, pulling me tighter to him. It was as if me being here was holding him together, preventing him from shattering. I wanted to be there for him. I wanted to be his person. The longing was acute; my breath came in short pants.

"Are you okay? I didn't hurt you, did I?"

He was so sweet, so caring, so attentive. How could he think he wasn't worthy of me?

"No. Of course not." I kissed the underside of his jaw, enjoying being able to touch him when I wanted. I wasn't sure I'd be as free tomorrow.

His fingers gripped my hair. It was a reassuring pressure.

In a few seconds, he relaxed, his breath evening out.

He wasn't leaving. He'd fallen asleep.

I thought being with him would be an escape, a chance to block out what was going on with me, instead, it opened me up to him and whatever he was struggling with. I hope I'd soothed him like he had me. I hoped he'd be here when I woke up.

CHAPTER FOURTEEN

JONAH

I woke up with hair tickling my chin. My shoulder was stiff, and my back was sore from sleeping in the same position all night. Callie's scent filled my senses. I wasn't ready to wake up. I wasn't ready for the morning after.

I never slept overnight with a woman. I usually left immediately after or woke up in the middle of the night. It must mean something that I was so comfortable with Callie I slept like a rock.

She shifted in my arms, snuggling closer to my side. Her hand drifted down to my stomach. My muscles clenched in response. Was she awake?

She kissed my chest. "You stayed."

I stiffened. I wasn't sure what to say. I had stayed, but it wasn't exactly intentional. In the bathroom, I'd worried about what to do. Leaving didn't feel right. Then when I came out to see her laying in the same spot I'd left her, I had to touch her. I felt compelled to climb back into bed with her. Then I'd said something I shouldn't have, but she didn't push me. It made me think I could be with her.

She lifted up on her elbow, her hair mussed from sleep.

My chest filled with something I hadn't felt in a while—happiness. "I'm glad I did."

Her lips tipped into a smile; her muscles relaxed. "I wasn't sure what to expect."

I ran my fingers through her hair, then down her bare back. "You're beautiful."

"You make me feel that way." She leaned down to kiss me.

She felt right. This felt right. I was going to enjoy this time with her as long as I could. She wasn't someone I'd fuck and walk away from. I had a good time with other women, but none of those relationships turned into anything serious.

I'd grabbed on to this little slice of happiness. I deepened the kiss, moving her knee across my hips so she straddled me. I groaned when her wet pussy rubbed against my erection. She ripped her lips from mine, throwing her head back as she slid back and forth, chasing her own pleasure. With each pass over my cock, I teased her entrance until I finally slid inside. Her wet walls surrounded my cock. It felt more intense than last night. She gasped when my fingers tightened on her hips, pulling her down.

She lifted up then slowly back down. Her lips slightly parted, her brown eyes glazed over with pleasure. I loved seeing her like this. Her blonde hair tumbling over her shoulders, her nipples playing peekaboo with the strands. I touched her flat stomach, kneading her breast as she moved up and down. She was so wet. She moved faster, biting her lip probably to hide her whimpers.

"Let me hear what I do to you."

I pulled her head down to mine, swallowing her moans as she rode out her orgasm. Her pussy spasmed around me, tight as a vice. Why did it feel so much better than last night? Was it because we'd slept together or because I felt closer to her than anyone in a long time?

She lay on top of me, her limbs loose. I lifted my hips, chasing my release. Burying myself deep, I exploded into her.

Coming down from the high, my skin still tingling, I felt wetter than usual.

"Jonah—" Callie lifted off of me. "Shit."

She must have realized the same thing I had—we'd forgotten a condom. I never went bareback with anyone.

She ran for the bathroom, slamming the door.

The compulsion to flee was strong, but I couldn't leave Callie.

Finally, she came out of the bathroom, her face stricken. She opened a drawer, pulling on panties and soft-looking pale pink pants, and a white tee.

Getting up, I touched her shoulder. She stiffened under my touch. I kissed the sensitive part of her neck. "I'm going to clean up. Then we can talk."

I didn't want her to worry even if I was freaking out inside. I couldn't have a child. I was always so careful. What happened this morning to make me forget why protection was a necessity? Is this what an addiction was like—you lost sight of all reason?

I washed up, trying to calm my racing heart, to quell the panic.

I washed my face, then walked out to find her scrolling through her phone. Pulling on my jeans, she looked up.

She looked calmer. "I don't think it's possible."

I knew without asking she meant pregnancy. "How do you know?"

"It's not the right time. Plus, I'm on the pill."

Relief flowed through my body. "Okay. That's good. I'm clean, so you don't need to worry about that."

"I am too."

I sat heavily on the bed next to her, relief making me light-headed. "I never lose control like that."

I wasn't sure what that said about me. Was it her?

"It's okay. Neither of us was thinking clearly." She offered me a small smile.

I nodded. Should I offer to pick up breakfast? I couldn't exactly offer to cook. This was her place. "Do you want to go out for brunch?"

Morning-after brunch probably meant something. That what we were doing was serious or at least qualified as dating. But I didn't want to think about rules or expectations. I was going to go with my gut. My gut was telling me to spend more time with her.

"Yeah." Her smile widened. "I'd like that."

The last thing I wanted to do was hurt this woman or treat her like she was just a one-time fuck, because she wasn't. I enjoyed spending time with her.

She stood, holding her hand out to me. "Shower first?"

I took her hand, following her into her small bathroom. The shower was small, but we'd fit. She turned on the water while I pushed off my jeans. Grabbing a condom, I placed it on a ledge inside the shower. I wasn't sure how long I'd have with her, but I'd make every moment count. I'd make her feel good.

I came up behind her while she held her hand under the stream of water, testing the temperature. I kissed her neck, placing a hand under her shirt on her stomach, pulling her back against me so she could feel me. She tipped her head, giving me better access. Gripping the end of her shirt, I pulled it slowly over her head.

I kissed her neck, cupping her breasts, flicking her nipples. She arched back against me, her ass nestled against my cock. Her pants were a thin barrier between us. One I wanted gone. She squirmed in my arms, throwing her head back against my shoulder. I wanted her with an intensity I'd never felt before.

I placed kisses down her spine, pulling her pants with me as I kneeled behind her, kissing one ass cheek then the other.

"Get in."

She glanced at me over her shoulder before stepping into

the shower. I stood, following her. My cock was hard and aching for her.

Grabbing the body wash, I soaped my hands, then her shoulders and breasts, and lower until my fingers were between her folds. Turning to rinse her off, I moved until I was in front of her, kneeling at her feet. Looking up at her, her skin flush with desire, her eyes begging for more, I gripped her thighs, encouraging her to widen her legs.

"I want to taste you."

This was different than last night. That felt like an escape. This felt like an intentional coming together. It was intimate.

Her hands gripped my shoulders tightly. I nudged her back against the tile, throwing one leg over my shoulder. My hand on her ass, I angled her pussy to my mouth.

I licked her; her lips parted when I sucked her clit into my mouth, her head falling back. Her fingers were in my hair, holding me tight to her. An overwhelming feeling of rightness, of belonging, swept through me.

How had I never felt this with anyone before? Was it her? Was I just desperate for any distraction from my injury? Was I reading more into it than it was?

I redoubled my efforts to make her come. I wanted her desperate for more, writhing against me, urging me on.

"Jonah." My name echoed in the small space, the room filling with warm steam.

With the scent of her sweet pussy on my tongue, I added one finger, then two. Her hips arched into me. I sucked hard, curling my fingers inside of her to find that elusive bundle of nerves. She moaned, her hips moving in tune with my tongue, chasing me. Her fingers tightened almost painfully before she jerked, tumbling over the precipice, chanting my name.

Her walls tightened around my fingers, spasming. She rode my fingers through her release, sagging against the wall. I kissed my way up her body, hovering over her lips. If I could love anyone, it would be her.

Water beaded on her lip. Before her tongue could dart out to clear it, I kissed her. I poured everything I was feeling into it. Lifting her, she wrapped her legs around me. Grabbing the condom, I ripped it open with my teeth, smoothing it down my cock before sliding into her. I resisted the urge to pump hard to claim her as mine. I wanted to go slow, to watch her crest again, to enjoy every second with her.

"You're so beautiful." I'd described other women I'd been with as hot and sexy, but Callie was so much more. She had a softer, more innocent look. I was the only one who got to see her ruffled from sleep, her eyes bright with desire. I was the only one who got to see her come undone.

Her arms tightened around my shoulders. I wanted her to hold on tight and never let go.

Pressure built in my chest, making me hope for more. More than I had a right to. More than I'd ever get.

I wasn't sure where these emotions were coming from. Was this why I never stayed overnight or brought anyone back to my condo? The extra moments were intimate.

I kissed her, getting lost in the feel of her arms around me, the water pouring down my back. This time, when we went over the edge, we did it together. It was sweet. Slowly lowering her to her feet, I ripped off the condom, tying it, then throwing it into the trash.

She soaped her hands, moving them across my shoulders, my chest, down my stomach, around to my ass, then down my legs. There was nothing more intimate than her washing me in the shower after sex, her caring for me. I liked it too much.

I quickly rinsed off, washing my hair while she did hers. We dried off, getting dressed in silence before leaving for brunch. Walking down the sidewalk to my SUV, fingers inter-laced, felt right. We drove to Fell's Point, parking in a lot before walking around for the right place to eat. Settling on a small bar, we walked inside, sitting at a table by the window.

We ordered, handing our menus to the waitress.

"This is nice." Callie looked from the people walking on the street to me.

My throat tightened because she'd echoed my feelings. "It is."

"I didn't think it could be like this with you." Her gaze was steady on me.

I shifted in my seat. "How'd you think it would be?"

"You keep to yourself. Never bring any women around. I kind of assumed you didn't do overnights or brunch."

Shame filled me even though it was the truth. "I don't treat women badly. They know what to expect."

Yeah, I didn't trust them in my space, but it was more than that.

Her eyes gentled. "I know this is new, but I like this thing with you. I thought I could handle one night, but this feels good. I'm sorry if that's crazy or out of line. I wasn't expecting to feel like this."

"I don't know what I'm doing." For the first time, I wanted to try. I wanted to be the man worthy of this woman. "But I like you. I don't want to hurt you."

Seemingly satisfied with my answer, she nodded. "We have the summer before you go back to playing full time. Let's make the most of it."

Her words were a challenge, one I wanted to meet. Something inside me bristled at the time limit, but if it made her feel better, I'd respect her wishes.

"I want to try with you." The wall I'd built around my heart since high school lowered, letting in the possibility of having this woman. It was an infinitesimal move for someone else, but monumental for me.

She leaned over, kissing me softly on the lips. Warmth flowed through me; my skin tingled.

The waitress placed our plates on the table.

We ate in silence. I wondered if I'd feel differently now

that I was in some sort of a relationship with Callie. Surprisingly, I felt lighter than I had in years.

"Should we tell Reid?"

If this was just for the summer, there was no need. "Can we keep it to ourselves?"

Callie's lips curled into a smile. "You're afraid of Reid, aren't you?"

"What? No." I laughed at the teasing expression on her face. "He's probably going to give me shit, but that's not the only reason."

"No?" Her head tilted as she considered me.

"This is new for me. Give me a bit of time, yeah?" I leaned across the table, covering her hand with mine. I was known for never being seen with anyone. Going public meant commitment. I wasn't ready for that.

Something passed through her eyes I couldn't quite catch. Maybe distrust? "Okay. Not for long though, okay?"

I nodded. I wanted to say or do something to earn her trust, but only time could do that. I couldn't tell her to trust me because I couldn't trust myself. I wasn't sure what the hell I was doing. I was literally riding the wave of feelings I had when I was with her. I'd stay with her as long as it felt good. It was that simple.

CHAPTER FIFTEEN

CALLIE

BEING WITH JONAH LAST NIGHT WAS IMPULSIVE. I'D FELT MORE alive last night than I had in a long time. I hadn't expected Jonah to stay the night, much less go to brunch the next morning. It was more than the one-night escape I was envisioning, but I wanted more.

It was like waking after being in a coma, everything was brighter, more vivid. The food tasted better; the sunshine was warmer.

We finished our food. Jonah picked up the tab. Walking out of the restaurant, I was reluctant for him to take me home. I wanted to spend more time with him.

We walked through Fell's Point in the general direction of his SUV. Jonah didn't seem in a hurry to get anywhere.

"Want to go to the movies?" Jonah nodded in the direction of the movie theater.

"Yeah, I'd like that." I had no idea what was playing. It didn't matter.

We chose the action movie, grabbing sodas and a tub of buttered popcorn to share. It reminded me of dates I'd gone on in high school before everything changed. I'd dated the college-bound preppy guys, the ones that picked me up in their car, meeting my parents, taking me to whatever the popular movie was at the time, then dropping me off before curfew. Back then, wondering if the guy would kiss me on my porch was my biggest concern.

We settled into the plush leather chairs in the back of the theater. Jonah lifted the armrest between us, placing his arm over my shoulder. With the tub in my lap, I rested my head on his shoulder. He kissed my temple before grabbing a handful of popcorn.

I wanted to thank him for the perfect day. He'd taken my mind off of my grandfather, letting me lean on someone besides myself. It was priceless.

The sound of the previews rumbled the walls, signaling the start of the movie. I settled in, enjoying Jonah's arm around me, his thigh pressed against mine.

At some point, he moved the mostly empty popcorn tub to the floor next to him, pulling me farther into his body. Listening to the steady beat of his heart, my eyes drifted shut. My head lifted and fell with each inhale and exhale. It was soothing.

"Callie. It's over."

I blinked, opening my eyes. The credits played on the screen; the lights came on.

"Did I fall asleep?" I took a sip of my lukewarm soda, soothing my dry throat.

Jonah's expression was affectionate. "Yup."

"Sorry." I yawned.

He smiled. "I didn't mind."

I wanted to ask if he meant the movie or holding me while I slept, but I didn't. I hoped it was the latter.

Jonah stood, holding out his hand. "You ready to go?"

I wasn't. I wanted to stay in this dark cocoon, not facing the outside world or reality, but most people were filing out.

"Sure." My voice was still raspy from sleep, my feet unsteady.

I stepped in front of Jonah. He placed his hands on my shoulders as we followed the line of people to the lobby. The heat hit us when we stepped outside. A contrast to the cool theater. Jonah pulled me close, walking with his arm around my shoulder. For a few minutes, I let myself believe the delusion that we were like any other boyfriend and girlfriend. Not coworkers or forbidden partners. That he wasn't a rich athlete, and I wasn't his employee. That we had longer than a summer.

I'd dated someone more seriously in college, but junior year, he'd transferred back to his home state to be closer to his family. I wasn't someone people stayed with.

"Are you going to see Frank today?"

"I usually go on Sundays, so I was planning on it."

"Mind if I go with?" he asked tentatively.

His wanting to be there for me filled my heart. It was close to bursting. No matter how many times I told myself to be careful, this one act of kindness had me wanting to throw caution to the wind, to be careless.

The closer we got to the personal care home, the more my stomach churned. I wasn't sure if it would be a good day or a bad one.

"Hey. It's going to be okay." Jonah's voice was warm and comforting. It wasn't the tone he used with fans. It was the one I'd started associating with the real Jonah.

I tried relaxing my muscles one limb at a time, taking deep breaths.

When Jonah parked, my hand moved to the door handle.

"Wait."

I turned to him. He leaned over, a hand on my neck pulling me closer, a tingle ran down my spine. Kissing me hard, it was a declaration that he was there for me no matter what we were walking into.

Facing whatever was on the other side of my grandfather's door was easier with Jonah here. It was nice having someone to talk to, someone who seemed to understand. This thing with Jonah felt too good to be true, even though I wanted it more with each passing minute.

Walking in, Jonah's hand landed on my lower back. It was comforting, and at the same time, it buoyed me, preparing me for whatever mood Grandpa would be in.

I paused by the doorway. "Grandpa."

He sat with his back to us in the chair by the door.

Turning, he said, "Callie."

Relief flooded my system as I lowered my shoulders. I went to him, hugging him. Tears flooded my eyes. I moved away, discreetly wiping the tears that fell.

"Hey, Frank." Jonah shook his hand. "What're you watching?"

Sports news played softly on the small TV.

I was grateful Jonah was here to distract him. I didn't want Grandpa to know how upset I was. That my moods went up and down based on whether he was having a good day or not. I couldn't imagine how much worse I'd feel as he moved through each stage of the disease.

I continued to relax as the evening went on. Grandpa was having a relatively good day, even though I knew these days would eventually stretch out longer between episodes where he didn't remember me. This was a brief reprieve, one I desperately needed.

We stayed for a couple of hours, playing cards and talking sports before saying good night.

On the walk out, Jonah's fingers twined with mine, his lips quirked up. "I'm pretty sure he was cheating."

I laughed, covering my mouth with my free hand. "Yeah. He totally took advantage of you."

He cocked a brow. "I'm a sucker, aren't I?"

I winked. "You kind of are, but it was for a good cause. Letting an old man win."

"I guess. I kind of feel like a schmuck though." His smile told me he didn't, not really. He'd enjoyed himself.

I shook my head. "You shouldn't. It was nice of you to come."

"I like spending time with you and him."

He wanted to be here with me. I let that sink in before I softly responded, "Thank you."

At my apartment, Jonah came inside to order takeout. He flicked on the TV, not saying anything about going back to his condo, which I was almost positive was more spacious and luxurious. Surprisingly, he seemed comfortable in my space. He fit here and, so far, in my life.

Today we felt like a couple, one that had been together for years. Being with him was comfortable, like putting on my softest comfortable T-shirt. I wanted to burrow into that softness, never letting go. I had to remind myself there was only an us for the next few weeks.

He flipped through channels, settling on a movie. "Is this okay?"

"Uh-huh."

I didn't ask if he was going to stay over, but I hoped he would.

When the movie was over, he turned off the TV, gathering our dishes from dinner, putting them away.

I stood at the counter, unsure how to ask him to stay.

Closing the dishwasher, he turned to ask, "Want to head to bed?"

I nodded, swallowing down my questions—what would happen on Monday, would we go back to coworkers, pretending this weekend didn't happen? Was I a secret summer fling? I brushed my teeth, washed my face, then changed into a tank and lounge pants.

Approaching my bed, Jonah seemed to take up all the space.

Jonah lifted the sheets for me so I could slide under the

coolness. My hand immediately went to his bare chest. His skin was warm under my fingers. I slid a leg over his, the hair on his legs rough as I rested my head on his shoulder. His body was like a furnace; warmth enveloped me as his arm tightened around me. I closed my eyes, content to be here with him.

I was exhausted from last night and the emotional ups and downs of worrying about Grandpa. I'd hold myself back from Jonah. We'd set an end date, and I couldn't quite push out the idea that he'd forget about me when he was cleared to play. He'd refocus on what mattered, and I couldn't blame him. Professional athletes were laser focused on their job. That's why they dated women who only wanted a good time.

CHAPTER SIXTEEN

JONAH

It was the weekend of the grand opening. The last couple of weeks were filled with getting ready for the opening, physical therapy, and visiting Frank.

I offered to tour the nursing home options with Callie, but she kept putting me off. I wasn't sure what was holding her back unless it was admitting that Frank had gotten to the point where he needed more specialized care. I let it go because it wasn't something that needed to be done imminently, even though his condition could change at any moment.

I set up the football field, complete with barrels of footballs wherever the task called for it. We'd set up the nets and field goals with signs for each activity so it was clear for the participants. Coolers of water and Gatorade sat by the front door. The walls were decorated with banners from the sponsoring businesses.

"Everything looks great." Callie's voice carried as she crossed the room toward me.

"It does." My stomach rolled with nerves like how I felt before a big game. When had this become so important to me?

"It'll be fun." Callie's eyes were bright with excitement,

her lips tipped into a permanent smile. She'd gotten more and more focused as the grand opening neared. It was as if she thrived on planning these kinds of events.

"I hope so." She touched my arm. I glanced around to see if anyone was paying attention. They weren't.

She dropped her hand, her bright expression dimmed at my reaction.

I wanted to say I was sorry. That being with her the last few weeks had been the happiest I'd been in forever, but I couldn't get the words out.

"Let me know if you need anything." She lifted her phone, her face a cool professional mask.

"Callie." I kept my voice low.

She smiled tightly. "Don't worry. I know you said you needed more time."

I flinched at her harsh description. "It's not that."

She raised her brow.

It was exactly that. Telling Reid made it real. Even if we had an end date, our relationship came with the weight of responsibility. Everything could come crashing down on me. Just the thought tightened a band around my chest, making it difficult to breathe.

She touched my chest; the pressure was light. Her eyes soft, she said, "Maybe if you could tell me what has you so scared, I'd understand."

I pulled in a shaky breath. "Now's not the time to discuss this." I could have closed my eyes, reveling in her touch, but instead, I was pushing her away.

"*This* might not be the right time, but we will discuss it," she hissed.

"The relationship's not that serious anyway." Irritation that I'd always have this albatross around my neck, holding me back, burst out in the form of words I didn't mean.

Her cheeks flushed with anger, she turned on a heel, walking away.

I could have handled that better. Rolling my shoulders back to relieve the tension coiled in my upper back, I went over to the check-in table, making sure the volunteers knew their jobs.

"We're about ready for the ribbon-cutting ceremony," Reid said.

I nodded, following him to the lobby and outside. Did he know about Callie and me? Did he suspect?

There was a large crowd waiting to enter the complex for the planned activities. Several media trucks were here. The entire team and most of the coaching staff came to support us. It was the last free weekend before training camp, so everyone was in town.

Reid shook hands before stepping up to the podium. I stood off to the side with Chase.

"Thank you all for coming out today. I had a vision of a place that would give local teams a place to play and would encourage more kids to pick up a sport. As a child, football was an escape for me. Something I desperately needed back then. It kept me out of trouble, but more than that, it gave me confidence."

I was impressed with how he was handling the speech. In the past, he'd answer questions reluctantly, only giving terse responses. He got a reputation as being grumpy and not forthcoming with reporters. Since he'd admitted to his struggle with his speech, talking in front of people seemed to be easier for him.

It made me think about how I was being a coward with Callie, keeping us a secret. There was no good reason not to tell Reid. I wasn't embarrassed by her. If anything, I worried someone would ask her what she was doing with me.

Callie stood at the front, her arms wrapped around a clipboard. It seemed wrong that she'd put so much effort into the complex and the opening for her not to get some credit.

"We planned this day to introduce you to some of the

things we're planning, and to give you an opportunity to try out the facility. We'd like every child to have the option to play a sport here, to join a team, or to learn new skills. If you'd like to donate new or used equipment or even a scholarship for athletes who can't afford the fees, you can meet with my manager, Callie. She'll be at a table in the lobby all day."

She smiled, her face flushed. She didn't like the attention.

He pointed at her. "She's my right hand around here. She'll be happy to answer any questions you have. Some of my teammates will be signing autographs in the lobby, others will be volunteering on the courts and fields with the various activities. The most important thing today is to have fun."

Then Reid pointed to one of the reporters who held up her hand. "Yes?"

"How involved do you plan to be at Rebel Sports with training camp starting next week?"

We'd expected this question.

"That's why I hired a manager I trust to oversee things." Reid glanced over at me. "Jonah has been involved too."

I shifted on my feet, not liking that he'd pointed that out. I didn't want fans to question my desire to come back.

"Speaking of Jonah, are you not planning on playing this year?" The same reporter directed her question at me.

I stepped forward, leaning toward the mic. "I'm working really hard to get out on the field as soon as possible. I'm part owner of Rebel Sports, but football comes first."

It was the right thing to say. The only thing to say. My coach and teammates were listening. I glanced over at Callie. She bit her lip, looking away. Was that hurt I saw on her face?

Had I said something wrong? She knew football came first. That all I wanted to do was get back on the field.

Reid stepped forward saying, "Sorry about that," under his breath. Reid cut the ribbon with Nolan and Cade Morrison, the owners of the construction company, watching. We

LEA COLL

took numerous pictures with the contractors, the team, and the coaches.

Callie eventually told us to get to our stations so the football competition could start. I was on the indoor football field, directing kids where to go, making sure everything ran smoothly. I wanted to talk to Callie to clear things up, but it would be a while before I could get her alone.

Some of the kids had played before, others were less experienced. Players manned the various stations. Each child was given a football when they entered for autographs.

One child was small for his age, but he made up for it in personality. "My grandma said I'm too small for football, but I want to play."

"You should try it." Size mattered in football, but this kid had a lot of years to grow.

His forehead scrunched. "I don't know if she'll let me."

"Want me to talk to her?" I asked flippantly, not expecting him to take me up on the offer.

"Would ya?" His expression was hopeful, I couldn't say no.

"Sure." What was I getting myself into?

"She said it was too dangerous. But you can talk to her, right?"

"I'll do my best, but if your parents or grandmother don't want you to play, you have to respect that decision."

His face fell.

I hated disappointing him, but it was his grandmother's or parents' decision, not mine. "Give your info to Ms. Callie. She's sitting at the front table."

Even if she wouldn't let him play football, maybe I could convince her to let him try something.

"JT, are you going to coach the football league?" another kid asked.

I wanted to say yes, but I hoped to be on the field before the football leagues here started.

"I think he's going to be playing this year," the kid's dad said.

"I tell you what, once I retire, I'd love to coach." I never thought much about what I'd do after football, but this felt right. I enjoyed working at the complex these last few weeks, but that was mainly due to my interactions with Callie. Being here with the kids was energizing.

"You getting the hard-hitting questions?" Reid handed me a Gatorade when the group moved to the next activity.

"You could say that." I tipped the bottle back.

"How's it going?"

"Great. I'm enjoying it more than I thought I would."

"You like working with the kids." It was a statement.

"I like their optimism. Their whole lives are laid out in front of them. They haven't made any mistakes yet."

Reid's eyes narrowed on me. "Are you talking about the playoff game?"

"I dropped the ball. I cost us the game. All anyone remembers is the play when the clock ran out. If I don't get back on the field, that will be my legacy." A therapist would probably tell me not to feel that way, but as part of a team, that's just the way it was.

"All I know is it'll be weird if you're not on the field."

There was nothing to say because everyone knew it was true. If I never stepped on the field again, the highlight of my career will be that dropped ball. It would erase everything that came before. "I'll stop by on Monday to support everyone."

"You can laugh at us while we're running in the heat."

"I have to get some joy being on the injured reserve list."

"I know you didn't want to work here, but how's it going?"

"It's good." If he'd asked me a month ago, I would have said the complex was a distraction I didn't need. My focus was only on football and training, anything else seemed superfluous. But working here, being with Callie, showed me there was more to life than football.

"You resolve your differences with Callie?"

I choked on the Gatorade. Water spewed out of my mouth.

"You alright, man?" Reid pounded on my back.

I held my chest as I recovered, hoping the worst of the coughing was over. "Sorry. I drank too quickly or something. Yeah, things are good with Callie. She's a hard worker."

I couldn't help but think this was my opportunity to tell him about us. In a few days, he'd be busy with training camp.

He touched my shoulder. "I'm glad you came around. Callie's important to me."

The band around my chest tightened again. There was no way I could tell him. Not yet. Was it worth upsetting Reid if we were just a summer fling? I ignored the nagging idea that I was the one holding us back.

My skin cooled despite the warm air in the arena.

Reid studied me carefully. "She told me you've been going with her to visit Frank."

His scrutiny made me wonder if he suspected something was going on between us. I shrugged as if it wasn't a big deal. "I was there when the nurse called. She was too upset to drive."

It was the truth, even if it felt flimsy to me.

"I'm worried about her. Frank's all she's got."

"Hey, Reid, someone has a question for you," Chase called from across the room.

I breathed a sigh of relief. I wouldn't hold up if Reid asked more questions. I'd cave, even knowing he'd be pissed. I hated lying to him, keeping something this important from him. I'd even told him and Chase about my past.

"How are you doing?" Callie appeared next to me, clutching the clipboard to her chest.

"Not great, honestly." Between fucking things up with her earlier and keeping something important from Reid, my stomach wasn't feeling great.

"Can I help you with something?" I hated that she was talking to me more like a coworker than her boyfriend, her lover.

I touched her elbow lightly. "Can we talk?"

Her face pinched. "I didn't think this was the right time."

It didn't feel great to have my words thrown back at me.

"I need to tell you something." I needed to make things clear with her, then we needed to talk to Reid.

I pulled her into a small locker room meant for the referees. I locked the door. "I'm sorry about earlier."

The cool mask slipped as her brow raised. "You are?"

"Yeah. You're right. We should tell Reid. I don't like keeping it from him. I almost told him, but then he said something about how special you are to him, and I chickened out."

The tension eased from her shoulders. "What changed your mind?"

"I hated lying to him, but it was more than that. I don't want to hurt you." I'd seen the pain in her eyes when I talked about going back to football during the press conference. I was worried Reid would have a problem with me dating Callie, that he wouldn't think I was worthy of her. I was still worried, but I didn't want to hurt her.

I cupped her cheek. "I'm not always going to do the right thing. My track record with relationships isn't the best. I know I don't deserve it, but can you please give me the benefit of the doubt when I screw it up?"

She smiled. "I can do that."

I leaned down, my lips touching hers softly. I didn't want there to be anything between us, hurt, resentment, secrets. I lost myself in her touch and her lips.

A few seconds later, she pulled back. "We should probably get back out there."

I tapped her nose. "No more hiding our relationship from Reid or anyone else. You're my girl."

I expected her to correct me, to tell me she wasn't a girl

and this wasn't high school, but her smile widened. "I'd like that."

"Yeah?" I kissed her again, this time harder. I wanted her to feel my mouth on hers for the rest of the day. She was mine.

When we broke away, her cheeks were flushed, her lips swollen. I traced the outline of her lips with my thumb.

"When we walk out at the same time, are we going to pretend we were working in here?" Her tone was uncertain.

I wanted to erase the uncertainty and pain I'd caused with my callous need to hide us from Reid. "Or we don't say anything. Let Reid figure it out."

Her forehead wrinkled.

I sighed. "I'll talk to him today."

I couldn't wait any longer. Not with training camp starting soon.

She popped up on tiptoes, kissing me lightly. My hands went to her hips. That one simple kissed warmed me, making me think we could do anything. Be in a relationship, survive training camp, and my eventual return to the game. We were strong enough to survive, weren't we? I couldn't imagine the alternative. Going back to how I was. After Callie, it would seem so much lonelier than before. Pointless even. She gave me a reason to play outside of escaping my past. I tried not to think about whether she wanted the same thing. She was the one who proposed the summer with the season being a natural end date.

Walking out, the gym was still bustling with kids. No one looked our way.

She wrapped a hand around my bicep.

I smiled at her, but when I glanced up, joy radiating in my chest, Reid stared at me from across the room, one brow raised. Sighing, I said, "It's time to face the music, pay the piper, whatever the saying is."

Her face fell as she followed my gaze to Reid's rigid one. "Ugh. I'm sorry."

"Don't be. You're worth pissing off my friend."

Looking down at her, I knew I was right. Reid could warn me off her all he wanted, but I'd still gravitate back to her. She was the sun that came up in the morning, the moon that was a steady presence all day. With her, I could do anything, be anyone.

Reid strode across the room, his gaze flickering from me to Callie. "You have something you wanted to tell me?"

"In your office?" There was no point in making people talk.

He nodded tightly.

I squeezed Callie's upper arm. "Keep things running smoothly. I'll be back."

Her expression was worried, but she let go of my arm. "Good luck."

I'd need it. I followed the tense set of Reid's shoulders to his office. I shut the door as Reid swung around, hands braced on his desk. "Were you going to tell me?"

Wondering if we'd made the right decision in coming out, I said, "We'd just decided to."

He braced his hands on the desk. "During the opening of the complex."

"I kept putting her off. Telling her I needed more time to tell you. It wasn't fair to her. I wanted to say something before training camp."

His expression softened slightly, but his tone was incredulous. "What are you doing with her, Jonah? You can't be serious about her."

I cringed at his assumption I wasn't anything more than a good-time guy. I'd made sure that was his impression, but it felt miserable having it thrown in my face.

He pushed off the table, pacing. "Hell. I don't even know why. Why don't you do serious?"

Answers filtered through my head… I didn't deserve it, it would end badly, I wasn't the right guy for anyone.

He stopped, his legs wide, his arms crossed over his chest.

Something slimy and cold settled in my stomach. He knew what happened to my ex, but I didn't want to talk about it. "I never met anyone I wanted to be serious with."

"And I'm supposed to believe Callie's the girl?"

"She is. I don't know what I'm doing, but I want to be with her."

"I don't like this." He tipped his head back, staring at the ceiling.

What could I say to alleviate his concern? I won't hurt her. That was the obvious answer, but I couldn't guarantee that. "I don't want to hurt her, but I know I'm not good enough for her."

His head bobbed in agreement. "I'm glad you recognize that. Look, she's vulnerable right now, susceptible to your charm. She's dealing with her grandfather's illness."

I didn't like his insinuation that Callie was only with me because of my football persona or my charm. I'd been more real with her than anyone else. "I know she is."

"I hope you know what you're doing." His voice was gentler.

"I'm in unchartered territory here." I spread my arms out to my side.

Reid's face relaxed. Something in my tone must have come across as sincere. "That's how I felt when I met Dylan. I pushed her away even when I wanted to pull her closer. In the end, I fucked up. I hurt her. I still regret that."

"I'm bound to fuck it up. I can't make any promises other than I care for her, and it's real." It felt good to clear the air with my friend. He hadn't reacted how I thought he would. I thought he'd agree I was a terrible choice for her, double down on his plea to stay away from her.

He studied me carefully, then nodded. "You know, that's all I can ask for. Take care of her."

"I will." His blessing settled in my chest, burrowing deeper, making me feel closer to the person who might deserve Callie Goodwin one day.

CHAPTER SEVENTEEN

CALLIE

THE DAY WAS A SUCCESS. THE COMPLEX LOOKED GREAT, AND the kids had fun. The best part of the day was Jonah pulling me into that locker room, telling me he wanted to tell Reid and everyone about us. I was still riding that high when Reid found me cleaning up one of the soccer fields. Someone got a hold of the confetti. It was a mess.

"You don't need to clean up."

Technically, cleaning wasn't part of my job description. We'd hired a crew, but I needed something to busy myself with. I had leftover adrenaline coursing through me from the day.

"I know."

Jonah was doing a more in-depth interview with a reporter in his office, but everyone else had gone home hours ago.

He stuffed his hands in his pockets. "Were you going to tell me?"

I dumped the dust bintrash in the garbage bag. "About Jonah?"

"Yeah." He winced, as if thinking about us together was difficult for him.

"I thought it was his place to tell you, and he didn't want to. Not at first anyway."

"I would have hoped you'd come to me about something like this. He's my teammate." Hurt tinged his voice.

"I never talk to you about who I date." That was never our relationship.

His face was pinched.

"I'm sorry if this makes things difficult for you." I couldn't promise to stay away from Jonah. I was in too deep at this point.

"It doesn't. I just don't want you to get hurt."

"You can't prevent that from happening." It was inevitable from where I stood. I'd already fallen for Jonah, the football player, his vulnerable side underneath, and for every sweet gesture in between.

"Is it so bad that I want to?"

I smiled at his honesty. "No. I'm glad you care."

"I promised Frank."

I knew it was more than that. Reid really did think of me as someone to protect, like one of his sisters. He felt responsible for me, even if that was ridiculous. "Well, you're off the hook because I'm an adult, and I make my own decisions."

He scowled. "Just be careful with him."

"Did you scare him away?" My heart pounded harder in my chest. I didn't think Jonah would stick around for the long haul. It's why I was so quick to offer up the summer as an option. I wouldn't be disappointed when it ended.

"No. I warned him to be careful, that's all. He seems sincere."

I smiled. "I think so too."

He'd been honest when he told me he'd was bound to screw things up, to give him time. It made me like him even more. I caught glimpses of the person underneath, and I wanted to dig deeper until I knew his very essence as a man.

"He doesn't talk about his past."

Something in his tone made me pause, made me think there was something he knew. "Is there something there?"

His expression looked guilty. "I shouldn't have said anything. It's none of my business."

"You're looking for things when there's nothing."

"Yeah, maybe I am." He shoved his hands in his pockets.

"What are you two talking about?" Jonah crossed the room, his smile bright, his expression relaxed.

Would he stand apart from me, acting like nothing had changed?

Jonah wrapped an arm around me, pulling me close. "Great job today. It went well. Don't ya think?"

He squeezed my shoulder then looked at Reid.

Joy surged through me, making me feel light, almost airy.

Reid had a pained expression on his face. "Yeah, it did. How was the interview?"

I guess our relationship would take some time for him to get used to.

"Good. I said I'm working hard. I hope to be back. That's all I can say."

Reid gestured around the room "Let the cleaning crew take care of this. You want to go out for a drink? Everyone's meeting at Federal House if it's not too busy."

"You want to?" Jonah asked me.

"Yeah, that would be nice." I was excited to go out as a couple.

We met Dylan and the rest of Reid's friends, Avery and Griffin, Cade and Hadley, Cade's brother, Nolan and Juliana, and Juliana's sister, Ava, who'd built our website, at the Federal House.

I sat next to Dylan; she leaned over to whisper, "When were you going to tell us?"

"It just happened." I'd talked to them about the kiss, but I hadn't seen them since.

Jonah sat next to me, throwing an arm around the back of

my chair. I was glad to see he was relaxed, that he didn't regret telling Reid. I didn't want this thing between us to affect their friendship.

I met his heated gaze. I thought I wanted to hang out with friends, but after being apart all day, and telling Reid about us, I wanted nothing more than to be alone with him.

"I can see things are going well." Dylan leaned over with a conspiratorial smile.

Reid cleared his throat as if expressing his displeasure.

Dylan elbowed him. "Ignore him. He's not a fan of things changing."

So many things were evolving around me, a new job, my grandfather's health, a new relationship. Was it too much at once?

"When will we get a chance to try out the facility?" Griffin asked. He'd invested in several small businesses and nonprofits in the area, but Reid hadn't needed his help with Rebel.

"With the season picking up, I'm not sure. I was hoping to have an after-hours party, but with training starting next week, I don't see how we'll fit it in."

"Maybe we can have a celebration after the season's over." My words rang hollow in my ears. Where would Jonah and I be in January? That was well past the deadline we'd set. Would I still be working with him, pretending he was nothing but a summer fling?

Dylan lightly bumped my shoulder with hers. "Let's work on it together."

"I won't turn down help." I was used to organizing Reid's life, but Dylan had only added to it when they started dating. She was amazing at event planning.

Talk turned to the day, the money raised, what local coaches had said about the facility being a necessity, something they'd wanted for a while. It was good to be doing something, not only good for my career, but for providing a much-needed service for the community.

Jonah was a constant presence next to me. His thigh resting against mine, his fingers playing with my hair. His touch sent tingles racing across my skin.

Something niggled in my brain about what Reid had said. He'd acted like there was something in his past that should concern me, but he'd been reluctant to say exactly what. Was there something there? He'd mentioned not having many serious relationships, had he had *any*? Was that something I could even ask without sounding like I was digging into his past?

I looked over at Jonah who'd shifted away, moving his hands as he talked animatedly to the guys. Affection swelled in my heart for him.

If there was something concerning in his past, he'd tell me eventually. He knew everything about me, my parents, and Grandpa, but that was different. I wore those wounds on my sleeve. Jonah was more reserved about his family. The only thing I knew was that he'd said his mom and sister visited when he was first injured.

Jonah caught my eye, leaning closer to whisper in my ear, "Everything okay?"

I smiled to cover my worries. "Yeah."

He kissed my cheek, taking my hand, placing it on his rock-hard thigh. The warmth radiated through my hand, zinging up my wrist to my elbow. I could get used to this. To being with him. I wouldn't waste our time together worrying about the past or what would happen if he was cleared to play. I'd enjoy him while I could.

No one stayed in your life permanently. You only got them for a short time.

"How's the bed-and-breakfast?" Dylan asked Juliana.

Juliana recently bought a bed-and-breakfast, hiring Cade and Nolan's contracting company to renovate it.

"It's really picking up for the fall. Ava's managing it for me." Juliana gestured at her sister.

I'd heard Ava wanted a career change, and Juliana couldn't live on site since she had young daughters.

Ava smiled. "My main job these days is managing the bed-and-breakfast. I do website design on the side."

"Do you like managing the bed-and-breakfast?" I asked her. She was so skilled with website designing, I was surprised she wasn't doing that as her full-time job.

"I'm single and young, so living at the bed-and-breakfast is perfect for me. I enjoy baking and cooking. I test out my creations on the guests."

"You should sell your baked goods. People would buy them." Juliana shot her a pointed look.

This sounded like something they'd discussed before.

"I'm happy doing what I am for now." Ava took a sip of her beer, seemingly uncomfortable with her sister's comment.

Jonah leaned over, kissing my cheek. "I'm going for a refill."

He picked up the pitcher, taking it to the bar.

Dylan shifted closer. "I'm so glad you came."

"Me too." The beginnings of a friendship with these people warmed my chest, easing the ache of loneliness I'd felt the last few years.

"I've been meaning to text you. How's Frank?" she asked, concern tinging her voice.

Dylan's mother suffered from MS. I wondered if she'd be helpful with my grandfather's situation. "I knew it was coming, but him forgetting things is upsetting."

"I dread when my mom's MS symptoms flare. It's devastating each time because I don't know if it's temporary or permanent. It throws me for a loop."

"With Alzheimer's, the symptoms come and go, he has good days and bad, but it's part of an inevitable progression." Just talking about it out loud to someone who'd gone through something similar helped.

"If you need company, I can go with you."

I'd wondered if she'd help me decide on a new home for him. "I actually need to choose a place for him to be moved to. I've narrowed it down to two. Will you go with me?"

"Of course."

"I think I've been putting it off because once he goes there, he won't be coming out. It's so final." I rested my head in my hand.

"You're doing the right thing."

"I can go with you." Jonah eased onto the stool, placing the pitcher in the middle of the table.

Was he hurt I hadn't asked him?

Avery asked Dylan a question, and she turned away from us to answer.

He shifted closer, resting his elbows on his knees. It was like we were the only two people in the room. "I thought you'd decided on one already."

I bit my lip. "I think I'll feel better about the decision if I see it in person."

"It's fine if you want to go with Dylan, but I can help out too."

"Are you sure? I figured with training camp starting, you might be busy going back and forth between that, PT, and Rebel."

He took my hands in both of his. "I'm positive. I'm in this with you."

The warm glow I'd gotten in the locker room spread bigger and brighter. The only thing that dimmed my joy was the thought that he'd change his mind once he got to camp and saw the other guys playing. I knew how professional athletes were; in the end, football reigned supreme. No girlfriend could compete with that.

I want to push back on that idea. I wanted to have Jonah to myself.

"You ready to get out of here?" I asked. I felt bold. I wanted to take what I wanted.

"Yes." He stood, pushing the stool under the table.

We said goodbye to our friends. The girls gave me knowing looks. I'm sure our desire to be alone was obvious.

When he pulled onto the highway, driving south instead of north, I was surprised. "Where are we going?"

"To my house." His hand tightened on the wheel. The look he shot me was uncertain.

"I thought you lived in the city."

Usually, only the family guys had a home outside the city.

"The condo is for in season. I bought a house on the water for the off-season. It's nice to have a place to escape to."

"I never knew."

"I haven't really talked about it with anyone. I liked having a place no one knows about. The media can't find me."

"Reid doesn't know?"

"No one does." His gaze was on the road.

"Have you ever brought anyone here?" I was trying to work out this new piece of information in my head.

"No."

"Not even your parents?"

"No. When I was injured, it was easier to stay in the city. The doctors and PT were there."

"That makes sense." I rested my head on the seat, studying his profile. I liked being the only one who got to see the real Jonah, the one he kept from everyone.

"Thank you for showing it to me." It might not have been a big deal for other people, but this was huge for him. I recognized the importance, even if he didn't.

He smiled. "I want you to myself. Plus, it's closer to Annapolis."

Twenty minutes later, we pulled down a long lane that ended at an elevated home on stilts. He parked underneath.

Getting out, the wind blew my hair. I could smell the bay.

He held out his hand.

Taking it, I walked with him to the front of the house. A

motion sensor light mounted on the side of the house turned on, making it easier to see.

We walked up the steps to a large deck off the back of the house. The water was inky black at night, the moon reflecting off the water.

We stood in silence for a minute, taking it in.

"It's beautiful. I'd live here all the time if it were mine." For the smell, the sound, the sense of peace I got standing here.

"But Frank lives north of the city." Jonah lightly bumped my shoulder.

Living somewhere like this—a beautiful house on the water—wasn't possible on my salary, especially with the cost of a specialized care home.

I shrugged. "I already planned to move him closer to Rebel Sports. Once I have him settled, I'll look for a place for myself."

I'd be looking for an apartment to rent. Not a house on the water. I'd never been to Jonah's condo, and I wondered if that was on purpose. I wasn't jealous of what he had, but seeing his home highlighted our differences.

He turned to face me, pulling me into his body. I flattened my hands on his chest, his heart beating a steady rhythm under my hand.

"I like you in my space." His expression was intense.

I tipped my chin up to maintain his gaze. "I like being here."

My hair blew across my face. He brushed it back. The movement was so tender my heart ached for more. My mind begged him to let me in.

He leaned down slowly, teasing my lips with light touches. Pressing my hips tight to his, he was hard everywhere. Jonah whispered across my lips, "I want to give you everything."

The sincerity in his words pulsed in the air between us.

If I could let go of my fears, I knew I'd want more than

sex. I'd want all of him. Not just the house he'd hid from everyone, but his past, his fears, his worries. "I want that too."

It was the only promise I could make in the moment.

He kissed me, increasing the pressure until my lips parted, his tongue sweeping into my mouth, claiming me as his.

I wanted to enjoy this for as long as it lasted. I should hold myself back, wait for him to give me more, but I felt like I was falling through quicksand. I wanted to grab onto something to stop my fall, but there was nothing to hold on to.

My hands moved from the soft material of his shirt to the hair on his neck. I sifted the soft strands through my fingers as his tongue tangled with mine.

He pulled back slightly, my weight supported entirely by him. "You always feel so good."

That's because we felt right together, but I didn't voice it out loud. He'd shown me a piece of himself today, he'd opened up. There was so much more to him he hid.

He grabbed my hand, tugging me toward a couch against the wall. It was darker here, secluded. The only sound was the water lapping at the shore. He sat, pulling me onto his lap.

His voice was low, rumbling through my body. "My neighbors can't see us here. I bought this lot for privacy."

"Well, aren't we lucky then?" I smiled mischievously, grinding down on his hardening cock.

He brushed a hair back from my forehead, holding it there. His touch was comforting. "I think I'm the lucky one."

"I'm not going to argue with you." I lowered my head, nipping his lip. I wanted to tease, not give him what he wanted. "You are."

He surged up, his cock creating necessary friction between my legs. I closed my eyes, reveling in the feel. Leaning back slightly, I reached down to unbutton his pants. Then I slid off his lap to my knees. The bite of the wood beneath me grounded me in this moment. I tugged his pants and briefs down over his hips, his cock popping out. He spread his legs wide, his hands diving in my hair.

He kept his hold light as if he wasn't sure he wanted this. I licked the head, keeping my gaze on him.

"Fuck, Callie. You don't have to——"

I sucked him into my mouth.

His eyes glazed over as he groaned. He lifted his hips as if wanting to be deeper.

Letting him out of my mouth with an audible pop, I said, "But I want to."

His eyes darkened, the moon reflecting off the water across his face. The fingers in my hair tightened. I rolled his balls with one hand, pumping him with the other. I drew on every trick I'd ever read about, wanting to make it good. I sucked him hard, basking in the desire I saw on his face.

"Your mouth feels so good." His voice was guttural, as if he was barely hanging on to his control.

I hummed in thanks, the vibration making him jerk in my mouth.

I knew he was close when his hips lifted, pushing his cock deeper. I welcomed him inside as he stilled. "Fuck, sorry."

I pulled off to say, "It's okay."

I didn't mind that he'd lost control with me.

His expression was full of desire. "I want to touch you."

I moved closer to make it easier for him. His hand drifted up my shirt, palming my breast. When his thumb passed over my nipple, I lost my focus. My core throbbed with need. I shifted restlessly as my rhythm faltered.

"I want you to ride me." He lifted up my shirt. I let his cock slide out of my mouth so he could pull it over my head. I reached around, unhooking my bra.

"You're so beautiful."

I stood, shrugging off my jeans and panties. I felt beautiful with him.

His hands on my breasts, rolling my nipples, drove me crazy with need.

"Get a condom from my wallet." I dug into his pocket, pulling out his leather wallet. I pulled one condom out, ripping it with my teeth as he sat sprawled on the couch, his cock jutting toward me.

I slowly slid the condom down, wanting to torture him. When it was on, I straddled him, sliding down one inch at a time, reveling in the stretch, the fullness when I took all of him.

"You feel amazing."

I wanted him filling me, my body, my soul. I rose then slid down, picking up my pace when he gripped my hips, thrusting up to meet me.

"So good." Everything with him was so good. Too good.

His hands drifted from my hips to my breasts, kneading them, sending lightning to my core. He pulled me closer, sucking a nipple into his mouth. I ground down hard, chasing my orgasm. The roughness of his jeans was a contrast to my nakedness. I wanted this feeling to last, the rise before the fall. The orgasm would feel amazing, but I didn't want to feel the inevitable crash.

He bit my nipple lightly, bringing me back to the moment. Watching his mouth work my nipple while he thrust his hips upward sent me over. I cried out, throwing my head back. His mouth moved to my other nipple, his hands at my ass, lifting me up and pulling me down. I was putty in his hands. He could do whatever he wanted to me. He thrust a few more times, finally growling his release against my chest.

What we'd just experienced was rawer than anything I'd ever felt.

I held him to me, never wanting this moment to end.

Eventually, he pulled off the condom, tying it off, and throwing it to the side. Then he pulled me close with my legs draped over his lap.

We gazed at the water, dark waves ebbing and flowing under the light of the moon. It was beautiful. I wished I could pause time, living in this moment forever. I felt the evidence of him inside me still, our heated skin cooling in the night air. I sank into his touch. His lips rested on my forehead. It wasn't a kiss so much as a touch, one reminding me he was here. I never wanted to leave.

CHAPTER EIGHTEEN

JONAH

A BREEZE BLEW IN THROUGH THE OPEN WINDOWS, COOLING the room. I loved the sound of the birds chirping in the morning and the sound of the water. It was quiet, peaceful. Callie lay with her head on my shoulder, her hand flat on my chest, as if holding me in place. I had no intention of going anywhere.

I lifted a strand of her hair, testing the weight and the softness. I liked having her in my space. I loved waking up to her. She shifted, her leg moving higher.

We had one day until training camp would start. I'd need to make an appearance and do some press. The pressure would come down like a guillotine.

I tried not to think about it even as my muscles stiffened.

Callie lifted her head. Her eyes were drowsy with sleep, her hair messy. "What time is it?"

"Seven."

"The birds are loud." She rolled off me, dragging the pillow over her head to block out the sound.

"This is living in the country." My tone was amused.

"Well, I don't like it." Her voice was muffled from the pillow.

I rested a hand on her sheet-covered ass. "I see you're not a morning person."

She grunted, shifting her position.

"I'll make some coffee and an omelet."

She was quiet, so I lifted off the bed, pulling on a pair of sweats. Padding to the kitchen, I wondered if I should get a dog, someone to follow me around in the morning. I brewed the coffee before cracking some eggs in a bowl. The water was gray this morning, probably a reflection of the clouds. My favorite was when the sun shone down, making the water a light blue.

Drinking coffee, I chopped veggies, sauteing them before adding the eggs, and finally, a little cheese. Making two omelets, I plated them. I'd finished covering her food to keep it warm when I heard footsteps on the ceiling above me.

Good. She was up. I didn't want to waste a minute of the day. I didn't know what she had planned, but I wanted to spend it with her.

She came down the steps in one of my button-down shirts cuffed at the wrist, the tail down to her knees. I reached her when she was on the last step.

"You look hot in my shirt."

She smiled, her face still sleepy. "I hope it's okay that I'm wearing it."

"I like it." I leaned in, kissing her softly.

Pulling back, I took her hand, leading her to the island. "Coffee?"

She slid onto the stool. "Yes, please."

I pushed the omelet toward her, taking off the cover, handing her a fork. Pouring her coffee into a purple mug with my team emblem, I asked, "Milk or sugar?"

"Milk, please."

I had someone local stock the fridge and clean once a week. I poured the milk, pushing the mug closer to her.

She blew on it, then took a small sip. "Thank you for this."

I wanted to say thank you for being here, thank you for being *you*, but I didn't. "You're welcome."

I took a large bite of the omelet. I was starving. Finished, I pulled out a container of cut-up fruit, digging in.

She took a few bites of her omelet, looking around. "This place is beautiful."

"I like it here. The quiet. The solitude." The kitchen was all white lines, modern, with a few pieces that depicted the bay; a wooden sign hung over the fireplace indicating the latitude and longitude of the home, saying *Home Sweet Home*. It was a gift from the realtor. A few colorful metal crabs my mom bought as a housewarming present, hung in the kitchen.

"I do too."

When she was finished, I cleared our plates. "Want to sit on the deck?"

"Yeah."

I refilled our coffee and opened the sliding door. "Grab a blanket from the couch."

This morning was unusually cool for July. I sat on the couch, placing our mugs on the end table.

She curled up next to me, the blanket wrapped around us.

"Camp starts tomorrow," she finally said.

I wondered if it was on her mind. If it was bothering her. "Yeah, I'll probably make an appearance. Do some interviews."

"Are you looking forward to it?"

"I can't say I am. It's the first time I'm not suiting up. There's this excitement the first week. There's competition, camaraderie, and the hope that anything can happen this year, no matter what the outcome was last season."

"Have you ever been?" I'd never seen her there, but maybe I hadn't been paying attention.

"No. Reid never needed me there. I loaded up on classes in the spring and summer because he needed me more in the fall and winter."

"Are you coming this time?"

She sat up, the blanket falling off her shoulder. "I don't have any need to. I'm not Reid's assistant anymore. He wanted me handling the day-to-day of Rebel Sports while he's playing."

"Would you come to see me?"

Her expression softened. "Of course."

I liked the idea of her coming to the regular-season games to watch me. "Will you wear my jersey when I'm cleared to play?"

"I'd be honored." She smiled, her cheeks pink.

"Will you wear it at home too?" I pulled her closer, my hand on her bare thigh. "With nothing underneath?"

Would her nipples be visible through the material? Would her skin look golden while wearing purple? "I like the idea of you wearing my number."

"Me too."

We were talking about something huge. Her wearing my jersey when no one had since my high school girlfriend. Back then, it meant you were going steady. "I'll get you one."

I just hoped I'd be wearing it again. "I kind of like the idea of you walking around my house in nothing but my jersey all day, maybe even all weekend."

Her cheeks flushed. "I do too."

I'd fought this level of intimacy with a woman for years. Now that I was here, I couldn't remember why. It felt easy. She fit here with me.

"I could stay here all day."

Sighing, she said, "Me too."

A while later, the sun had moved higher in the sky, the air was warmer. "You want to go see Frank?"

"Do you mind?" Her expression was relieved.

"Of course not."

She stood, wrapping the blanket around her. "I can't help

but think there are easier girls for you to date. Ones that don't come with baggage."

I chuckled. "Right now, you come with my shirt. I don't see any baggage."

I had baggage too. She just didn't know about it. I pushed back the dark thoughts, not wanting my past to intrude on the best thing to ever happen to me.

"You know what I mean. There are less complicated women out there."

"There are women who throw themselves at me, they say and do what they think I want. If that's what you mean."

She nodded tightly.

"That's not what I want. I like you." That was the thing with Callie, I wasn't looking for anything when she sat next to me at the bar. I hadn't thought of her as anything other than Reid's assistant. Off-limits. But she'd opened up the possibility of having a relationship, a connection with someone. The concept settled in my muscles, making me feel loose and free.

"For how long?"

I stilled. "What do you mean?"

"I can't help but think that things will change with training camp. Your priorities will change."

"I'll be more focused on recovery, on getting back to my team. That's my job. But my feelings for you won't change."

I liked her. I enjoyed spending time with her, but I wasn't sure what this feeling in my chest was. Sometimes, it grew so big it threatened to overwhelm me. It was a mix of happiness, contentment, excitement, anticipation for more. At the same time, I was worried about training camp. How that would fit into my current existence.

Working at Rebel Sports, spending time with Callie, was the best time I'd had in forever.

"Your job is important to you. I understand that." It was like she wanted to say more but held back.

"You're important to me too."

She bit her lip.

"You think football is more important." I didn't want her to think she ranked under football.

"It should be." Her gaze lowered.

"It has been. It was a lifesaver in a lot of ways."

"How so?"

I didn't want to tell her about the accident, but I could tell her something real. "My high school coach told me I could go all the way. He gave me something to focus on, to turn the negative energy into something good. I doubled down on football. Never strayed from my lane."

I didn't think I deserved to go to college on a scholarship. After everything that happened, I didn't deserve anything good in my life. Instead, I proved I was worthy of it each day by showing up, training hard, taking rookie players under my wing, and mentoring kids.

This was the first time I'd let in something—*someone* good for me. Could I hold on to her and have football at the same time?

Her expression was tentative. "You don't talk much about your past."

I'd just told her more than I told other people. "What's to talk about?"

"Your family, your hometown."

This right here was why I'd never let anyone in. "I already told you about my family. I didn't have a good time in high school. I was happy to leave."

"A football star in high school who didn't have a good time?" She was teasing, but there was a hint of something else there too.

I shifted on the couch, pushing off the blanket. It was too hot suddenly. I stood, bracing my hands on the railing, wishing there was a breeze off the water to cool my brewing temper.

Her hand touched my back. I hadn't heard her bare feet on the planks. "I'm sorry. I shouldn't have pushed."

I tensed. I enjoyed high school. Too much. "I don't like to talk about it."

I straightened, turning to face her.

"I get that." Her face was pensive.

I was grateful she wouldn't push more now, but I wasn't dumb enough to think I was completely in the clear on this topic. I needed to tell her something, to make her feel like I wasn't shutting her out.

"My family usually comes for the first game. You could meet them."

Her shoulders relaxed. "I'd like that."

Hopefully meeting my family would show her what she meant to me without revealing all of me. I wasn't naive enough to think I could keep my past from her forever, but selfishly, I'd try as long as I could. If she found out, she'd be gone. There was no way she wouldn't blame me for what happened. I already did.

"We should probably get ready if we're going to see Frank."

We spent the rest of the day avoiding any mention of training camp and what would happen. It was like we were living in this bubble. Was Callie right, would my priorities change when football was an option? Did I want them to? Did I want to go back to who I was last year when I was so focused on football I couldn't see anything else?

Frank had another good day. We talked about training camp, the rookies, who would make it, and who probably didn't have what it takes. Frank didn't talk much about the wide receiver rookies. He must have sensed it was a sore subject.

Walking outside into the bright sun, I asked, "Want to head to your place?"

I didn't want to show her my condo. It was the ultimate bachelor pad, sleek modern lines, black leather, and a large-screen TV. When I was in season, I didn't care about my surroundings. With her, I did.

"Can we go to your house?" Her tone was tentative.

I could go for one more peaceful night. "We can stop and get your things."

We were quiet on the drive, lost in our thoughts. I didn't want to think about tomorrow, only about her hand in mine.

When we got home, I unlocked the door, letting her in. "Are you hungry? I can cook."

She smiled, her face relaxed. "*You* can cook something besides breakfast?"

"I can't eat out all the time or it affects my performance." I wiggled my brow. "All self-respecting men should be able to grill."

I got out steak, potatoes, and veggies to grill. I chopped the veggies while Callie cleaned the potatoes.

"I learned more out of necessity after my parents died. Grandpa wasn't the best cook."

I placed the veggies into a bowl to marinate them. "I hate you lost your parents so young."

I wished I could go back and change it for her. I wondered how the experience had changed her. Was she more cautious? Was she afraid to take risks? She'd stayed closer to home to be there for Frank. That made her an amazing person. She wasn't selfish. She didn't always put herself first. She deserved a man who'd put her first, not someone whose career was so demanding.

"Help me carry these out?" I picked up the platter of steaks and potatoes. I'd prepped more than we'd probably eat, but it would be good leftovers for the week.

She sat on the couch while I grilled, talking about her hopes for Rebel Sports. How she never thought she'd be in this position so young. It was all because of Reid. How much he believed in her.

"I had my doubts at first, but you're a hard worker, a go-getter. You're organized, efficient, and you have great ideas. Others would have seen it too." I closed the space between us, tipping up her chin.

"Thank you." Her eyes swam with emotion.

She didn't have parents to lift her up. I wanted to be that person for her. The idea surprised me because I never thought I'd be in the position of being anyone's partner or cheerleader. I'd resigned myself to a sideline role in most people's lives. The good-time guy.

I kissed her, pouring everything I was feeling into that kiss.

"The steak smells done."

"It does." She made me forget about everything when I was with her. Other things seemed less important.

We ate on the deck while the sun set, commenting on the boats we saw.

It was nice, comfortable. I wanted more nights like this.

"You should get a boat. You have a dock."

"The realtor insisted on me buying a property with one. She'd said it was a necessity in this area. I could have put one in later, but it's nice to have one now."

Cleaning up our plates, I asked, "Do you want to walk down there?"

She nodded eagerly. I cleaned up the plates, putting the leftovers in containers in the fridge.

We walked through the long grass down to the dock. "If we're going to be coming here often, I'll need to hire someone to cut the grass."

"Why not do it yourself?" It was a flippant comment, except there seemed to be more behind it. It felt like a test.

"I guess I could. I do like the idea of taking care of something myself." Of making something besides football a priority. I could take pride in other things.

"I'd need to buy a mower." We walked onto the dock. There was a bench on one side, but Callie sat on the edge, her feet dangling in the water.

"It could be fun buying things for your house." She smiled at me as I sat next to her.

It would make it mine. It wouldn't be as easy to pick up and leave or to think of Maryland as a temporary home. If I wasn't cleared to play, I could stay or go somewhere else. Other than my hometown, I'd never lived anywhere else.

"The water's cool." She kicked her feet in the water.

"Want to jump in?" I wanted to show Callie what it was like to let loose. To live a little.

She shook her head. "I don't know."

"I'll get in first." I stood, lifting my shirt over my head, then shoving down my briefs and shorts.

"You're crazy." She laughed as she watched me.

"I think you mean fun." I stepped off the dock, falling into the water. Coming up, I slicked back my hair.

Callie wiped her face. "Hey! You got me wet."

"That was the point." I swam closer to her.

"Oh no you don't." She lifted her feet as if she was going to move away from me.

I grabbed onto her ankle. "Come in with me, Callie."

She laughed uneasily. "No."

"The water feels good. I promise." I grinned.

She shook her head. "I don't believe you."

"Come in for me?" I lowered my voice.

"Ugh. With that charm, you can convince anyone to do anything."

I tilted my head to the side. "Yet it doesn't seem to be working with you."

She licked her lips.

"Please, Callie." My hand slid up her calf, to her thigh. "Think how much fun we could have."

Her breath hitched.

I changed tactics. "Callie, come in or I'm pulling you in— clothes and all."

"You wouldn't." Her voice had an edge to it.

I slid her closer to me. "I would."

"Ugh. Fine." She pulled her shirt over her head.

"Your bra too."

She glanced around as if worried someone would see.

"There's no one here. No boats. No neighbors."

"Oh, all right." She unhooked her bra, her breasts perky.

I lost my train of thought. Bracing myself on the edge of the dock, I leaned over to suck on her nipple. She arched into me. The water wasn't so cool anymore. I pulled down her shorts and panties, pulling her into my arms.

She inhaled sharply when her legs encountered the water. "It's cold."

I kissed her, slowly lowering her until she straddled my cock.

She moaned into my mouth.

"I told you it would be good."

I'd never expose her or hurt her, but I wanted her to have fun. To let loose. So much had been taken from her at a young age. I wanted her to feel like the girl she was—carefree with no worries.

I wanted her to be happy. Feelings for this woman coursed through me, happiness, desire, longing, and affection. I wasn't in love with her. It was too soon. She didn't know me, and how much did I really know about her?

I pushed those thoughts away, focusing on the feel of her pussy gliding over my cock. Her eyes glazed over as I slowly lowered her inch by inch.

"Put your hands on the dock for leverage." Her eyes refocused as she complied.

I thrust inside her to the hilt, pausing when I was fully seated. The position itself was awkward, but it heightened everything I was experiencing.

"Fuck." There was an explosion of sensations in my body as the feel of her pussy walls surrounded me. The white globes of her breasts pressed against my chest. The cool lap of water on my exposed chest, the hard nubs of her nipples, her legs tightening around my waist. The relative quiet of the night around us. The feeling of being completely alone yet wrapped up in one person.

She kissed me. It was passionate, yet messy. She finally ripped her lips from mine, tugging on my ear lobe, her lips trailing a path down my neck. Every muscle in my body tensed. The pace was almost frantic as I chased that feeling I only got with her—a sense of rightness, belonging, and a desire to claim her as mine.

On the edge, I stilled my movement, wanting her to go over first. I pressed my thumb against her clit. When she spasmed around me, I pumped inside her, roaring my release.

"Ohmygod." Callie rested her head against my shoulder.

I stilled. "We didn't use a condom."

She shrugged. "I'm on the pill. You said you were clean."

"I am." I enjoyed the feel of her in my arms as the coolness of the water registered. Goose bumps erupted over her skin. She began to shiver.

"Let's get inside." She needed a towel and dry clothes. And a fire to warm up.

It was summer but the air was unseasonably cool. I lifted her onto the dock. She quickly gathered her clothes as I pulled myself out, water pouring off me, dripping into my eyes. She threw my shirt in my direction. I used it to dry my face.

"Come on. I'm freezing." She gathered her clothes to her chest, running toward the house.

I followed at a slower pace, enjoying the view.

I couldn't believe she was here in my sanctuary, and she was perfect. The feelings swirling in my chest were bigger and more beautiful than before. They threatened to overwhelm me with their intensity, illuminating every sensation.

Callie threw open the back door to the house, scrambling inside. I closed and locked it behind us. Grabbing a blanket from the laundry room, I wrapped it around her shoulders. Her teeth were chattering.

"Let's take a hot shower." I lifted her into my arms, carrying her through the family room and up the stairs. Flicking on the gas fireplace in my bedroom, I set her down outside the shower. Turning the knob to hot, I waited for the water to warm the room before pulling the blanket off her and guiding her underneath the stream.

"Aren't you cold?"

"A little." The truth was, I was warm all over, either from the emotions swirling in my gut or from what we'd just shared. But I couldn't say that. What if she wasn't ready or didn't feel the same way? I wasn't sure how to handle it.

I stepped behind her, reaching for the shampoo to wash her hair. Her head tipped back, and she moaned in ecstasy. Turning her so the water rinsed the soap out, I grabbed the body wash, efficiently scrubbing her, warming her skin as I went.

I wanted her warm. I wanted her relaxed. "What about you?"

"I'm warming up." A slow smile spread over her face. Her voice didn't waver from the cold. Her skin was a healthy shade of pink, not blue.

"Why don't you grab a towel and get dressed? The bedroom should be warm."

"Yeah, okay." She moved to comply, covering her body with a large towel, then wrapping her wet hair with a second.

She was probably still feeling a chill. Jumping in the water was impulsive, and probably a little bit stupid. But I felt invigorated, almost giddy with anticipation for the future.

"Go lie down. I'll be right there."

"Don't take long," she teased.

I couldn't resist leaning over to kiss her softly on the mouth.

She giggled, tightening the towel around her. "You're all wet."

She stepped backward, smiling wide with happiness before disappearing into the bedroom.

I'd been so ambivalent about anything other than football, never allowing myself to feel anything. Now that I let the feelings in, everything was more intense. I closed my eyes, letting the water flow over my face and body. No matter how good this felt, I didn't deserve her. I didn't deserve anyone.

CHAPTER NINETEEN

CALLIE

I WOKE UP WARM AND COZY AFTER THE HOT SHOWER WITH THE fire and Jonah's arms around me. I never wanted to leave this house. Here, nothing could get to us, not training camp, the season, or our friends. There were no outside forces or worries creeping in.

I didn't want the night to end. Reality would be back as soon as I opened my eyes to the sunshine I saw under my lids.

Lips touched my shoulder, causing me to arch back into Jonah's hard cock. Another kiss along my spine. His fingers expertly rolled my nipples. His knee slipped between my legs.

"Good morning, beautiful." The words whispered across my ear.

Moving so I could see his face, I said, "Morning."

He kissed me, his cock nudging my entrance. I widened my legs, allowing him better access. There was no better way to wake up than this. I wanted to tell him everything I was feeling, but we were too new. We were untested. We'd lived in a cocoon the past few weeks, pretending nothing else existed.

He slid inside, impaling me on his cock. I was putty in his hands as he used the force of his hips to make me feel good.

One hand moved from my nipple and down my stomach to where we were joined.

"You're so wet."

It was all for him. Only he could make me this needy, this desired. When he circled my clit lightly, I moaned, "More."

"Whatever you want." He bit my neck lightly. The combined sensation of his cock, his fingers, and his teeth sent me over the edge too soon. I'd wanted to drag this out all morning, never getting out of bed. He pumped a few more times before pausing deep inside me, his cock jerking.

"I love waking up to you." He pulled out, moving to the bathroom.

I wanted to say *me too*, but he was already gone. The cool air drifted over my back, my fingers finding the sheets warm from the heat of his body. I was too tired to move. I lay there until he came back, cleaning me with a warm washcloth.

"You didn't need to do that." Between last night and now, I felt spoiled, cherished.

"I want to." He kissed my shoulder then threw the wash-cloth toward the hamper by the wall.

He tightened his arms around me, pulling me back against him. I didn't want to turn and face him. I didn't want him to see the emotions in my eyes. I couldn't hide them. I felt too raw.

"Nothing's going to change."

"Of course not." It was a lie. We both knew it. Everything was going to change.

We took our time that morning, me getting ready for work at Rebel Sports, him in athletic gear to go to training camp. He would continue his PT there so he was close to his team. It made sense.

The pressure of training camp was tremendous. The expectations were overwhelming.

Getting into Jonah's SUV, he said, "I'll drop you off on the way. I can pick you up tonight."

"Oh, you don't have to do that." I fastened my seat belt.

"How are you going to get home? Uber?" He glanced over at me, his expression incredulous.

"Well, yeah." It was far. I couldn't afford to Uber from work to home often. It wasn't practical.

He shook his head. "That's ridiculous. I'll pick you up."

His reaction warmed me more than the hot shower last night. "Okay."

In the parking lot, he gripped the back of my head, pulling me over the console. He kissed me like a man possessed, like a couple saying goodbye at the airport before a long separation or a soldier deploying for a long tour of duty.

"Have a good day."

I wanted the intensity of his touch, his lips, and the expression on his face to stay with me the rest of the day. "Good luck today."

"It's just another day of PT."

I smiled to cover my concern. It was much more than that, but neither of us admitted it out loud. "See you tonight."

He leaned over, kissing me one more time.

I closed the door, heading inside. It was the first day I was one hundred percent in charge. Reid and Jonah were at training camp. The facility was open for personal training and workouts, but the busy time would be when school and work let out.

With the facility open, I wondered if my hours should shift. Should I work in the evening more, visit with my grandfather in the morning when it was quieter? I'd have to talk to Reid about it.

I sat down to review the sign-ups for the fall sports to start assigning players and coaches, acquiring sponsorships for the teams. I got lost in the work. It was hard to believe this was my life, that this was my job. It was like a dream come true.

At lunchtime, my phone buzzed with an incoming text.

Dylan: Want to meet for lunch?

Callie: I'd love to. I don't have a car though.

Should I explain that Jonah dropped me off?

Dylan: No problem. I'll pick you up.

Thirty minutes later, we were on our way downtown.

"I love that you work so close now. We can have lunch or cocktails after work."

"Yeah, it's perfect." I just needed to pick a facility for Grandpa and get him moved closer. And find a new place to live.

"Are you still living in Baltimore?"

"For now. I need to get Grandpa moved closer before I find my own place."

"That commute is tough. Is your car in the shop?"

"No. Jonah dropped me off."

She shot me a knowing look. "Really? Are things getting serious between you two?"

"It feels serious." I just didn't know if Jonah felt the same way. The reverent way he'd handled me after sex in the river, and again this morning, made me think he did.

"That's good, right?"

"Training camp starts today."

"Football season is tough. They're so focused, but Reid still makes me feel important. He already sent me flowers at work saying he misses me."

"That's sweet." I wasn't even sure if Jonah was the flower sending type.

"Jonah will have his own way to make you feel special."

"I'm sure. He's picking me up tonight."

"Oh good. I wasn't sure if he'd have to stay at camp with the other guys or not."

Even if it wasn't required, would he feel obligated to stay?

She parked by the city dock and we walked to one of the restaurants by the water. "Want to eat outside?"

"Sure." It was a mild summer day.

"We should stick together during the season."

"I'm worried he's going to see his teammates playing or that rookie everyone's talking about vying for his position, and he's going to freak out. He's going to be so worried about keeping his job, he'll go back too soon, before he's healed."

"The trainers and doctors are good at seeing through that kind of thing. They won't put him out there before he's ready."

"I hope you're right."

"Just be there to support him. He's a professional. This is something they all have to deal with at one time or another."

Something told me Jonah might take it harder. He was more obsessed with football than Reid was. Reid had his family he wanted to help and support, but football wasn't his life in the same way. It was almost as if it was tied to Jonah's self-worth. I wondered why that was. "Do you know much about his past?"

"Jonah's?"

I nodded.

"Just where he's from, and that his family's nice. They visit when they can. Why?"

"I don't know. It's just—I get this feeling he's hiding something. Or he's not exactly who he seems. Like he's one person in front of his friends and fans, and another with me. It makes me wonder what else is different or why he feels the need to put on a front."

She shrugged. "He's a professional athlete. Everything he does is scrutinized."

I sighed. "Yeah, I'm probably overthinking it."

I took a few bites of my crab cake sandwich, determined to put it out of my mind.

A few seconds later, Dylan snapped her fingers. "Are you comparing Jonah to Reid's situation? Maybe you're projecting Reid's issues onto Jonah."

"Yeah, maybe." Just because Reid was hiding something didn't mean Jonah was too.

She looked at me sympathetically. "Or you're waiting for the other shoe to drop. You've been through a lot, and maybe you don't trust something good coming into your life."

I sucked in a breath. Was she right? Was I so jaded from my parents' accident that I couldn't enjoy a good thing when I had it?

"Have you had any serious relationships recently?"

We'd never discussed our past relationships with each other. It felt good to have a friend to talk things over with. "No. I was a little wild in high school after my parents' accident."

"That's understandable. I can't even imagine."

"I dated someone in college, but he transferred closer to home because he missed his family." He hadn't wanted to try long distance. It hurt. I'd let myself think we could be something more. When he'd left me behind so easily, I questioned everything. Why did people always seem to leave me? Why wasn't I enough for them to stay?

"If I were you, I'd take it day by day. Try not to jump to conclusions. See how things go. You're still new."

I picked up a fry, dipping it in ketchup. "That's good advice."

"That's what friends are for." She smiled triumphantly.

"We're having a get-together at the end of training camp to celebrate the start of the new season. I'd love it if you'd come. I'm sure Jonah would have invited you, but you're our friend too."

"I'd love to go." Maybe I'd held myself apart from people because I was worried I'd lose them too. The thought of losing Jonah sent a pang of unease through my chest.

Talk turned to their group of friends and how they played pickup football when they get together. Apparently, there was a lot of trash talk between the boyfriends and girlfriends. It sounded fun.

It felt good to be part of a group of friends. To feel like I belonged.

I said goodbye to Dylan when she dropped me off, determined not to worry about Jonah. I'd have faith that things would continue as they had so far.

I got lost in work, calling the tech guy to figure out an issue with the sign-up page. When dinner came and went without a text from Jonah, I got worried. I sent a text asking if he was still planning on coming. I could get an Uber, but he'd been adamant I wait for him.

When the minutes ticked by without a response, I searched online for any news about camp. There was an article on the rookie wide receiver. The reporter claimed this wide receiver was similar in playing style to Jonah. The speculation was that the coaches could easily replace him. There was more speculation about whether he'd ever perform at the same level again. The picture was one of the rookie catching a pass while Jonah looked on stone-faced.

Jonah never seemed like a jealous guy to me. He was confident in his abilities; he'd always given credit where it was due. So, I wasn't sure the reporter's comment about Jonah being short with reporters was true. I wanted to talk to Jonah. To make sure he was okay.

Finally, my screen lit up.

Jonah: Sorry, I'm running late. We're watching tapes. Can you get another ride home?

The anxiety about the future I'd felt before I talked to Dylan was back full force. I wouldn't be the jealous, clingy girlfriend. This was his career. It was important to him, and I'm sure he wanted to prove to the coaches he was determined to come back stronger than ever. I'd never get in the way of that.

Callie: Of course. No worries.

My vision blurred as I stared at the words I'd typed. It

wasn't true. I was worried about us, wondering whether our relationship could survive.

I shouldn't have gotten in so deep with him. I should have held myself back.

I pulled up my app, ordering a car. I'd go back to my small apartment in the city. I'd start the process of pushing back my feelings. I'd lower my expectations. That way I wouldn't get hurt.

I hated this. The push and pull of a relationship. The worry about whether you were enough or if the person would one day get sick of you and walk away. Being single was so much easier. You didn't set yourself up for heartache.

Then there was the saying—without risk, there were no rewards.

It sounded tempting, amazing even, but I needed a guarantee that things would work out. That the guy wouldn't walk away.

Checking the app, the car would be arriving soon. I headed outside to wait. When the small car pulled to the curb, I checked to make sure it matched the description before opening the door to get inside. I wrinkled my nose at the body odor the driver was giving off. I'd gone from a high this morning, lying in Jonah's arms, to knowing exactly where I stood. Football came first for Jonah when I wanted someone to put me first.

I knew what I was getting into when I started seeing Jonah. There was a possibility lurking in my mind that he'd get sucked back into his career. I'd let his touch and his sweet words seduce me, making me think we could transcend the stresses of a professional athlete's schedule and focus. I should have known better.

The love Reid had for Dylan—she was confident he'd quit if she needed him—was rare. That devotion didn't exist for me. I was always the one left behind and made to adjust to the new reality.

I'd focus on Rebel Sports so Reid wouldn't have to stress about a thing. Then I'd make sure Grandpa was taken care of. People depended on me. I wouldn't let them down. I was stupid to think I could depend on anyone else but myself.

I closed my eyes, remembering the warmth I'd felt last night. The feeling that I belonged, that Jonah was mine. It was nice for a moment, but I couldn't get used to it. Nothing lasted.

CHAPTER TWENTY

JONAH

WALKING TO MY SUV AFTER A DRAINING DAY AT CAMP, FANS yelled out, "Are you going to play again, JT?"

I opened my mouth to say, *as soon as I'm cleared,* but another asked, "When are you going to start earning that paycheck?"

I tensed, the back of my neck aching with tension. I should have taken the team massage therapist up on her offer for a massage, but I hadn't wanted to miss a meeting. It was the least I could do if I couldn't run on the field.

I smiled, but it felt brittle. "I want to get out there as soon as I'm cleared. I'm just as eager as you are."

"I bet you are. You'll be riding that bench until Baltimore releases you."

The cold trickle of fear slipped down my spine, but I refused to rise to the bait. I was better than getting down and dirty with some asshole fans. I tried to remember the kids' faces at Rebel's opening. That was who I played for, not these guys.

A security guard approached. "I'll walk you to your car, sir."

"Thanks, Hector." I made a point to remember everyone's names.

When my car door shut behind me, my shoulders relaxed. I threw the SUV in reverse, eager to go home. I had a few hours until I had to do this all over again.

The fans were unforgiving. The sports commentators acted like I had something to prove. I did, but how could I?

The uncomfortable reality was no one's position on the team was guaranteed, especially when on the injured reserve. I couldn't prove anything except I was devoted to the team and to getting back onto the field. I'd watch every film, attend every meeting, do every single thing the trainer asked of me until I was cleared to play.

My feet itched to be on the field, running faster than the rookies, catching every pass thrown at me if I had a chance of erasing my last game. I needed to replace the memory of that dropped ball with new ones.

The fans were fickle. I just needed one big play. Then last year would be forgotten.

I didn't want that one play to define the rest of my life. Panic made my throat tighten. If I wasn't cleared to play, it was unlikely I'd get picked up by another team. My career would end with me dropping the game-winning touchdown pass. Anytime my name came up, there'd be the film of me screwing up. I'd always wonder what if.

When I pulled into my driveway, I remembered how I was supposed to pick up Callie from work. I'd promised her I would, but that was before I realized I'd need to be a presence at camp. As much as listening to the questions and doubt bothered me, being absent would be worse.

Chase took me aside at lunch, telling me I needed to be present, the veteran there for his team.

When Callie's text came through, I was watching film. The pressure to be at every meeting was intense. I felt bad I'd forgotten my promise, but I'd make it up to her. She'd understand. This was what it was like dating an athlete. My job wasn't nine to five. It was doing whatever it took.

I showered, letting the stench of the day dissipate. Tomorrow would be better. I knew what to expect. Sliding into the sheets, Callie's smell surrounded me. Exhausted, I video-called her before I fell asleep.

"Hey." Her face filled my screen.

I couldn't tell from her expression whether she was upset.

I scrubbed a hand over my face. "I'm sorry about today. I didn't realize how intense it would be."

"I got home fine. Don't worry about me."

I shouldn't have promised her a ride not knowing how the day would go. Now that I was alone, surrounded by her scent on the sheets and the memory of this morning, I wanted to be there for her.

"I'm sorry. I got caught up. I thought I'd be able to come and go, but Chase thinks I need to be there to support the team."

"Of course, you do. I get it."

Did she? Or was she placating me?

"I miss you."

Her face softened. "I miss you too."

Should I ask for space? Was it fair to date her when I was so consumed by work?

I yawned, the stress of the day weighing me down.

"You should get some sleep."

"Yeah. I'm exhausted."

"Good night, Jonah." She hung up.

I should have asked about her day. If anything had come up at work. For the first time in a while, what was happening at Rebel Sports hadn't crossed my mind.

CHAPTER TWENTY-ONE

CALLIE

AFTER HIS CALL ON THE FIRST DAY OF CAMP, I WAS CAUTIOUSLY optimistic we'd be okay. At the end of that first week, I wasn't so confident. More often than not, he was too busy or too tired to call or text. I felt like an afterthought.

Resigned not to depend on him, I handled the tech issues with the website at work. I scheduled nursing home tours that weekend, inviting Dylan along.

At the first one, I got out of my car when I saw Dylan approaching. "Hey, thanks for coming."

"Of course. I'm happy to help."

It was nice to have a friend here, but I wished it was Jonah. Remembering how he'd offered to accompany me, I'd texted to ask if he'd join me, but he said he had a meeting with the wide receivers this morning. I understood the pressure, but at the same time, I hated that he'd forgotten about me so easily.

We went inside, checking in. Waiting in the lobby for a tour guide, I asked, "How's Reid doing at camp?"

"Good. He's feeling confident going into this season. I think coming out about his speech issues made him more confident overall. He's playing better than ever."

"That's great." I was happy for them, but my tone fell flat.

"How's Jonah doing?"

"Good. He's been pretty busy." My gaze snagged on the bulletin board by the front desk that outlined activities for the residents.

"It's only my first training camp while involved with a player, but it seems like a lot. There's so much scrutiny by the fans and the press. I bet Jonah's feeling pressure about when he'll be cleared to play." Dylan's tone was gentle.

I nodded. "Right."

"They get so focused. It's normal, I promise."

The difference was that Dylan and Reid were more established in their relationship, they'd been tested by her car accident and had come out better for it on the other side.

Jonah and I were new, still in the honeymoon stage of the relationship. I wasn't sure how many bumps we'd survive. Or if it was worth hanging on for the ride anymore.

"You're here to see the facility?" A woman in her thirties approached. She was dressed professionally in a suit.

"I am. It's for my grandfather."

"Of course. I'll show you around. Feel free to ask any questions."

The place was amazing. Clean and bright. The staff seemed engaged and determined to make the patients' stay enjoyable.

As we walked around, my stress eased. I felt better about the idea of moving him. He'd be closer to my work. I could stop by at lunch and when I got off. I felt excited about the possibility.

"Here's the brochure with everything you need to make a decision."

I skimmed the top sheet as we followed her back to the lobby. My gaze snagged on the price listed at the bottom of the page.

She paused in the lobby, her smile warm. "What do you think?"

"It's great. I'd feel good about placing him here—"

"What's holding you back?"

"Honestly? The price. I'm not sure if this is doable." Insurance paid eighty percent. It was the other twenty I was worried about.

She flipped through the pages in my hands. "This is a list of options for you. There are a few assistance programs that might be a possibility."

The disappointment was acute. This was why I hadn't visited any of the locations. It was the financial part that had me panicked. How could I afford the rest of his care and his medications when I needed to pay rent?

Dylan's arm wrapped around my shoulder. "We'll take a look at it and call with any questions."

"I'm happy to help. I think your grandfather would be a good fit here."

Dylan guided me out. "I'll look into these places for you."

"Would you?" I could do it myself, but help sounded better.

"Yeah, this is what I do. I find funds for people who need it."

"Thanks, Dylan."

She paused at my car. "Are you okay?"

"I'm just feeling a little overwhelmed." I was light-headed all morning. I thought it was stress, but maybe I was coming down with something.

"Why don't you lie down when you get home?"

"I should." Exhaustion pulled at me. I wanted nothing more than to cover my head with a blanket and fall asleep.

She held the paper with the financial assistance information in her hand. "If it's all right, I'll take this, research some options, and we can talk about it."

The relief was acute. "Thanks. I really appreciate it."

"Of course." She hugged me quickly. "It'll be okay."

It wasn't just the financial part. It was the fact that moving

Grandpa here was admitting his disease was progressing. It felt out of my control. I hated it.

I visited Grandpa that afternoon, not expecting to see Jonah. He'd mentioned they were volunteering as a team with a local group of kids.

I understood his work commitments, but I wished he'd make seeing me a priority at some point. Would I not see him for the duration of the camp? If I'd known that going in, maybe I wouldn't be so bothered by it. Or if he called me each day, but he didn't.

"How is Jonah doing at camp?"

"He's focused on getting better."

"Is he worried about that rookie?" Grandpa's voice was rough.

I pushed his cup over to him, hoping he'd drink. "I think so, but he hasn't said much to me."

He nodded toward the TV where sports news played. "The commentators are trying to make it look like a rivalry."

"I haven't talked to him much since camp started, so I'm not sure."

He looked at me. "I thought you two were together?"

"We are." Kind of. Or I thought we were.

"Then why don't you know more about what's going on?"

"He's really focused on football. I think that crowds out anything else."

"He's young. Football's important to him. I can understand that." Grandpa nodded like it was no big deal. Like my heart wasn't breaking in two.

"Things were so great when he was working at Rebel Sports. I wasn't prepared I guess."

"It's an adjustment anytime you start a new job. Why don't you help him like you did Reid?"

"Be his personal assistant?" I didn't like that idea at all.

Grandpa nodded.

"That's not what I want to do. It was a good job when I

was in school, but I need something in my field, something I'd be proud of." I wouldn't feel great following him around.

What would I do when our relationship was over? I'd have a front-row seat to women coming onto him. Of course, it was still happening, I just didn't see it. That made me uneasy too.

Jonah never had a girlfriend during his career. What if he decided I wasn't worth it? Maybe he'd decide he wanted one of the groupies instead. They were less trouble. You didn't have to call them at the end of your day. Not that he was calling me.

"If you're not happy, you should talk to him." This was the grandpa I knew. He saw through the bullshit.

I looked out the window. "I don't want to be clingy when he should be focused on football."

"Maybe he needs you too but doesn't know how to ask for help."

The idea gave me hope. Was he in over his head? Was he stressed about the rookie? I'd been so wrapped up in feeling left out I hadn't considered that he might need someone to talk to. He might not even realize it.

Grandpa turned his attention back to the TV, turning up the volume.

I paid close attention to when he talked, tucking away his advice to pull out later because I wasn't sure how long he would have to dole out advice. There would come a time when he wouldn't remember me at all, when he wouldn't be coherent.

I texted Jonah, asking if he'd have time to talk or get together. I didn't want to be needy, but if we were in a relationship, then we should be able to talk about things. We needed to work out something for the season that made sense. If he wanted to take a step back, then it would be nice to know that so I could move on.

Surprisingly, Jonah responded right away, saying he could meet me at his house in Southern Maryland later.

When dinner arrived for Grandpa, I kissed his cheek, saying goodbye.

Tonight, I'd talk to Jonah. The drive to his home seemed longer by myself. I was exhausted from worrying about Grandpa and the situation with Jonah.

I could probably swing the nursing home, especially if Dylan found us some assistance, but I couldn't afford to move. Rent in the city was cheaper than in the county, plus I'd need the security deposit and first month's rent. I'd just started paying back my student loans.

The realization I couldn't afford more loans struck me in the chest. Even if I was accepted into the MBA program, I probably couldn't go, not yet. I loved my grandfather, but sometimes I resented having to grow up at such a young age.

Turning into Jonah's driveway, I questioned talking to him when I was so upset, especially when I was frustrated with more than just the situation with him.

I knocked on the door, wondering if I should have gone home.

Opening the door, he said, "Callie."

He looked so good in workout pants, a T-shirt, and bare feet. He held his hand out, pulling me inside into his arms.

I rested my head against his chest, breathing him in. His arms tightened around me. "I missed this. I missed you."

"I did too." There were so many things I should have asked like, *why haven't you called to check in with me?* But I squeezed my eyes shut, enjoying the moment.

"I didn't realize how much until now."

That comment had my shoulders stiffening. It sounded too much like an out-of-sight, out-of-mind notion. It made me feel forgettable. I pulled away from him.

"Come here." I reluctantly took his hand as he led me to a stool in the kitchen. I stood between his legs, a hand on his chest, his heart beating a steady rhythm beneath my fingers.

FALLING FOR YOU

His mouth by my hair, he said, "I lost my mind a little this week."

I tipped my head back to see his face. "What do you mean?"

He brushed a hair out of my face. "I got caught up in the hype. The reporters kept asking how I felt about the rookie gunning for my position until I was convinced I was in competition with that guy."

"Aren't you?"

His lips pressed into a tight line. "My record should speak for itself. I have nothing to prove."

"It's hard not to get caught up in the negative energy." I'd been at enough press conferences to know reporters' questions could burrow into a player's psyche, messing him up.

"I know better. I've been doing this a long time."

He'd opened things up for me to talk about what had bothered me this week. "Is that what happened? You just got caught up in the hype?"

"Yeah. I'm not proud of it. I felt like I had to be at every meeting, watch every minute of film."

"What made you change your mind?" I wanted him to say he missed me.

"Coach pulled me aside, said my responsibility was PT, eating healthy, getting enough sleep, and getting better."

"That's good advice." I waited for him to acknowledge he'd neglected me.

"I forgot what's important."

"Not really. You wanted to do a good job. Football's important to you."

"*You're* important to me. I went to camp and did exactly what I said I wasn't going to do. I got lost. I didn't have time to call you, to see how you were doing. I hated being stressed out."

I leaned into him. "I was wondering if you'd changed your

mind about us. If a relationship was too much for you right now."

"I want to be able to call you at the end of the day to talk about it. I want to send you a text just because." He buried his head in my hair.

"I want that too."

"How've you been?" His lips brushed my hair.

"I went with Dylan to check out one of the places on my list for Grandpa."

His arms tightened around me. "I hate that you went without me. I wanted to be there."

"I'd put it off for too long."

"Did you like it?"

"Yeah, it's a great place. It sucks to even have to be making this decision."

"You're doing the right thing for him."

"Thanks." I relaxed into his hold. It felt good to unburden myself, but I wasn't ready to talk about the financial stress. Like Reid, he'd want to step in and fix it, but I wanted to do it on my own.

"Are you going to move closer to work now?"

I hesitated, not sure what to say. "I'll think about it more once he's settled."

That would be a few weeks. Maybe things will look better. Give Dylan a little time to work her magic.

"I'm so sorry that I wasn't there for you this week."

I pulled back so I could see his face. "I want to be there for you too. If you'd talked to me about what was going on, I could have helped."

"You're right. I'm not used to having someone to talk to. Someone who's there for me."

"You're used to relying on yourself."

Something crossed his face that looked like regret. He covered it so quickly I thought I'd imagined it. "I have a day off tomorrow. Let's spend it together."

"That sounds perfect."

He kissed me softly. It felt like coming home. All the worries and unease from the week faded away. We'd handled our first issue without too much fuss. We'd need to communicate better in the future, but for now, we were okay.

His hand in my hair, the other on my waist, he deepened the kiss. Pulling back slightly, he asked, "Are you hungry?"

"No." I hadn't eaten anything since lunch, but I wanted to be with him. I needed this assurance that we were okay.

"Good." He dove back in, kissing me like he'd been starved for me this past week. I wanted to believe that was true. That despite his infrequent texts, he'd missed me. That this was real.

"I can't get enough of you." He stood, cradling my jaw, his voice tinged with emotion.

"Me either." When he was like this, open and vulnerable, I felt like I was in a free fall.

He picked me up, carrying me to his bedroom. He undressed me slowly, using his mouth and hands to trail a path across my body. I felt cherished, loved.

I arched into him, begging for more contact, more of him. I pushed away the doubts and insecurities to stay in this moment with him.

He moved down the bed, spreading my legs with his broad shoulders, sucking my clit into his mouth. This wasn't a slow seduction. It was a takeover. The sensations rolled over me one after the other, the tight grip of his fingers on my thighs, the suction of his mouth, the scrape of his scruff.

I tugged on his hair. "More."

He renewed his efforts, using a firmer touch.

I cried out, arching into his mouth, spasming around him. Boneless, I dropped back to the bed, spent. Exhaustion from the stress of the week washed over me. He quickly shucked off his clothes, kneeling between my splayed legs. He interlaced his fingers with mine on either side of my head, lowering his cock to my entrance. He slowly entered me while he kissed me. I couldn't escape him, the feel of his naked skin on me, his scent, his touch. He was everywhere, overwhelming me, consuming me.

I wanted to get lost in this moment, forgetting everything else.

Everything in my body tightened when he found the spot inside, the one that burned only for him. He started a slow glide, whispering across my lips, "Go over, baby. I want to go with you."

I whimpered before the orgasm crashed into me like a wave on the rocks, devastating and refreshing. He was chipping away at my defenses, softening out my edges, making me smooth, making me his.

He pounded into me. I lifted my hips, meeting every thrust. I wanted to be enough for him.

He thrust deep, growling into my neck. I longed to be enough for him. It was asking a lot, probably too much for a guy like him. I had to keep those feelings to myself. They'd ruin everything.

He rolled away from me, going to the bathroom. When he returned, he slipped beside me, pulling me into his chest. He kissed my temple, his breath evening out.

I didn't want to be a stop for him. A distraction or a good time. I wanted to be more than that. I wanted to be everything.

CHAPTER TWENTY-TWO

JONAH

IT FELT GOOD TO BE HOME. I DIDN'T HAVE TO OPEN MY EYES to know Callie was here. Her hair tickled my arm, her scent invading my nose.

When she moved, kissing my shoulder, I said, "I did something crazy."

I opened my eyes to her resting her chin on her hand.

"What's that?" Her eyes were soft, not full of the shadows I'd seen when she was at my door.

"I bought a boat."

"You did?" Her eyes widened.

"I wanted to do something with you this weekend by ourselves. No friends. No distractions. Just you and me."

"Where is it?"

"At the dock."

"Here?" She scrambled out of bed, hurrying to the window to pull back the curtains. "Holy shit. You did."

I came up behind her, pushing her hair off her shoulder, kissing her skin. "Want to take her out today?"

"I'd love to." The sun was shining on the water. It made me hopeful for more than one perfect day. It made me think a future was possible with Callie.

"Let's eat, pack a lunch, and go."

I wanted a full day of nothing but us on the water, enjoying each other's company before I had to be back at work tomorrow.

She threw her hair in a messy bun and put on shorts and a T-shirt before following me downstairs.

"I can't believe you bought a boat." Her tone was full of wonder as she pulled down mugs for coffee.

There was something else there too, was it jealousy? She'd never hinted that my wealth bothered her before. I figured she was used to it being surrounded by athletes.

I enjoyed what I had, but I didn't flaunt it. "Do you think it was impulsive?"

I pushed the brew button on the coffee machine, pressing a hip against the counter. She bustled around the kitchen, pulling out eggs and milk.

"Definitely." Her smile was teasing.

Maybe I'd imagined any jealousy. "I work hard. I want to enjoy my free time."

It was worth the extra cost to expedite the sale and have it delivered.

"Of course."

Something was still bothering me about her tone. I pushed it aside. I wanted to enjoy today, not assuming there were problems when there weren't. Too soon, I'd be feeling the pressure of getting back on the field.

When we were together, it faded away. I liked that feeling. I wanted to hold on to it.

She whisked the eggs and milk in a bowl. "I can't wait to be out on the water. It's the perfect day for it."

I moved closer, wanting to touch her while she cooked.

She poured the eggs into the frying pan.

"I like you cooking in my kitchen." She hadn't asked, she'd just done it on her own.

Her smile was sheepish. "Sorry, I was hungry."

"I don't mind." I kissed her upturned lips before packing a lunch and snacks while she finished breakfast. We made a good team.

If only my job didn't take over so much of my life. If only we'd met when I was retired, I'd have the time to put into our relationship.

Unease slid down my spine. Was it wrong to get more involved with her when the season was just starting? Could I give her what she needed? I'd handled this week badly. I'd have to see how things went the next few weeks.

She slid a plate over to me, dropping two slices of wheat toast next to it.

"I could get used to this." I took a bite of the warm eggs.

"What? Someone taking care of you?"

Affection for her flowed over me, making me warm from more than the fresh-brewed coffee. "You being here in my space."

She should move in. The idea hit me like a ball to my stomach. Hard and sharp, stealing my breath. It was too soon. We barely knew each other. If this week was any indication, I wasn't ready for a serious relationship. I was shit at juggling my priorities. I got too focused on one, ignoring the other.

She grinned, then leaned over to kiss me softly.

We ate quickly, eager to get out on the water. I followed behind her, carrying towels and our food.

She paused on the dock, taking it in.

It was a sleek motorboat. Something I could use as a pleasure boat or for fishing.

"I love it."

I stowed our stuff then held out my hand to her to get on board. I turned on the engine, prepping the boat to leave.

Untying the lines, we headed out on the water. I never thought I'd feel this kind of peace. It was like having my own slice of heaven, the house, the boat, being on the water with Callie. This felt right. This was where I was supposed to be.

For the first time, the thought of a long season of practices, games, and travel wasn't appealing.

I wanted to be with Callie, building this thing between us until it was so strong nothing could break it. My fingers tightened on the wheel. The only issue was my past. Was it possible she wouldn't find out?

We didn't have to visit my hometown. My parents never brought up what happened. I assumed they were ashamed.

I drove to a quiet spot and turned off the engine, letting the boat drift.

"Is everything okay?" Callie shifted closer, her hand on my thigh.

I placed my hand over hers. "I'm happy you're here. This week was crazy."

"I can't imagine the pressure you're under. I feel bad for thinking—" She moved away, looking over the water.

"For thinking what?"

She bit her lip. "For thinking you'd changed your mind about us."

"That never entered my mind." The scary part was when I was focused on football, not much else entered it.

She still looked uneasy.

"I want to be with you. I'll try to do better this week."

"I don't want to be clingy. I just like to touch base with you. Know you're okay."

"I don't think you're being clingy." I hadn't been in many relationships. But the one serious one I'd had, we'd talked every day.

"I like being with you." I pulled her close, wrapping an arm around her.

"Me too."

"Let's enjoy this thing between us. I'll make a better effort to touch base with you while I'm working."

"I don't want to be a task on your to-do list." She moved

her finger like she was crossing off a box. "I checked in with Callie today."

"Don't ever think that." She was important to me. I didn't want her worried about her place in my life. There had to be a way to show her she was a priority.

"Why don't you come and watch camp sometime this week?"

"I'm supposed to be managing Rebel Sports."

"Work doesn't pick up until the afternoon or evening, right?" She nodded.

I could see her thinking about the possibility. "You could stop by in the morning."

She licked her lips. "Won't it be an issue for the media coverage there?"

"I don't care if they know we're dating. It might be a good thing. Maybe they'll go easy on me."

Her forehead wrinkled. "I doubt that. It could make things harder for you."

"I like you. I'm with you. End of story."

She smiled like she liked that explanation.

"Are you ready to fish?"

We spent the day fishing, then eating, then driving around to see different spots on the river. We got back in the evening. We were tired and in need of a shower. I quickly cleaned everything up while she went upstairs to shower first.

Things between us would be easier if I could figure out my job. That was on me. I needed to be more attentive. At first, I was worried she'd be a distraction. She was, but she was the best kind there was. She'd be there for me if I remembered to reach out. When the reporters were stressing me out, I could talk to her. She'd be a sounding board.

I headed upstairs, intending to join her in the shower. I pushed open the door to see her eyes closed and head tipped back as she stood in the water. I undressed, stepping in behind her. My hands skimmed her shoulders. When she startled, I kissed her neck.

"I didn't hear you come in." She turned to face me, a smile on her face.

I was falling for her. The words were on the tip of my tongue. I needed her more each day. Instead, I kissed her. Cupping her breasts, I rubbed a thumb over her nipple. They pebbled under my touch, the water making her skin slick.

I wanted her at training camp, in the stands at my games, with our friends. I wanted her, and I wouldn't stop until she was mine.

She arched her back, pressing her nipples into my hands.

I leaned down, kissing the globes of her breasts, tracing the moisture with my tongue. I vowed to make sure she felt special this week. I'd send her flowers, I'd video call, maybe even add in a little phone sex. Next week, she wouldn't doubt where she stood. I'd overwhelm her senses, even if we couldn't see each other often.

Her head tipped back; her eyes closed as my mouth sucked on her nipple. "You're intense tonight."

I lifted my head, waiting until her eyes opened. "I don't want you to doubt me."

"I won't." Her eyes were clear of the worry and doubt I'd seen earlier.

"I'll make sure of it." No more leaving things to chance or thinking she'd figure out she was too good for me and walk away.

I hoisted her in my arms, pressing her back against the tiles. Her legs wrapped around my waist, her arms around my neck. When I thrust inside, her head fell back against the wall.

I loved the way her pussy clamped around me. I liked her hot and needy for me.

"Jonah." She ran her fingers through my hair.

The tenderness in her voice combined with her touch sent tingles down my spine. I covered her mouth with mine so I wouldn't say the words popping into my head. Be with me. Don't leave.

The thoughts swirled in my head, getting stronger and more insistent with each rotation, but it was too soon. It would trigger a fight-or-flight response in her. Instead, I'd keep it cool, be a good boyfriend, make her a priority. Everything else would fall into place.

I convinced myself she never had to find out about my past. No reporter had ever brought it up. My parents didn't talk about it. My secret was safe.

I remembered my coach's advice from high school when I left to play in college. He'd said not to get too cocky. Always work like you were the underdog, like nothing was guaranteed. I'd do the same with Callie. She'd never doubt where my priorities stood again.

I moved my hand between us, pressing her clit. Callie tensed before she moaned, her skin flush and pink from the heat of the water, her pussy spasming around my cock, setting off my own release. I bit her neck lightly, soothing it with my tongue.

"You feel so good." She felt like coming home. It wasn't the house. It was her being here. She could take care of herself, but I wanted her here with me whenever I had a spare moment. I didn't want to waste time waiting for her to travel from the city when we'd have so little time together during the season.

Her arms and legs tightened around me as if she wasn't ready to let me go. We stood like that for a few minutes until the water ran cold and Callie began to shiver.

"Let's get you out of here." I carefully placed her on the floor, grabbing a thick towel to wrap around her.

Her expression was so vulnerable, I leaned down, promising to take care of her with my kisses. My touch. I'd ask her to move in soon.

CHAPTER TWENTY-THREE

CALLIE

FIRST THING MONDAY MORNING, FLOWERS WERE DELIVERED TO work. The note said: *I miss you. Every time you see these roses, think of me. —Jonah.*

I breathed in the scent of the flowers as my heart skipped a beat at his sweet words. I snapped a pic, sending him a text with the caption: **I love them. Thank you.**

Jonah: Are they working? Are you thinking of me?

I only hesitated a second before telling him the truth.

Callie: I'm always thinking of you.

My heart raced. Was it too much too soon? Had I misread the intensity of this weekend or the flowers?

Jonah: Me too.

A few seconds later, he sent a selfie of him at camp with Chase and Reid. He looked relaxed and happy. I hoped that meant he hadn't let the reporters get to him. For his sake, I hope he was cleared to play before the season started.

This weekend things seemed to catapult into serious territory. He'd seemed intense yet at the same time holding back. Was he worried he'd come on too strong?

I wasn't looking for a serious relationship, but that was because I was afraid I'd have something to lose. I still felt that way about Jonah, but I wanted to risk it, to see where it would go.

That night, Jonah called to video chat before bed.

"Hey, you." I couldn't stop the smile from spreading across my face.

"Hey. I wanted to say good night."

Disappointment coursed through me. I'd hoped we could talk about our day too.

"You're tired?" I asked, unable to keep the disappointment out of my voice.

"Not too tired to talk to you."

That earlier fullness I'd felt in my chest was close to bursting. "How was camp?"

"Good."

"Yeah? Did the reporters back off?"

"No. I just acted like the old Jonah, the one who knew he belonged there. No rookie's taking over my position."

I wanted to say *that a boy*, but that would have been cheesy. "That's great. I'm confident you'll be back on the field soon."

I knew how reporters operated. If they sniffed out insecurities, they'd capitalize on them. If Jonah exuded confidence, they wouldn't gain much by prodding him.

"Thanks for supporting me even when I was being an ass."

My face heated at his words. "You were just knocked down a bit."

"You're good for me."

I couldn't tell him I was afraid I'd lose to football or a groupie. It was hard to let go of those fears, but I wanted to for him. "I think you're good for me too."

"I want you here."

"At training camp?" He'd mentioned it over the weekend, but I wasn't sure he was serious.

"Yeah."

"I'd like that."

I didn't ask what he'd told the other players or whether they'd assume I worked for him or Reid. I wouldn't assume the worst-case scenario. I'd trust him.

I yawned.

"I'll let you get to bed."

"Thanks for calling." It was the little things like this I'd missed last week. It was crazy how not calling or texting made you feel less important.

"I missed you today. I got used to having you around."

"Me too." We'd spent part of the weekend together but I'd felt the same. Eating together, going boating, sleeping over, it felt good. It felt natural. Nothing was forced.

"Sleep tight, Calliope."

I smiled, loving the sound of my full name on his lips. It held none of the mock teasing kids had used when I was young. It sounded beautiful coming from him. "You too."

I snuggled into bed, anticipating seeing him made it difficult to settle down for sleep.

I WOKE UP TO GOOD MORNING TEXTS AND A PICTURE OF whatever Jonah was doing that day, working out, physical therapy, or watching film. Each night, we video chatted before we went to sleep.

On Thursday morning, Dylan stopped by for lunch. She was waiting for me in the lobby when I came out to meet her.

A delivery man was at the front desk where the new receptionist was working. "It's for a Calliope Goodwin."

"Oh, she's right there."

He walked toward me. "Ms. Goodwin?"

"Yes."

"You'll need to sign for this."

Dylan took the package while I signed his electronic pad. "Have a good day."

"You too."

"What is it? The return address is the team offices." She handed the package to me.

I'd mailed numerous packages for Reid over the years, like jerseys and signed balls for his fans. I almost wished Dylan wasn't here so I could open it in private.

"I'll just put this in my office before we go."

She followed me. "I want to know what Jonah sent you."

"We don't know it's from Jonah. It could be something for Reid. Lena probably forgot I'm not his PA anymore."

"I bet it's from Jonah."

My heart was beating heavily in my ears. I wanted it to be from Jonah. I placed it on my desk to deal with it later, turning to go.

Dylan stood in the doorway. "Oh no you don't. I want to know what's in there."

"Friends are so annoying."

"You know it." She moved closer, rubbing her hands together.

"You know it's probably nothing." I reluctantly turned it over, my finger sliding between the seams.

"You won't know if you never open it."

I opened it slowly, trying to tell myself it was just someone mistaking me for the guys' PA, or the team donating something to the office, it wasn't for me specifically.

The paper fell away, revealing shiny purple and black material.

Dylan squealed. "It's his jersey."

My heart stuttered. It was. I lifted it in the air, his number, eighty-three, and the name Templeton in bold print above it. A paper fell to the floor.

Dylan leaned down to pick it up. "Oh look, a note."

It was handwritten.

Callie, When you come to training camp, please wear this. I can't wait to see you in it...

Dylan leaned closer.

"I'm assuming it's from Jonah, but it doesn't say." I turned the paper over. **And nothing else. Jonah** was written on the back.

My face heated. I shoved the note in my purse to examine later when I was alone.

"You have to put it on and send a pic to him. I'll help you."

"I don't know if that's a good idea."

"Trust me. He's going to love it. It'll guarantee he's thinking of you."

"Fine." I wanted to get this over with, but at the same time, I loved the idea of sending him a pic because he was always sending me ones of him. I pulled the jersey over my head.

Dylan tied the jersey in a knot at my waist so a sliver of my belly was showing.

"This is perfect."

She held out her hand. "Phone, please."

I gave it over.

"Stand like this." Dylan cocked her hip in a sexy pose.

"I don't know if I can pull that off."

"Oh, you can, trust me." She dug through her purse, throwing a tube of lipstick at me. "Put this on."

It was candy apple red.

She fluffed my hair.

She gestured at me while holding up the phone. "Come on. Give me a come-hither look."

"This is ridiculous."

She lowered her phone. "You're right. You should stand in front of the Rebel Sports sign in the front."

"That's not what I meant." I'd been talking about the impromptu photo-shoot session, not the location.

But she was already grabbing her purse, walking quickly back to the lobby.

The receptionist, Laura, raised a brow when we returned, our high heels clicking on the floor.

Dylan waved a hand at her. "Oh, don't mind us. We're sending sexy pics to Callie's boyfriend."

My cheeks flushed hotter.

"Go stand in front of the sign," Dylan said while she fiddled with the settings on my phone.

I reluctantly moved in front of it, cocking a hip to copy her seductive pose. She'd made it look effortless, but it felt awkward.

Dylan looked at me through the lens, then came over to move me where she wanted.

She smiled, holding up the phone again. "I like your cheeks flushed. You look like you're thinking of something naughty."

"Just take the pic." I felt ridiculous standing here.

"Can you think of something you've done with Jonah recently that was super naughty? When he gets this pic, it will be the first thing he thinks of."

My mind skipped back to Monday morning when I'd dropped to my knees in the shower, sucking on Jonah's cock. I'd never felt sexier, more powerful. My panties got wet thinking of it, my shoulders relaxed, my hip pushed farther out.

"Purse those lips. Perfect." She took several shots, taking a second to scroll through.

"Just don't post these online. These are so hot. Reid will have a conniption."

I stepped closer, looking over her shoulder. I looked sexy. There was a challenge in my eyes, a seductive pout on my lips.

"He's going to love it." She sent it to him, then put my phone in my hand.

"There. It's sent."

"He could be with his trainer, his coach, his teammates…"

"Even better. Trust me, guys love this stuff. It's not like you were naked. It's classy." I couldn't help but think he would have preferred me in nothing but the jersey.

We headed back to my office so I could change. "I don't remember you sending Reid naughty pics."

"Not back when we were first dating. But I did when we knew we were forever." Her eyes softened.

"We just started dating." I took the jersey off and carefully folded it, holding it to my chest as we headed outside to go to lunch.

"Trust me. He won't be annoyed you sent this during work hours. He's going to love it and pounce on you the next time he sees you. Don't be surprised if he shows up tonight."

My skin tingled with anticipation. "I doubt it. He's pretty busy."

I slid into Dylan's sedan. My phone buzzed as she pulled out of the lot.

Jonah: I love it.

I closed my eyes. *I loved him.* Where had that come from? We'd only been dating a few weeks. A few deliveries of flowers and a football jersey, and I was putty in his hands.

Jonah: You're so beautiful.

He hadn't said sexy or hot, the two words I would have expected.

Callie: Thank you. For the jersey and for saying I'm beautiful.

Jonah called. I held the phone to my ear, feeling Dylan's gaze on the side of my face. "Hey."

"Hey, beautiful. I'm going to make it my screensaver."

"You are not." I couldn't keep the incredulous tone out of my voice.

"You can't stop me."

"Anyone will be able to see it."

"I was standing next to Coach Ackerman when you sent it." His tone was teasing.

I sank farther into my seat, wanting to disappear. "Dylan sent it. Not me."

"You have nothing to be embarrassed about."

Would his coach or his teammates think I was just another cleat chaser, a groupie? That I was Reid's assistant trying to get to one of the players?

"Now everyone knows you're mine."

"*Everyone* saw?"

"Well, Chase was here too. You know how it is, the locker room is a bunch of women gossiping all day. No offense."

"None taken." I did know how it was. "You don't mind them teasing you?"

"Not as long as they know you're off-limits, and not because Reid said so, but because you're mine."

His words settled deep in my chest. "I like that."

I could feel the curiosity emanating from Dylan. She was dying to know what we were talking about.

"I'm going to lunch with Dylan."

"Have fun. Thanks for the spank bank."

"Ugh. I knew it." For all of his pretty words, he'd thought it was hot too.

"I miss you, Callie." His tone was serious. I wondered if he was around the guys now or by himself.

"I miss you too."

"Call you later. Wear the jersey tomorrow."

Feeling bold I said, "I'll wear it to bed tonight."

"Fuck. Are you serious?" His voice was low, sending the best kind of shiver down my spine.

"Yes." I liked this game we were playing. It was naughty and thrilling.

"And nothing else." His tone was commanding.

I loved it. "You'll have to wait and see."

He growled over the line.

I said goodbye, grinning at his reaction

"Well, did he like it?"

I settled back in my seat. "He loved it."

"I knew he would. How are you guys doing?"

"Good. Things last week were a little weird. But I think we've figured out the time away thing."

Of course, he wasn't that far away. In season, he'd be flying across the country.

"You get used to it. You can fly to the games."

I couldn't afford to do that. It was no secret Dylan came from money. She didn't flaunt it, but she didn't worry about money either. She had her trust fund to fall back on.

"We'll see how it goes." As hard as I was falling for him, I was still cautious.

"Jonah's never been like this with anyone. He's never brought anyone to training camp or a game."

"Why is that?"

"I assume most guys are careful about who they date and bring around the organization. So many women are just looking for a hookup with a player, a few minutes of fame, and expensive presents."

I liked that I was different for him. I just wondered if there was another reason he'd been so private.

CHAPTER TWENTY-FOUR

JONAH

.

EVER SINCE CALLIE SENT ME THAT PICTURE, I'VE BEEN imagining sinking my cock into her while she was only wearing my jersey. I could practically see her nipples poking through the material, my hands gliding up her thighs, cupping her mound. I was constantly adjusting my junk.

It was the pose, the sliver of belly she'd exposed, the slight pout to her lips, and the challenge in her eyes. It was like she was thinking about me when she took that picture. Thinking about doing naughty things to me, maybe even remembering how she sucked my cock in the shower.

As soon as I got back to my room, I showered then video called her. I was staying in the dorm with the other guys because it didn't make sense to commute every day.

"Jonah." Callie's face filled the screen. Her voice lifted on my name as if she was excited to talk to me.

"Hey, Calliope. What are you wearing?"

She moved the phone so I could see more of her. She was in my jersey. Her fingernails were painted purple to match. The numbers eight and three were painted individually on two fingers. As amazing as that was, I had to know if she was wearing anything underneath.

"Are you—" I couldn't choke the words out; I grabbed my cock through my briefs. I was already hard at just the thought of her naked underneath.

She spread her legs. "Want to find out?"

Where had this Callie come from? The one who oozed confidence, who went for what she wanted. I loved it.

I nodded, not caring how eager it made me look. I was crazy for this girl.

Her hand glided up her thigh, pulling up her jersey until I saw her pink pussy.

I pulled my cock out of my briefs, stroking it. My head was tingly; my heart raced in anticipation.

"Are you touching yourself?" Callie's tone wavered.

"Yes. Will you?"

This was our first time having phone sex. Heck, it was my first time doing something like this with anyone. I was hesitant to order her around even if I wanted to.

She licked her lips, her finger separating her folds, one purple nail slid inside.

"Fuck, Callie. That's hot."

She added a second finger, and I squeezed my cock harder.

"Imagine they're my fingers. Thicker than yours. I'd pump harder."

Her thighs were shaking, her pussy glistening, her eyes glazed with lust as she pistoned her fingers faster. "I wish you were here."

"If I was, I'd push that jersey over your breasts so I could see your pretty nipples."

She set the phone down, making sure it was steady before scrambling to push up the jersey; her fingers were still buried deep.

I groaned, not caring if anyone heard.

"Rub your nipples." Pinch them, pull them.

She whimpered. I wasn't sure whether it was from her fingers touching her nipples or my dirty words.

"I can't hold back." Callie's voice was strained.

"Come with me." I jacked myself harder at the sight of her orgasm. She arched, pumping frantically now. Her nipples were rock hard, her chest flushed.

Cum spurted over my stomach. I grabbed the towel I'd thrown off after my shower. Cleaning up, I threw it on the floor and pulled up my briefs. "That was so hot."

She'd pulled her jersey down, covering her gorgeous body. She had a lazy smile on her face. "I feel closer to you somehow."

"Yeah, phone sex is the next step in intimacy," I teased, but I knew what she meant. I did feel closer to her. Everything we shared, everything we did, only solidified her in my mind as the person I wanted to be with.

"I love you in my jersey." My voice was rough.

She bit her lip. "Yeah?"

It was then I realized what I'd almost said. *I love you.* It was too soon. Enjoying her was enough. I was falling so hard for this woman. When I landed, there'd be no one to soften the fall.

"I haven't wanted to see anyone in my jersey for a long time." My high school girlfriend wore it. Back then, it was a statement that we were going steady.

"I feel like a lucky girl then."

"I'm pretty sure I'm the lucky one in this relationship." My tone was teasing, but I was dead serious. If she ever found out about my past, she'd be gone.

~

THE BEST THING ABOUT CALLIE ATTENDING TRAINING CAMP was that I could stand on the sideline next to her.

I found her standing by the fence watching the guys run plays when I was done with physical therapy.

I came up behind her, whispering in her ear. "You're going to make the reporters talk wearing that."

She startled at the sound of my voice, her eyes wide. "You told me to wear it."

My hands settled on her hips. "I know."

Pride filled my chest that she was here for me.

Reid stopped in front of us, arching a brow at me. "Don't you have work to do?"

"I'm done with PT. Thought I'd see how you guys are holding up."

He wiped his face with a towel. "It's fucking hot out." Then to Callie, he said, "Sorry."

She smiled. "I can handle a little swearing."

"So, you two are official?" He nodded at my number stretched across her chest.

I pulled her tighter against me. "Yes."

She tipped her head back, smiling up at me.

I leaned down to kiss her. I felt light, as if nothing could get to me. When I pulled back, Reid's expression was concerned, his gaze on the guys on the field.

"The reporters are going to say you're not focused."

I lowered my voice. "Fuck them. I'm a little sick of this game they're playing."

Reid drank from his water bottle.

"Besides, I met with the team doctor this morning. They're looking to clear me at the end of preseason."

"Seriously?" Reid pushed off the fence to face me.

I nodded.

"That's great, man. Can't wait to have you back out there." Then he lowered his voice. "There's something about having the tried and true on the field with us."

"I know exactly what you mean." I was young. I had a few good years left in me. It was too soon for me to make my exit.

Callie looked at me quietly, not saying anything.

I wondered what was going through her head. Was she happy for me?

Coach called Reid over to the field. Reid slapped the fence with this hand. "See you two later."

"Are you really being cleared?" she turned in my arms so her back was against the fence.

"Yeah. I have a twinge of pain here and there, but otherwise, I feel great."

"Being out on the field is different." She looked worried.

It meant being vulnerable to tackles. I was more likely to be injured. I loved that she was worried for me. "I'll be ready."

She laid a hand on my chest. "Then I'm happy for you."

I kissed her because I wanted to, because she was mine, even if it was just for a few more weeks.

When I pulled back, she turned in my arms so she leaned against me. We watched in silence for a while, the sounds of the coaches calling out plays, and the thuds of bodies striking each other filling the air. The satisfying smack of the ball when a receiver caught it made me want to be out there with them. For a distraction, I asked, "Did the reporters say anything to you?"

She sucked in a breath. "I think the jersey caught their attention."

"What did they say?" My words were clipped.

She winced. "One asked if I'd moved on from Reid to you."

"You were never dating Reid." I hadn't expected that.

"You know they say things to get a rise out of you. I didn't say anything."

Every muscle in my body pulled taut. "If they say something to me, I might."

"No. It's not worth it. You have your job to worry about. You shouldn't be getting into fights with reporters right now."

"If they're coming after you, I won't ignore it." My tone brooked no argument.

She turned, looking up at me, her eyes pleading. "I'm asking you to. Please."

"I don't like it." My jaw was tight, my teeth clenched.

"I know, and it's sweet you care, but you forget I'm used to this stuff."

That didn't mean I couldn't protect her. "You're not used to being the one questioned."

"True." Her lips drew into a line.

Maybe it was a bad idea to have her wear my jersey. I hadn't thought much about the repercussions beyond claiming her as mine.

They were accusing her of player hopping. No woman wanted to be accused of being passed around from player to player. "If it comes up in a press conference, I will address it. I'll say you're my girlfriend. You worked for Reid."

I wrapped an arm around her, wanting to protect her from anyone who wanted to hurt her.

"That's reasonable. Just keep a level head." Her tone was chiding.

That, I couldn't promise. If one of them accused her of sleeping around, I might see red.

She left an hour later to get to work.

Her being present didn't distract me. If anything, she motivated me to work harder. Seeing her and talking to her throughout the week settled me. It made me think we could handle being apart during the season. We could survive anything, even reporters who wanted to tear us down for entertainment.

Over the next few weeks, my knee felt even better. I felt stronger. The doctor and trainers were optimistic I'd be cleared in time for the first regular-season game, if not a preseason game. Callie visited me one or two mornings a week; I texted her throughout the day and called her at night.

I had flowers and something else delivered to her, like pastries or cupcakes, each week. I also arranged for Dylan to take her to the spa one Saturday for a massage.

I wanted to take care of her. I wanted her to know she was my girl, and nothing would come between us. We were stronger than this small separation. We spent most weekends together at my house. We went boating, enjoying each other's company.

I couldn't help out much with the mentor program until the post-season, but I called that kid's grandmother, talking to her about the benefits of sports. How it kept me out of trouble. She made me promise to keep an eye on him. It felt good to be a positive influence in someone's life. It made me hope for more than just the summer with Callie.

I wasn't able to help much with Frank's move to the new home, which was closer to Rebel Sports, but I knew Callie felt better having him nearby. The only thing still bothering me was Callie living in the city. There was no need for her to commute with Frank being near her work. I wanted her close during the season. Anytime I brought up the idea of her moving, she made an excuse. She hadn't found a nice place yet, or she wanted to focus on work.

Those were all good reasons, but I felt like there was something I was missing. At the end of training camp, Reid hosted the team at his house.

Pulling up to his house, I said, "Before Dylan, he never would have hosted something like this."

"No. He's changed for sure."

I looked over at Callie. Had she changed me too? Or had I always been this guy waiting for the right girl to show up? "Ready to go in?"

At her nod, I walked around the SUV, taking the tray of brownies from her lap. She stood, smoothing out the wrinkles in the skirt of her sundress.

"Are you nervous?"

She licked her lips. "A little. I'm not attending as anyone's employee. It's different."

I pulled her into my side, kissing her head. "Everyone's accepted that we're dating."

Walking in, Dylan immediately greeted her, pulling her over to her friends, Avery and Hadley. They weren't dating players, but they were usually around when Dylan hosted.

I headed out to the deck. There was a spread of crab, corn on the cob, hushpuppies, and cold salads. The picnic tables were covered with blue and white checked table cloths in the backyard overlooking the water.

Reid came over, handing me a beer. "Things with you and Callie are serious?"

"Yeah." Last time, he'd asked me that question with Callie standing next to me. He wanted my unfiltered response, but it wouldn't change no matter who I was standing next to. The only thing was I couldn't tell him we'd agreed to just the summer.

"You ready to be back?"

"So ready." Things were looking up. I was getting stronger every day. The twinges of pain were days apart. Hopefully, it would only get better.

Reid clapped me on the back. "Hope to have you on the field soon."

No one wanted that more than me. We ate at picnic tables on the lawn, drinking, talking, and laughing. I never enjoyed these events before. I tolerated them. With Callie by my side, things were different. I wanted to stay into the evening when the sun set over the water.

When the pickup game formed, it was girls against guys. The girls' choice. I liked the idea of being paired against Callie. After a few snaps, Callie looked a little sluggish.

"Are you okay?"

She held a hand over her stomach. "Maybe it was something I ate."

"Was the crab bad?" I guided her to a chair on the lawn, having her sit.

I looked around. No one else seems to be sick.

Her face was pinched and pale.

Dylan came by with a water bottle. "Are you okay?"

Callie breathed in and out slowly as if she was trying not to throw up. "I'm just hot."

It was warm but not overly hot for August. Sweat beaded her forehead.

I took the bottle from Dylan, twisting it open, then crouched down next to her. "Here, drink this."

Callie smiled at me, but it felt forced. "I'll be okay."

The game resumed, but I stayed on the sidelines with her.

When her color came back, I relaxed. She probably had too much to eat, then overdid it by running around in the heat.

She brought out my protective instincts. I wanted to take care of her. It was scary because if I did, I'd feel responsible for her. I wasn't sure I was ready for that.

CHAPTER TWENTY-FIVE

CALLIE

THE LAST FEW WEEKS HAD BEEN EXHAUSTING. I WASN'T SURE IF it was the problems we'd had at work with the website, the extra hours I was working, or trying to divide my time between work, Grandpa, and Jonah. I didn't want to stress out Jonah while they were busy with the team, so I kept most of the issues to myself.

Occasionally, I felt slightly nauseous, like that party at Reid's house, but I'd brushed it off due to lack of sleep. I used to feel sick when I pulled all-nighters in college.

Dylan stopped by for lunch on the Friday before the first game of the regular season.

"Are you nervous to meet Jonah's family?" she asked when I slid inside her car.

"No. I'm excited about it." I was hoping I'd get a glimpse into Jonah.

"How are things going with Rebel Sports?" she asked, driving toward the downtown area.

"I think we finally ironed out the issues with the website. People were signing up, but it wasn't registering them." My stomach seemed to be in a constant knot, slowly unraveling, then tightening with each new problem.

"I know Reid's happy to have you working there."

Sighing, I said, "I wish I didn't have to report problems to him anytime he calls."

"He gets it. There are bound to be issues when you're opening a new business. It's not your job to build the website."

"Just to make sure things run smoothly, which hasn't happened lately."

"Let him know if you need any help. You've been too busy to even hang out."

"It's not just work. I'm visiting Grandpa, making sure he's settled in okay, and then Jonah." It wasn't going to get easier because Jonah would be living in the city once the official season started.

She glanced over at me. "I'm worried about you. You look tired."

I was so tired I could easily fall asleep, and I wasn't one for daytime naps.

She parked at the city dock parking lot which was packed with lunchtime visitors. "Is something else going on?"

"No. Why?"

"You look like you're not feeling well."

"I'm just tired." Something had been troubling me. The exhaustion and sickness, I could pass off as being too busy to take care of myself, but this week, my breasts were feeling heavier, my nipples painful. I'd blame it on my period, but I usually skipped them by continually taking the active pills and throwing out the inactive.

"There's something else."

Dylan was a new friend, but ever since her car accident, I felt closer to her. I could trust her. I blew out a breath. "I'm worried I might be pregnant."

"Have you taken a pregnancy test?" Her gaze was focused on me.

"I'm scared." If I don't, I can pretend everything's fine.

"You might feel better if you knew one way or the other."

"Then it'll be real. I'll have to tell Jonah." It was awful timing. He'd been cleared to play in the first regular-season game this weekend, and I wasn't sure how he'd react. We'd foregone condoms because I was on birth control. Would he blame me?

I wasn't in a place to even consider having kids. I couldn't afford to move into a new apartment, much less find a bigger space to accommodate a baby and everything they need.

"I'll go with you. Let's grab some subs to eat at my place." I nodded because I was grateful to have someone to go through this with.

We walked to the pharmacy on Main Street. Dylan took charge, grabbing several different brands before taking me to her house. She'd moved in with Reid but hadn't rented her old house out yet.

Taking the boxes into the bathroom, I read the instructions, wondering if I was ready for my life to change. Could I be responsible for another human being? My chest constricted painfully. I've never felt so alone. How I wished I had my parents for this. They could've been here as a sounding board, a support system.

I peed on the stick, waiting for the time to be up to check the window. With each passing second, I felt more agitated. How could I raise a baby? I wanted to pay off my student loans, get my MBA, prove myself to Reid. How could I fit a baby in the mix? Would Jonah even want one? Or would I raise a baby alone?

I couldn't stop the anxiety.

I opened my eyes. Lifting the stick with shaking fingers, the window said *Pregnant.* Trying not to panic any more than I already was, I took two more tests with the same results.

Dylan knocked softly on the door. "Is everything okay?"

"I'm not sure." Would Jonah welcome this baby? Or would he toss me and him or her aside?

I unlocked the door for Dylan, my eyes filling with tears.

"You're pregnant?" she asked as soon as she saw my face.

I nodded miserably, gesturing at the tests lining the sink. "What am I going to do?"

I wrapped my arms around my middle.

She hugged me. "We'll figure this out."

"I have to tell Jonah." The question was when. He had his parents visiting this weekend for his first game. I didn't want to be the reason his comeback didn't go as planned.

"It will be okay."

I was grateful she was here. That I wasn't alone, but telling Jonah was this crushing weight. I felt like I was going to suffocate.

"I'm here for you. No matter what happens."

Dylan helped me clean up then drove me back to work.

I tried to be productive, but it was impossible. I searched online for ways to tell your unsuspecting partner you were pregnant. It didn't help. The negative stories only increased my anxiety.

This baby would change everything. My relationship with Jonah, maybe even my new friends. I might be alone again raising this baby.

I wiped away the tears, trying to think about it rationally. I was old enough to care for this baby. I knew Reid would be supportive.

I laid a hand on my stomach. The baby was a tiny speck at this point, but I wanted to protect him or her. Love washed over me for the life growing inside me. The baby was unexpected, but he or she would be my family. They'd love me unconditionally. The thought of that love would hopefully get me through the next few days. Having someone so helpless rely on me was scary, but I could do it.

I left work determined to take care of the baby, to keep him or her, no matter how Jonah reacted. I had both the baby and my health to consider now.

I fell asleep before Jonah called to say good night. The

next morning, I had a text from him saying he was sorry he missed me, and he'd meet me at his condo in the city to meet his parents.

I couldn't tell him yet. I couldn't drop this bomb on him when his parents were visiting. We needed time to talk about it. He needed space to think. I'd have to hold it inside and pretend everything was okay. I hoped I could pull it off.

I'd never been to his condo, although he lived in the same building as Reid. When I knocked, an older woman with brown hair and Jonah's eyes opened it.

"You must be Callie."

Stepping inside, I wished I'd been here before. I wouldn't feel like such an outsider. Holding my hand out to her, I said, "It's so nice to meet you."

"I'm Tasha, Jonah's mother. My husband, Rick, ran out to grab some coffee. This is my daughter, Elodie." Her tone was friendly.

A younger woman came up to us. She was tall with long brown hair and blue eyes. "Nice to meet you. Jonah hasn't brought a girlfriend home since—"

Then she glanced at her mother.

I didn't miss the tight shake of Tasha's head. She didn't want Elodie to bring up this ex. All I could remember was that he'd only had a few relationships, but maybe I'd assumed that. I wish I had more background information on him so I didn't feel so lost.

"Where's Jonah?" I asked, desperate for an ally. So far, Tasha and Elodie were friendly, but I felt unsteady not knowing his history.

"He's getting ready. Do you live in the city?" Elodie asked.

"I have an apartment here. I work at Rebel Sports." My face heated. I hadn't thought much about him being my boss in a while. I hoped his parents didn't think less of me.

"Is that how you met?" his mother sat on the couch next to Elodie, so I sat across from them.

"I used to be Reid Everson's personal assistant, but we hadn't talked much before. We got to know each other better while working at Rebel."

We hadn't really discussed what to say or not to say.

Jonah walked in. Grateful, I stood as he crossed the room toward me. "There you are."

His hands touched my shoulders, comforting me as he kissed me lightly on the lips. It was chaste, but I was pleased he'd done it in front of his family.

"My dad will be back in a minute with food and coffee. I see you met Mom and El?" His voice was rough. I wondered if he'd gotten much sleep with his first game today.

"I did. They've been very nice."

"Good." He sat, pulling me down next to him.

"We were just discussing how you met," his mom said.

His arm tightened around me. "Ah. Through work. She's been my rock while I've been injured."

His compliment warmed me. I wasn't sure what to expect, if he'd act differently in front of his parents or not. But I liked this. I wished I could tell him about the baby. I didn't like keeping it from him.

His dad walked in then. His mom and sister stood to help him with the bags.

He opened his mouth, but I interrupted before he could ask how I was. I didn't want to lie and say I was fine. My stomach was in knots.

"How are you feeling about the game?"

"Great. I'm excited to get out there."

It was something he'd say to a reporter or maybe his family, but I could feel the barely restrained energy flowing from him. He wanted to be on the field.

I lowered my voice. "How's your knee?"

He touched my forehead with his. "It feels great. No twinges in a week."

"That's great, Jonah. I'm so happy for you." I was happy

for him that his career would be back on track, hopefully after today's game. Even if my future was tenuous at the moment, I wouldn't do anything to derail his.

"I'm so happy you're here. I missed talking to you last night."

My face heated. "I'm sorry. I was so tired last night. I fell asleep early."

"That's okay. It's just I don't like not talking to you before I go to bed."

"Me either." I relaxed, relieved he wasn't upset I'd missed our call.

"Reid said work has been tough lately."

I sighed. "Yeah, the website had some kinks we had to work out."

"Why do I get the impression you're not telling me everything?"

I hadn't told him about the late nights because I was supposed to handle things at Rebel Sports so they could focus on football. "It's fixed now. That's all that matters."

His dad came to stand in front of us. "Hi. I'm Rick, Jonah's dad."

I smiled, holding my hand out to him.

Elodie handed coffees out while Tasha dumped the cubed fruit into a clear bowl. He had a nice family. I couldn't believe I thought he was embarrassed by them or hiding something about his past. They seemed nice.

They'd make amazing grandparents. A longing so acute throbbed in my chest. I wanted this baby to have family. I only had Grandpa. Would he get to know the baby?

"Do you want coffee?" Elodie asked.

"Oh, no thank you." I was allowed to have small amounts of caffeine, but the smell was turning my stomach. "I'll get some water."

I went to the kitchen, pulling down a glass from the cabinet, filling it.

Jonah and Rick discussed the opposing team's chances.

"How long have you been dating?" Tasha's tone was nothing but friendly.

"I guess a couple of months now." I took a sip of water, hoping it would help my churning stomach. I wasn't sure if it was nerves or the baby making me slightly ill.

"You know, in season, Jonah's pretty busy with games, practices, and travel." She pushed a small bowl of watermelon in front of me. I took the fork she offered, popping a cube in my mouth. The flavor burst in my mouth. It tasted so good.

I turned to face her. "I remember how it was when I worked with Reid."

"He won't have as much free time."

Why was she warning me? Did she think I wasn't a good influence, or I'd be a distraction for her son?

"I'd never demand anything of him." A sharp pang hit my heart. I didn't want to be a burden or a distraction for him. Would his parents think I was a gold digger or got pregnant on purpose to trap him?

The piece of watermelon I ate settled like a rock in my gut.

"Is everything okay over here?" Jonah asked.

"Just fine." I smiled to cover my worries.

I wished we had time alone so I could talk to him. He wrapped an arm around me, pulling me into his chest. I closed my eyes, suddenly exhausted.

"You feeling okay?"

"Yeah, just a little tired."

Concern sparked in his eyes. First, I was exhausted last night, then this morning. I needed to filter my words until I had an opportunity to talk to him. I didn't want him to guess what was going on with me.

"You're working too hard."

My first inclination was to deny that, but I didn't want him to ask more questions about why I was so tired. "Yeah, probably."

"If this keeps up, we might need to hire more staff. You're probably doing the work of three people."

What I'd read said I'd be really tired the first few months. It might be difficult to work late in the evenings. "That might be a good idea."

"Don't you need to get to the stadium?" Rick asked.

Jonah checked the time on his phone. "I do." Then to me, "Walk me out?"

"Sure." I waited while he said goodbye to his family.

Following him downstairs to the underground garage, he turned to me, pulling me against his body. "I wish we were alone."

I smiled. "Me too."

The knowledge I was carrying his baby was burning a hole in my gut. I needed to tell him soon. I worried how he'd react. If it would affect our relationship.

"Good luck out there today." I loved being the one who supported him. He'd let very few people take this role in his life. I didn't take it lightly.

"I love having you here, wearing my jersey." He cupped my ass, pulling me into him. "I wish we had more time."

"Me too. How long are your parents in town?"

"Until Monday."

It would be tough to get any time alone with him this weekend. I wasn't sure what his schedule would look like next week. I couldn't put off telling him for too long. My stomach was uneasy.

He kissed me. "I'll look for you in the seats."

I was sitting with his family in the stands. They didn't want to sit in the box.

"I'll be the one cheering for you the loudest." I couldn't wait to see him play. Should I wish him good luck or tell him to be careful out there? I knew athletes were superstitious about things like that. I settled for, "Have fun out there."

He smiled as if it was the right thing to say. "I will. I have to go."

I pulled away, reluctant to leave the comfort of his arms. I wanted his reassurance we were in this together, that a baby wouldn't change anything.

A cold feeling swept over me. What if he was angry about the baby? What if he wanted nothing to do with me when he found out? I swayed on my feet.

Thankfully, Jonah didn't see. He waved at me as he backed out of the parking lot.

When he was gone, I rested a hand on my belly, murmuring, "I'll protect you. I'll be there for you." No matter what, I'd be a good mom to this baby.

Since we'd started dating, Jonah had been attentive and sweet. He hadn't given me any reason to think he'd walk away, but I couldn't forget how he was before me. He was known for a good time. Would he see this baby as an albatross around his neck, someone holding him back or restricting his lifestyle? Nothing was permanent.

I headed back to his condo. I hated the uncertainty.

CHAPTER TWENTY-SIX

JONAH

I WISHED MY PARENTS WEREN'T HERE SO I COULD SPEND SOME time with Callie. Something was going on with her. I hoped it wasn't Frank's health. She probably didn't want to burden me with things going on in her life, but that was the definition of a relationship.

The commentators were calling this my comeback game. It was a lot of pressure. People would be talking about my knee all day—was I performing at the same level, did I limp after the tackle? I wanted to block it all out and focus on Callie.

Her beautiful face, her encouraging words. I wanted to sink inside her and forget everything else. I wanted to tell her I loved her. I couldn't do any of those things with my parents in town. I couldn't give her the attention a declaration like that required. With the season officially starting, I wasn't sure how much time I'd have to be with her.

It would be a struggle juggling my team obligations with spending quality time with her, but I needed her. I'd optimize whatever time we got. I needed to convince her to move in with me. I let the excitement fuel me. I was energized, eager to get on the field, then to Callie.

Hopefully, we'd have some time tonight. Maybe I could convince her to stay overnight even with my parents visiting.

Once I got to the stadium, I focused on football, getting into my usual pregame routine. Music played through my earbuds while I dressed and warmed up with the trainer. Then I lined up with the rest of the team, waiting to take the field. I breathed in the familiar scents, internalizing the roar of the crowd as the announcer pumped them up. I was proud to be wearing number eighty-three.

"Are you ready?" Reid asked.

When he asked, it was different than the trainer, the coach, or the reporters. I didn't have to put on a front.

"I am. I feel great."

"Go out there like you're one hundred percent. Like you weren't injured. The last game never happened. Got it?"

Liking the sound of that, the pressure in my chest eased. "Got it."

Chase slapped my shoulder pads. "I'm throwing to you."

"On the first play." I pulled on my helmet, determined to erase the doubt and speculation.

Reid nodded. "You got it."

My friends' support buoyed me, making me think I could do anything. I visualized running, dodging the defenders, catching the ball, and going in for the touchdown.

I let the crowd's energy flow through me when we ran out onto the field. This was any other game. I was ready.

On our first possession, Chase threw the ball to me as promised. I caught it easily, running for fifteen yards. The crowd seemed louder than usual. They wanted me to do well too.

After that, I was in the zone—run the play, dodge the defender, catch the ball. At the end of the first half, I ran long for a touchdown. The crowd surged to its feet. It was like a tidal wave of support. Chase ran toward me, bear-hugged me, then lifted me above our teammates. I raised my hands to the crowd, taking in the noise, the cheers, the energy. I hadn't yet won the game, but I'd beaten back the doubt and the fear that I couldn't play at the same level. I was back.

Chase let me down, the other guys slapping my back, saying great catch. I held on to the touchdown ball, scanning the crowd for Callie. Their seats were in the front row at the thirty-yard line. Callie was on her feet, yelling for me. Meeting her gaze, I lifted the ball, indicating I wanted to throw it to her.

She nodded, her cheeks red. The cameras were probably on her. I tossed it lightly to her. She caught it before holding it up in one hand—the universal sign of victory. The crowd cheered louder.

Our gaze locked while the crowd continued to cheer around us. It was a dull roar in my ears when I mouthed *I love you.*

She smiled wide before I turned, jogging back to the sidelines with my team. It might have been too soon, or the wrong moment, but it sure as hell felt right.

I wanted her in the stands, my condo, my life. Finally, I had everything I never thought I deserved. A football career and a woman by my side.

During the second half, Cleveland met each score with one of their own. We were up by a field goal at the end of the fourth quarter. It felt eerily similar to the playoff game when I dropped the ball. That game hovered in my subconscious, threatening to break through my confidence.

Reid stepped in front of me, hands on my pads. "New season. New game. Nothing's changed."

"Of course, it hasn't," I promised.

Reid nodded, satisfied with my answer. I hadn't faltered all day. I'd been consistent, reliable. I wouldn't let the doubts creep in. The reporters' questions swirled unanswered in my head. I was back. No one could stop me. Not the other team. Not an injury. Nothing.

We watched as our defense stopped their drive. We were up by three, one minute left. We just had to maintain possession. Chase would be handing it off to the running backs, playing it safe.

We lined up. The first three downs ended in small gains. The next play was supposed to be a short pass to me. If I performed, I'd prove I could handle the pressure. I wouldn't let anything get to me.

The center hiked the ball to Chase, I pivoted away from my defender, holding my hands up in a silent request for the ball, remembering what my high school coach had told me— *only winners want the ball when the game's on the line.*

Chase threw the ball high. I jumped up with tunnel vision on the ball. When my hands closed around it, I braced myself for a hard impact. I landed on my feet. No one was near me. I took off running down the sidelines so I could easily step out of bounds to stop the clock. When a defender ran toward me, I jumped out of bounds as he dove for my legs. It was more than enough yardage for the first down.

Chase kneeled with the ball on the next play, running out the clock, ending the game. I'd won playoff games before but I've never felt better than this. I'd proven everyone wrong. I'd squashed the doubts. I had Callie waiting for me.

I showered, getting ready for the press conference.

Lena met me outside the locker room. "You're ready for this?"

"Of course." I never shied away from the press. I didn't appreciate them while I was injured, but everything went great today. I didn't anticipate any hard questions.

She lowered her voice. "Be vague about your injury. You don't want them reading into anything. You feel great. You're happy to be back."

"All true." I pulled out every ounce of charm to smile at her.

"I'm glad you're back. I haven't seen this guy in a while."

"It feels good to be back." The guy she referred to was scared he'd never play again. Everything had turned around the last few weeks, first with Callie, then being cleared to play.

We walked into the room where Coach was giving a rundown of the game and his hopes for the season. "We're glad JT's back."

Coach looked at me. "I'm sure you have a few questions for the man of the hour."

He stepped back, laying a hand on my shoulder. "Good job out there today."

"Thanks, Coach."

Standing at the podium, the reporters poised with questions, I felt great.

"JT, you looked like your old self out there," a reporter in the front said.

"Thanks," I looked at his press lanyard, reading his name, "Mark."

"Any pain from your injury last season?"

"None." I kept my answer short, remembering Lena's advice. My mind was on Callie, wanting to know what her reaction was to my declaration.

"Does your performance have anything to do with the woman you gave the touchdown ball to?"

"She's my girlfriend." I didn't hesitate. I wanted everyone to know she was mine.

"She the same blonde you were seen with at training camp?"

I bristled at reducing her to her hair color. "Callie's the only blonde I'm with."

"Is she your good luck charm?" another reporter called out to a few chuckles.

The demeanor of the room was relaxed. These guys weren't looking to tear me down today.

"I don't know that I believe in good luck charms. She's

been an amazing support throughout my recovery. I'm happy to have her by my side, cheering me on."

"Are there any other questions about football?" I kept my tone light, steering the focus back where it should be. I publicly declared her as mine even if I didn't say her full name. I answered a few more questions about the game before a reporter asked, "Is your girlfriend, Callie Goodwin, Reid's assistant?"

"She was." I looked over at Lena. I didn't like this line of questions. I wasn't sure how much of Callie's past she wanted out there.

"She dated Reid then you?"

My jaw tightened. I wouldn't usually address these kinds of questions, but I didn't want reporters hounding Callie. She didn't deserve that. "Callie Goodwin never dated Reid, and she was never my personal assistant."

I hoped I got my point across. There was no story.

Lena stepped in. "I'm sure you have a few questions for Chase."

I stepped back, grateful for the interruption. I kept my head down, walking toward the lounge area where friends and family members waited. I didn't slow until I saw Callie standing with my parents.

There were dark circles under her eyes. I needed to talk to Reid about getting some help at the complex during the season.

She still held the football in her hands. "Thank you for the ball."

I hugged her, whispering in her ear, "Did you know what I said?" The press conference was playing on several screens around the room, but I was talking about me mouthing *I love you* on the field.

She smiled. "I did."

"I meant it." Maybe I shouldn't have told her that way, but it was how I felt at the moment.

It wasn't the time to discuss it.

"Great job out there, son," Dad said.

We headed home. When I pulled into the parking spot, my parents and sister got out.

"You should go out and celebrate," Dad said when I moved to get out.

"Yeah?" I did want Callie to myself. "You want to?" I asked her.

The dark circles under her eyes concerned me, but she nodded. "Sure."

"Text me if you need anything," I said to Dad.

When we were alone, I asked, "Are you sure you're up for this?"

Her forehead wrinkled. "Do you mind if we go to my place?"

My shoulders relaxed. "It would be nice to be alone."

It was the perfect solution. I could tell her how I felt in person, then show her.

CHAPTER TWENTY-SEVEN
CALLIE

It was nice getting to know Jonah's family, but the entire time I felt like a fraud. I was hiding this big thing from Jonah, from them. I wanted to unload the news as soon as possible. I didn't want to say I was tired from work or lie anymore. Even though I'd only kept the secret for a day, I had to tell him.

He'd mouthed that he loved me, and I thought my heart couldn't swell anymore. His mother thought it was sweet. Both her and his sister seemed hopeful, yet surprised we were serious so quickly. After his declaration, they asked more questions about our relationship. The scrutiny made me more curious about him.

Jonah was practically vibrating with excitement on the way to my apartment. He had to be high on his performance. It made me wonder if he'd said he loved me because he was caught up in the moment. The thought deflated me a little. Would he see this baby as a problem for the season? Would he refocus on his career and push me away?

Telling your girlfriend you loved her was one thing, finding out she was pregnant was another.

He was so happy. I hated to bring up something so serious

and life-changing. Maybe I should wait. Enjoy this night. Tell him another day.

"Everything okay?" He smiled crookedly at me.

I couldn't continue to keep it from him. "Yeah."

He parked down the street from my apartment. "You find a place to move to yet?"

I stiffened. "No. I've been so busy I haven't even looked."

"I don't like you walking so far to your apartment at night. It's not safe."

It was sweet he was worried.

"When is your lease up?"

"I pay month to month." I switched over a few months ago when my lease was up, knowing I wanted to be closer to work.

Jonah flashed me one of his signature smiles. "You should move in with me."

"Are you serious?" The offer took the air out of my lungs.

"Yeah. I don't get a lot of time at home during the season. I don't want to waste it traveling back and forth. I want you there when I get home."

"I'll have to think about it." It was nice that he wanted to take that step, but he didn't know the whole story.

We walked up the steps to the third floor. This wasn't the ideal apartment for a baby. There was no elevator for a stroller, parking close by was difficult to find, and it wasn't in the best area.

I unlocked the door, letting him in. "You played great today."

I wasn't sure how to talk to him about the pregnancy. Did you just come out and say, I'm pregnant, or was there a good lead-up to something like that?

I wiped my sweaty hands on my jeans.

"I'm sorry if telling you on national TV I loved you was upsetting."

"I'm not upset. It was nice."

"Nice?"

"It was more than nice." How would it have felt if I wasn't pregnant? "It was sweet. But your parents seemed a little surprised you were so serious with anyone."

I didn't get the impression it had anything to do with me specifically.

"Really?" He rolled his shoulders back. "It's probably because I don't bring many women home."

That was a reasonable explanation, even if I wanted to clarify whether he'd brought *any* women home over the years. I would expect professional ballplayers to be careful. "There's something I need to talk to you about."

I felt light-headed. Maybe I hadn't eaten enough today. "I don't know how to say this."

His brow furrowed. "Is it too much too soon? We can forget I said anything. There's no pressure. I get it. We just started dating."

I shook my head. "No. It's not that."

"Then what is it? The moving in with me part? You don't have to. It was just an idea."

"It's not that either." I licked my lips. "I'm pregnant. I just found out yesterday."

He stilled.

"I didn't want to tell you this morning with your parents around. Maybe I should have waited to tell you. It's a big day for you," I rambled on, nervous.

He sat there motionless, his face a mask I couldn't read. I rubbed my arms to ward off the chill.

"Say something." Anything. Tell me you still love me, you'll be there for me. My whole world was changing. I needed him by my side.

He stood abruptly, running his hands through his hair. "I don't understand."

"I don't know exactly how it happened. I was on the pill.

We stopped using condoms. Birth control isn't one hundred percent."

"Did you plan this?"

"What? No. Of course not." I wasn't in the right place to start a family, but maybe he thought I was trying to trap him.

The bottom dropped out of my stomach. Blood pounded in my ears.

"I'm the wrong guy for this. I can't have a kid." His words felt like a bomb dropping.

The headache that had been threatening all day came on full force.

"I don't understand what you're saying."

Was he saying he couldn't be a dad or didn't want to be?

"I'm telling you I'm pregnant with your child because you have a right to know. You can be part of this child's life if you want to be. Otherwise, I'll do it without you." I stood, my head reeling, my words were cool. I wrapped an arm around my stomach. "I don't care what you decide, but I'm keeping this child. *Our* child."

He was quiet for so long I wasn't sure he was going to say anything else.

"You said you loved me. I tell you I'm pregnant, and... what? You're just going to walk away like I mean nothing to you?"

"This has nothing to do with you."

I was so confused. It had everything to do with *us*.

"I'm not the right guy. I can't be a dad."

"I get that this is a lot to take in, but we don't have to figure everything out tonight." If he needed time to process, I could understand that.

He shook his head. "You don't know. If you did, you wouldn't want me in your life or anywhere near a baby."

He only stood a few feet away, but it felt farther. "What are you talking about?"

He turned, walking toward the door. "I can't do this. My family's in town."

"You didn't mind spending time with me a few minutes ago." I felt desperate. If he walked away like this, I wasn't sure he'd be back.

He grabbed the doorknob. "Everything's changed. I can't have kids. I should have told you."

His voice was resigned.

"I'm already having your child. What do you mean you can't?" Was he going to walk away?

"I'll talk to you later." Then he was gone. The click of the door was the only thing I heard above the pounding in my head.

I crumpled to the floor, the emotion from the day over-whelming me. The tears fell as I clutched my stomach. I felt like I was being torn apart. I thought I could do this on my own, but I didn't want to. I wanted to go back to that moment when he'd mouthed I love you. I wanted him to say it to me while we were alone. I wanted him to show me one more time.

Eventually, I pulled myself off the hard floor to lay in bed. My body ached from the position I'd held for so long, but I reveled in the pain, preferring to focus on that instead of the chasm in my chest.

He didn't call. Not that I expected him to.

CHAPTER TWENTY-EIGHT

JONAH

I CAN'T BE A FATHER. THE WORDS RAN ON REPEAT IN MY HEAD. I pulled into my parking spot, not wanting to go upstairs and face my parents. I texted Reid and Chase on our group message chain.

I hoped they were staying in the city and could meet up. They responded right away. I wondered if Reid already knew. If Callie told Dylan.

I suggested a bar within walking distance, knowing I was going to drink. I headed that direction, sitting at the bar, ordering a shot. Then another.

"What's going on?" Chase asked, sliding onto the stool next to me.

"She's pregnant."

Chase exchanged a look with Reid who sat next to him.

"Why are you here and not with her?" Reid tipped his head toward the bartender.

"I think you know the answer to that." I drank the last shot, slamming the glass down harder than necessary.

Reid and Chase ordered a beer, placing it on my tab.

Then Reid said, "I don't. Explain it to me."

"I can't be a father." It was the same thing that kept repeating in my head.

Chase faced me, his brow furrowed. "Why not?"

"I can't be responsible for anyone." I'd proven that. I'd fucked up in the worst way possible.

"Does she know?" Chase lowered his voice.

"I never told her." I took a long pull of my beer, my gaze on the chipped bar.

Reid rubbed his chin. "How did you react when she told you about the baby?"

I couldn't remember my exact words. "I think I said I couldn't do it."

"That's it. No explanation?" There was a deep crease in Reid's forehead.

Chase tapped the bar top rhythmically. "You told her you were in love with her in front of an entire stadium of people—"

"And everyone watching at home," Reid interjected.

"Then you break up with her because she told you she's pregnant." Chase tapped his fingers on the bar.

The sound was beating like a drum in my head, making it pound with tiny explosions of pain.

"That's right." I tipped the beer bottle to my lips, hoping the liquid would soothe the burning sensation in my gut.

"Was she upset?"

I hadn't looked at her face. I couldn't. "I don't know."

My stomach pitched.

Reid's fingers were flying over his phone.

"Who are you texting?" What could be more important than this conversation? I felt like I'd been rocked off my axis, thrown back in that moment when the police said she was gone. She wasn't coming back, and it was all my fault.

Reid shot me an annoyed look. "I told Dylan to go to Callie."

Someone else being there for her tugged painfully at my heart. I rubbed my chest to stop the ache.

Chase took a long pull of his beer, pushing it toward the bartender. "You're not thinking clearly."

I shrugged. "I'm drunk."

"You weren't drunk when you talked to Callie," Reid said reasonably.

"I went over there to tell her I loved her. Then everything went to shit."

Chase leaned back on the stool. "Maybe it would help if she knew what happened."

That was the only thing they'd said that made any sense. "If I tell her, she'll understand why I can't be a dad."

"You can apologize. Then tell her you want to be a good dad, but you need her help."

"What are you talking about?"

"Promise her you'll get it together. You'll read books if you have to. You'll be there for her." Reid's tone was stern.

"What? No. I told you I can't be a dad." Why didn't anyone get it? It was so obvious.

"Can't or won't?" Reid asked pointedly.

"What happened wasn't your fault," Chase said carefully as if he was worried I'd blow up.

"It was." This argument was futile. I don't know why I'd asked them to come. I thought they'd agree with me. The whole thing was ridiculous.

Chase tipped his head to the side. "Has anyone ever said it was your fault?"

The familiar pain unfurled in my chest, spreading to every part of my body. I'd never forget that moment when I apologized to Amanda's mother in the receiving line of the funeral. She hadn't been able to speak, but her father pulled me to the side. With barely contained fury, he'd said it was all my fault. I encouraged her to speed. I was the one pushing the gas pedal that day even if I wasn't in the car. I'd apologized profusely, knowing the only way I could help was getting out of their sight, leaving town, and rarely returning.

"That was when everything was fresh. You need to talk to them for closure. I doubt they still feel the same way."

I kind of wanted to punch him. Rage poured through me.

I scoffed. "I was young and stupid, but I dared her to do it."

Chase gave me a pointed looked. "It was her choice. Like it was her choice to hit the gas when she saw the red and blue lights."

"I was the one who set everything into motion." There was no getting around it.

Reid stared at me thoughtfully. "You need to talk to her parents. You need closure."

"You need peace, or you're going to continue to close yourself off to anything good in your life. You think Amanda would want you to avoid relationships forever? You think she'd want you to reject your child?"

"Me being responsible for another human being is ridiculous. You know that." Although, I didn't feel as sure as I had when they arrived.

"You're impossible to talk to right now." Chase sipped his beer.

Reid called the bartender over to ask him to close out my tab. Then he said to me, "You're going to regret this in the morning."

Was I? I couldn't even look at Callie when I said whatever I said. She was probably pissed at me. There was no coming back from this. I should destroy any chance of anything between us. She had to know I was no good for her or the baby. I was kidding myself to think I could be in a real relationship with her. It was always going to lead to this—kids, marriage, everything I'd always avoided.

Reid stood, pulling out cash and throwing it on the

counter. "I think you should talk to her and explain what happened back then. She'll understand."

"She'll hate me." Like I hated myself.

"I don't think you give her enough credit." Chase shoved his hands in his pockets.

Reid braced his hand on the back of the barstool. "If you don't talk to her, you'll make things worse for yourself. You're going to wake up one day and want a relationship with that kid. Don't let this go too far."

I didn't respond because there was nothing to say. He was dead wrong on that count.

We walked outside. The air was warm.

"Fix this," Reid said before nodding at Chase and stepping off the curb. I watched him get into his black SUV.

"Don't let this go on too long or it will be too late." Chase squeezed my shoulder.

I shrugged him off. My only regret was falling for Callie. I blamed it on her. It was easy to love her. She was everything good and right in this world. I should have trusted my first instincts: I didn't deserve someone like her. I was destined to be alone.

THE NEXT MORNING, POTS BANGED IN THE KITCHEN. MY HEAD pounded. My mouth was dry. I tried to open my eyes, but the sun was too bright. I groaned, rolling over. My bed was empty.

It came back to me in a rush of blinding pain. I'd broken things off with Callie.

The coffee machine whirred. My parents were here.

The loud banging, laughing, and talking continued to drift down the hall from the kitchen. I wished I could be alone to wallow.

I got up and pulled on sweats and a tee from the floor.

Sniffing myself, I declared it was good enough. Maybe if I stunk, they'd leave early.

I threw some water on my face, not looking in the mirror. Fucking things up with Callie was inevitable. It was better to end things now than to screw up my kid. He or she deserved better than me.

Resigned, I walked slowly down the hall, rubbing my face. I was exhausted. I'd tossed and turned all night, repeating that scene with Callie, wincing each time the words fell out of my mouth.

"Oh! I figured you'd be at Callie's." Mom lifted her head when I came into the room.

What could I say? That was done. She was having a baby, but I wanted no part of it.

She was having a baby. I don't think that had truly sunk in last night. She was carrying my child, my parents' first grand-kid. My chest compressed. I couldn't breathe.

"Are you okay?" Elodie asked.

"Yeah. No. I don't know."

"You get into a fight or something?" Mom asked, pushing a plate of eggs and bacon across the counter.

I took a bite of the crispy bacon. "Something like that."

I couldn't talk to them about this. I couldn't talk to anyone.

"I'm going to get in the shower," Elodie said, walking down the hall.

Dad sat in the living room watching the news.

I ate a few more bites, drinking the entire glass of water she placed in front of me. Could I talk to them about what happened back then? The thought of how Callie was feeling right now threatened to split me in two. I was an asshole. I'd walked out on her when she needed me. She was pregnant and alone.

If there was a way I could be deserving of her, I wanted to be.

"Ever since Amanda, you haven't introduced anyone to us."

I flinched at the use of her name. My mom hadn't referenced her by name since the accident. It was like she was afraid to bring it up. "No one was serious."

"Callie is."

"She was." The words stuck in my throat. I drank some more water, hoping to clear out the black in my soul.

"What happened wasn't your fault." Her words were so soft they almost didn't register.

I carefully placed my glass on the counter, my hand shaking. "How can you be so sure?"

My parents knew exactly what happened. I'd confessed to them as soon as I saw them.

"You were kids. You made bad choices."

"I feel responsible."

"Anyone would, but you have to forgive yourself or it's going to poison the rest of your life. Is that why you had a fight with Callie?"

"She's pregnant." Saying the words out loud made them real.

Mom sucked in a breath, her eyes filling with tears.

"How can I be responsible for a human being, one that's so vulnerable?" My voice cracked. I could be strong in front of Callie, in front of the guys, but not my mom.

"You can't hold yourself accountable the rest of your life. You both made a mistake. Amanda paid the price for it. But she'd want you to keep living your life. She wouldn't want you to miss out on everything good that comes your way."

She was saying the same sentiments as Chase and Reid, but I couldn't get past the fact that Amanda's parents blamed me.

"The Reynolds blame me." I was holding on to the things I'd believed over the years. Tossing them back at my mom, I wasn't sure if I wanted her to agree or disagree with me.

"They don't. I have had several conversations with them over the years. They don't blame you. It's hard for them. The pain of her death won't ever go away, but they wouldn't begrudge you living your life, being happy. They'd want you to have what Amanda couldn't."

I let those words roll around in my head, testing their weight, their veracity.

"Do you want to be a part of this baby's life?"

I think I did. "I want to be there for Callie."

"You have a while to prepare for the baby coming. We'll be there for you, your friends, and Callie."

"If I haven't screwed everything up with her…" The situation felt hopeless.

"Nothing is unfixable. Not when you come from a place of caring. You're worried you won't be a good dad. That you'll make mistakes. That's being a parent. It's normal."

I shook my head. "I have to apologize."

She bustled around the kitchen, cleaning the already spotless counters with a cloth. "You do, but you have to deal with this thing with the Reynolds first. I think you should talk to them."

Would I get closure by talking to them? Would I finally be able to move on, to let myself be happy? It sounded too good to be true.

Maybe I could go to the gravesite, talk to Amanda. It was something I did whenever I returned to town. I never stayed long, worried I'd run into her parents.

"What if they won't see me?" I didn't think I could handle that. It would be a confirmation that they blamed me.

"They go to her gravesite every Tuesday evening."

A chill ran through me. The accident happened on a Tuesday. It was an opportunity to get some answers, maybe even closure. "Okay."

Her shoulders lowered. "You'll go back?"

"I have to." I wanted to apologize to Callie, but I needed

to take care of this first. Hopefully, she'd understand once I explained everything to her.

"I'm proud of you."

"Thanks, Mom." I wasn't sure I deserved her praise. At least not yet. Everything hung in the balance—my past, my present, and my future. An image of a baby with a tuft of blond hair on his head popped into my head. I wanted to be a good father.

Finally, she turned to me. "Congratulations."

I let it sink in that I was going to be a dad. It was terrifying. At the same time, I was bursting with love for Callie and our baby.

"Do you want this baby?"

"Of course, I do." I couldn't believe I'd said otherwise last night. I'd panicked.

"Then go make things right. We'll be here."

"Shouldn't I plan how I'm going to make it up to her?" Didn't I need to bring a gift or make some amazing gesture to fix it?

"Don't let her think you're not going to be there for her."

Adrenaline coursed through me. I pulled up the airline website. I had to go home, the one place I'd run from. I had to face what I'd avoided my whole life. Booking the first flight back, I texted Callie.

Jonah: I'm so sorry about last night. I want to see you. I want to talk to you, but there's something I need to do first. I have to go home. Can we talk when I get back? I'll explain everything.

I didn't expect an answer right away. The fact that I had a plan fueled me to pack and get on that plane. It was the first time I was returning to my hometown as a man, not the shell of the boy I was. I hoped Amanda's parents would see that.

CHAPTER TWENTY-NINE

JONAH

I CALLED COACH, EXPLAINING THAT I WOULDN'T BE AT practice on Tuesday. Monday was a rest day. I told him everything—Callie's pregnancy, my past, and my need to speak to the Reynolds. I needed closure even if they didn't forgive me. If they still blamed me for what happened, I'd understand. Dealing with the death of a child was difficult.

Facing the prospect of being a father, I was worried about Callie and the baby's health. I wished I'd asked more questions. I wanted to be there for Callie, be at her doctor's appointments. Instead, I'd read everything I could on the plane to catch up.

I'd pushed what happened to Amanda and my guilt so far down, I'd failed to actually deal with it in any meaningful way. I'd let it interfere with my personal relationships, rarely getting close to anyone. I'd allowed it to steamroll, potentially ruining my future with Callie and my child. I wouldn't continue to make that mistake.

My parents came with me, wanting to support me in my decision. Walking around town on Monday was surreal. In the past, when I'd visited, I'd go straight to my parents' home, never venturing out. I was afraid of what people might say, afraid of running into the Reynolds. Fear kept me frozen. At this point, no one would know who I was or what had happened, but it was important for me to move past the idea that I wasn't welcome in my hometown.

To my surprise, several people approached me, congratulating me on my accomplishments. It wasn't that accolades overshadowed what happened, but I was starting to think people didn't blame me for the accident. Maybe I'd been too harsh on myself all along. Yeah, I set things into motion, but she didn't have to go along with it. I never told her to speed over the limit or accelerate if she encountered a police officer. Those were her decisions.

Tuesday evening, I went to the gravesite with a bouquet of flowers. I'd been careful in the past not to leave a trace of my visits, but this time, I wanted to. The air was heavy with moisture, the grass wet from earlier rain. The sky was overcast. I carefully arranged the sunflowers, Amanda's favorite in high school, in the vase that was part of the gravestone. I stood, not wanting to get wet, closing my eyes.

I'm so sorry that we made the decision we made that night. I never wanted this to happen.

I stood there, my eyes closed, listening to the drip-drip of water on the leaves of a nearby tree. I pushed out the guilt and shame, letting in peace.

"Jonah," a woman's voice wavered.

Opening my eyes, I saw the Reynolds.

"My parents said you'd be here. I hope it's okay. I thought we should talk."

Mrs. Reynolds's expression was pained. Mr. Reynolds nodded.

I took a deep breath, trying to remember what I'd planned to say. The actual speech eluded me. Instead, I went with my gut. "I'm so sorry for my part in Amanda's accident. I never meant for it to happen."

"We know you didn't," Mr. Reynolds finally said, his voice

gruff with emotion. "We've had a lot of time to think, to reflect, to regret."

I waited, letting him gather his thoughts. "I'm sorry for what I said to you at the funeral. I was distraught, out of my mind with grief, but it didn't excuse it. We don't blame you— not anymore. Amanda made her own decisions that night." Mr. Reynolds broke off.

"Amanda wasn't wearing a seat belt. She made several poor decisions that night, but that was the one I couldn't get over."

My heart sped up. "She always wore her seat belt."

Mrs. Reynolds shook her head. "I know. I don't understand it."

Mr. Reynolds opened a black umbrella, holding it over his wife's head to protect her from the drizzle. "The officer said she wouldn't have hit the windshield had she been wearing it. She most likely wouldn't have died."

The cool rain landing on my forehead kept me anchored in the moment, not spiraling back to that night. I wasn't that kid anymore. "That's—" horrible, "I don't know what to say."

"We don't blame you."

"I'm sorry I ever suggested racing home."

"Did you?"

"Yeah, I was the one who said let's see who can get home first—or maybe it was which route was the fastest." Had I not said the word race? Did it matter?

"We know you loved her. You wouldn't have wanted her to be hurt."

I shook my head. I never wanted this outcome. Now that I was in love with Callie, I could see my love for Amanda was young and untested. I doubt we would have lasted through college, but I wished she'd had a future. "I'm sorry. I'm going to talk to someone to try and get past it. I'm seeing someone now. She's pregnant. For me to be there for her, I need closure."

"You need to forgive yourself."

"Yeah."

"Know this—we don't blame you. She chose not to put her seat belt on that night. She pushed the accelerator when she saw that officer. That's on her."

I swallowed over the lump in my throat. Was it that easy? If I could forgive myself, would the shame and guilt ease over time?

"You deserve to live your life to the fullest. Amanda would want that."

"Thank you." I sensed they wanted to be alone with her.

I moved closer, shaking Mr. Reynolds's hand, patting Mrs. Reynolds's shoulder. "Thank you for sharing that with me. It helps."

"I hope so."

I nodded one more time, then moved toward my car. There was nothing left to say. It was time to heal. With each step I took away from Amanda's tombstone and her parents, I felt lighter. I drove around for a while before I headed to my parents' house.

Walking inside, I felt different. The heavy weight of guilt had lifted. I was eager to get back to the city, to Callie. I needed to make things right. I wanted to tell her what happened, why I'd reacted the way I had. There was no excuse for my behavior, but I hoped she'd give me another chance.

"How'd it go?" Mom asked when I walked into the kitchen.

"She wasn't wearing a seat belt."

"I wondered about that. How she'd—"

She couldn't say it. How Amanda had died from blunt force trauma to her head. Her car was old. It didn't have airbags, but the seat belt might have prevented her from striking the windshield.

"I take it you talked to Amanda's parents?"

FALLING FOR YOU

Hearing her name didn't pierce my heart like it usually did. Coming back and talking to the Reynolds hadn't made anything worse. It was almost as if I'd filed the car accident, and the experience, into a folder. I could pull it out to examine it if I wanted, but it no longer was at the front of my mind. The pain wasn't as raw. It was more muted.

"Yeah. It helped." I'd never forget the look of pain on their face—pain they'd probably always feel. "I apologized. They said they didn't blame me. She made poor decisions too. They reminded me that I have a future—one that Amanda would want me to live to the fullest."

Mom bobbed her head in agreement. "Blaming yourself doesn't get you anywhere. All we can do is move on and not make the same mistakes in the future. You do a lot of good with the football program and the charities. You mentor kids."

"Maybe it was my way of making up for my mistakes."

Mom gave me a pointed look. "It's good to pay it forward, but I hope you don't blame yourself anymore."

"I think it will be hard to let go of everything, but I want to talk to a therapist, see how I can move past it."

"I think that's a great idea." Mom poured some tea from the kettle into a cup, then pushed it toward me. "You need to get back."

"Yeah, I have an early flight tomorrow, then practice." Then I'd talk to Callie. I hoped she'd forgive me.

"I hope you make things right with Callie. I think she'll forgive you if you explain everything."

I sighed. "I hope so."

Mom leaned over, covering my hand with hers. "You have a big heart. She'll see that."

I wanted her to see who I was now, not the boy I was back then. We'd all done things in our past that we weren't proud of. I'd allowed mine to dictate my future. No more. I'd make myself worthy of Callie and our baby. Even if she didn't take me back right away, I wasn't going anywhere.

CHAPTER THIRTY

CALLIE

DYLAN STAYED OVER FOR A COUPLE OF DAYS. I COULDN'T STOP the tears from flowing. I blamed it on the peanut in my belly. He or she was so tiny, but she was wreaking havoc already.

I couldn't tell Dylan what Jonah said. Repeating his words, his rejection out loud made them real. His text gave me a glimmer of hope, but I quickly tapped it down. He'd walked out. He wasn't here. That's all that mattered.

We called out of work on Monday, watching mindless TV while I replayed the scene in my head.

Was there a better way I could have handled things? Should I have softened the blow? On Wednesday, I sent Dylan home, showered, and went to work. I was grateful for Dylan's support, but I needed the distraction only work could provide.

That night, I drove home, exhausted. For the first time, I let myself think about raising this child on my own. Staying in my current apartment wasn't a good idea. I needed to find something closer to my work. Maybe Dylan would let me rent her old home in Annapolis. Letting myself in, I pulled on comfy lounge pants and an oversized tee, wanting nothing more than to watch mindless TV before I passed out.

My phone rang with Dylan's name on the screen.

"Hey." I tensed, expecting her to ask how I was doing.

"You're never going to believe it!" Her excitement was evident through the phone.

"What?" I smiled despite how down I'd been the last few days.

"I was able to get you some help for your grandfather." She went through the details of the aid I qualified for. It would cover the portion that insurance didn't.

"Thank you. I really needed something good."

"Happy to help. Have you thought more about what *you're* going to do?"

I knew she meant with the baby—maybe even Jonah, but I wasn't ready to talk about him yet. "I need to move close to work and my grandfather. Are you thinking of renting out your home in Annapolis?"

"I was going to rent it out but then was worried I wouldn't be able to trust anyone with the home. I'd love to have you living there. This is perfect."

"Thank you." The words weren't enough. Dylan had become a friend—a connection to the area and Reid. I wouldn't think about her ties to Jonah.

"I'm happy to help. You're probably overwhelmed with everything." She hesitated.

I knew she wanted to ask about Jonah, but I wasn't ready to talk about him walking out, or the possibility he didn't want to be part of our baby's life. It was one thing to reject me, but another to turn his back on his child. I glanced at the time on the clock, yawning. "I'm getting tired."

Using exhaustion from the pregnancy was a good excuse to cut the conversation short.

"Of course, but Callie, I'm here if you need to talk— about whatever."

"I appreciate that." Gratitude for the people who were present in my life flowed through me, giving me strength.

I hung up with her, feeling better. I covered my stomach

with my hand. Things were coming together. I didn't need Jonah. I'd be okay on my own.

If I was accepted into the MBA program, I'd take classes, even if it was one a semester. I'd show this baby that education and hard work were important. You didn't give up on your dreams because things were hard.

I turned on the TV for a few minutes of mindless entertainment, when a knock sounded on the door, making me jump.

My heart skipped a beat. Was it Jonah? I hadn't expected to see him so soon when he'd said he'd left town. When the second knock sounded, I stood, wiping my hands on my pants. Opening the door, the sight of him standing in the doorway sent tendrils of pain curling through my body. I wouldn't survive a repeat of the other night.

"Jonah." I crossed my arms over my chest.

"Can we talk?" His hair was mussed as if he'd run his fingers through it multiple times. His shirt was rumpled. He smelled like an airplane. Had he come here straight from his flight?

I swallowed, stepping back so he could enter. I deserved an explanation. I was curious about what he'd meant in his text. What did he have to take care of that he needed to go home before he talked to me?

He closed the door softly. "Callie."

My heart skipped a beat, then picked up at the sound of my name on his lips. I sat on the couch, closing my eyes against the pain I saw in his. Why was he hurt?

"I'm so sorry for the other night. For what I said. For leaving." His voice cracked.

The couch dipped as he sat next to me.

I dropped my head into my hands, squeezing my eyes tighter, knowing if I saw his expression, I'd cave. I'd give in to whatever explanation he fed me. I deserved more than that. Our child deserved more.

"My reaction was unacceptable." He sighed as if the memory was too much for him.

Slowly opening my eyes and lifting my head, I studied him.

His elbows rested on his thighs, his gaze on my coffee table.

I wasn't ready to let go. I held the pain close to my chest. Everyone always left. It was better he go now before I depended on him.

He glanced at me briefly before averting his gaze. "I have to tell you something, then I'll leave if you want me to."

I remained silent. I wanted to hear what he had to say. I couldn't imagine there was an excuse for his behavior. Not one that was believable.

He was quiet for a few seconds, gathering his thoughts. "My high school girlfriend died in a car accident. I'd always believed it was my fault."

He'd said it matter-of-factly, but pain tinged his tone.

I sucked in a sharp breath.

His body tensed as if anticipating a blow. "That night, I'd met her at the mall when she got off work. We drove separately. I thought it would be fun to race home. I dared her to do it."

He shook his head, his expression disgusted. He was quiet for so long I wasn't sure he'd continue.

I remained quiet, waiting for him to go on.

"We each took a different route home except when I got to her house, she wasn't there. She never showed up."

Laying a hand on his arm, my heart ached to comfort him.

He didn't acknowledge my touch. "She was speeding. The police tried to pull her over, but instead of slowing down, she sped up. She lost control of her car, hitting a tree. The police said she died on impact."

Had he been holding this inside since? I couldn't imagine bearing the weight of that guilt.

"You blamed yourself." This was what he'd been hiding. This was why I never felt like I had all of him. He'd held himself back from me. Did he think he wasn't worthy of me? That he wasn't deserving of happiness? My heart skipped in my chest. I couldn't get ahead of myself. I needed to protect myself and the baby from him until I was sure of what he was saying.

He looked at me, his eyes pleading with me to understand. "That's why I don't want—I *didn't* want kids. I wasn't prepared the other night."

I laughed without any humor, remembering the pain of him walking out. "I'm not prepared to be pregnant either, but I'll figure it out."

"I didn't think I'd be good for a kid. A child would depend on me." He fell silent.

"What happened was horrible, but she was the one speeding, she was the one who chose to go faster when she saw the cops."

"It wouldn't have happened if I hadn't dared her."

"You were a kid. Yeah, you made a bad choice, but so did she. You have to forgive yourself. Give yourself permission to make better choices going forward, to be happy. I doubt she'd want you to be miserable. Or to walk away from your child."

"That's what everyone keeps saying." His voice was resigned.

Were we getting through to him, or would he always be thinking this one mistake dictated his entire life? "Maybe you should take their advice. You deserve to be happy."

"You think I deserve someone as good as you?" His expression was so vulnerable.

Tears pricked my eyes. I couldn't answer because the man who walked out on me was different than the guy I'd gotten to know.

"I'm sorry I overreacted the other night."

"I understand why you did. Thank you for telling me." It solidified what I'd suspected all along. There was something or someone holding him back from relationships. I just hadn't realized it affected him this much.

"Is that why you went back home?"

"I thought her parents blamed me. I needed to talk to them. To get some closure. I went to the gravesite. They were there. They told me they were angry at first and blamed me. They said it was easier to blame someone else for what happened. But after a while, they went to therapy and realized their daughter made her own choices that night. I never knew she wasn't wearing a seat belt. The cops said if she had been, her head wouldn't have hit the windshield. I don't understand it because she always wore her seat belt."

"You'll probably never know why." Second-guessing that night was tearing himself up inside.

"The Reynolds were able to let go of the anger and get some peace."

"Do you think you can let go of the guilt?" I saw the situation with clarity now. He couldn't be there for us if he was harboring guilt for his past decisions. It was tainting everything around him. He was sabotaging his happiness because he didn't think he deserved it.

"I'm trying. I think I should talk to someone about it." He looked so vulnerable, I wanted to reach out and touch him.

"Like a therapist?"

"My past is standing in the way of me being there for you and our baby. I'll do anything to be there for you both."

My heart picked up at *our baby*.

"Can we start over?" His tone was hopeful.

"Like, hi, I'm Callie Goodwin?" I wished I'd washed my face or brushed my hair.

His expression was serious. "Maybe start with *I'm pregnant.*

I wouldn't want to erase anything else that happened between us."

Was it that simple? Could we erase that moment when he'd reacted so horribly and walked out? I understood why he did it. I closed my eyes, remembering the man I fell in love with—the one who vowed to make me a priority in his life. "I'm pregnant."

Blood rushed to my head. I was standing on a precipice, taking a chance on him. Handing him my heart and hoping he would protect it.

"May I?" He held his hand out as if to touch my belly.

Leaning back on the couch, I nodded.

I bit my lip as he pressed his hand to my still flat stomach. "You're really pregnant."

His tone was filled with awe. I'd had a bit more time to get used to the idea.

"According to the tests we got at the pharmacy. They're supposed to be pretty accurate." I'd researched to make sure. False positives weren't common.

"Are you happy?" His gaze rested on me.

"I was shocked at first, but now that I've had time to think about it, I am. This baby will be my family, someone to love unconditionally. Maybe I'm too young, not established enough in my career to raise a child, but sometimes the best things are unexpected."

The truth of that statement curled around my heart.

"Everything, since you came into my life, has been the best kind of unexpected. I love you, Callie. I love our baby. I want to be part of this family." His hand rested on my stomach, the warmth seeping through my shirt into my skin.

A part of me was screaming yes, but the other part, the logical, reasonable part wondered if he'd walk away again. "Will you leave if things get tough or you get overwhelmed?"

I had to know his answer. Everything hinged on it—my present, our future.

His face pinched. "I won't. I won't let my past dictate my future anymore. I want to be with you. I want this baby. But I understand you need time. I hope you'll give me time to show you I've changed."

He'd gone to his hometown, spoken to the Reynolds, he'd said he wanted to see a therapist. He was doing what he needed to do to move on. He was showing me that our baby and I were a priority.

He moved his hand away, standing. His gaze uncertain, he took a few steps back. "Let me know if you need anything. If it's okay, I'd like to come to the doctor's appointments."

He turned and walked out.

My heart pounded in my head. What was I doing? Was I willing to let him walk out that door thinking that I hadn't already forgiven him? That the moment he told me his past, his reality, my heart broke for him? He bore the weight of that guilt his entire adult life. He thought he didn't deserve love, me, or our child.

Was there anything more heartbreaking than that?

I wanted to give him everything he'd never allowed himself. "Jonah, wait."

I stood and ran to the door, throwing it open. Tearing down the hallway, I came to an abrupt stop a few feet away from him.

His expression was subdued. He didn't expect me to forgive him.

"I forgive you."

He tilted his head to the side like he'd heard wrong. "You do?"

"Of course. I love you."

"Are you sure?"

I stepped closer, wrapping my arms around his neck. "That's what love is, taking you as you are, your past, your flaws, everything. I'm willing to help you work through it if you are."

He opened his mouth, but I placed a finger over his lips. "But if you ever act like you did the other night—walking away without telling me what's going on—I won't give you another chance."

"I get that."

He squeezed me tight, burying his head in my neck. "I didn't think I deserved you."

"You deserve everything."

He pulled back. "I love you so much."

"I love you."

Something seemed to snap inside him when I declared my love for the second time. He crushed his lips to mine. Relief coursed through me. He was here. I wouldn't have to do this on my own. We'd be a family.

EPILOGUE

JONAH

I couldn't believe she was here in my arms. I'd never take her for granted again. I'd prove to her every day that I loved her, I wanted to be here for her.

Callie worked hard to make sure Rebel Sports was running smoothly. She worked with Ava to fix the issues with the website, proving to Reid she was more than a capable manager. The fall sports season was in full swing, and Callie was already planning instructional clinics for the spring sports with former pro athletes. Ava helped her to build online buzz and generate interest to field more than enough athletes for the leagues. Callie was worried she wouldn't be able to keep up when she had the baby, but Reid hired more people to assist her.

She turned over, her belly seemingly growing bigger each day. I couldn't resist covering it with my hand. I tried to imagine what our baby would look like—would he have brown hair and tan skin like me or be blond and fair like Callie?

My heart tripped over itself at the idea of a little boy or girl with Callie's blonde hair and sweet smile. Either way, I imagined teaching them how to throw a football, carrying them on my shoulders, tickling them until they giggled. I was so lucky.

Callie's hand circled my wrist, a smile playing on her lips. "Will I always wake with your hand on my stomach?"

She was finally in my bed every night because she'd recently moved out of her apartment, splitting time with me between my condo in the city and my house on the river.

I smiled. "Just until he or she's born."

"Are you okay not knowing the sex until birth?"

"I'm happy with whatever you want." That was true, but there was one thing that was making me edgier each day.

"Everything?" She cocked a brow.

I took a deep breath. I was waiting for the right moment, but I'd told her I loved her spontaneously, maybe that was the best approach. "Not everything. I want to make you mine before the baby comes."

"I am yours."

We'd helped Frank move into his new place a few months ago. He was lucid and Callie was getting something from the car, so I took the opportunity to ask him for his blessing to marry her. He teared up when he admitted he'd been worried about leaving her alone. He'd clasped my shoulder tightly, then said having me in her life, knowing I would take care of her, eased his mind. Knowing I had his support was everything.

I leaned over, kissing her. "It might be old-fashioned, but I want you to be Mrs. Jonah Templeton before our baby's born."

I wanted Frank to attend the wedding too.

She opened her mouth as if to respond, her expression wary.

"I don't want to marry you because you're pregnant." I thought back to that moment when I told her I loved her for the first time in front of everyone—my family, a stadium full of people, and viewers at home. If she hadn't told me she was pregnant, I still would have wanted to be with her forever.

"I knew you were the one before we made this baby. I knew you were the one when I said I loved you." There was a flutter under my hand.

We both stilled.

"Was that a kick?" I looked at her in wonder.

She bit her lip. "Yeah, they're getting stronger."

At first, she said it felt like bubbles or popcorn popping. "He or she's so strong."

"Just like you."

"And you. Callie Goodwin, will you marry me. Will you be my family?"

Tears glistened in her eyes.

"Will you let me take care of you, our babies, and our family for the rest of my life?"

She nodded, tears streaming down her face. "I'm sorry. These hormones are the worst."

I kissed her cheeks, wiping away the tears. "I love you more than I ever thought possible. Yet, it feels like it could still get bigger, like it knows no bounds, it's limitless."

Our love was endless. Tingles erupted over my skin. This was happiness. This was acceptance. I loved her, our baby, and this life we were building together one step at a time.

She touched my cheek. "I feel the same way."

"What do you say, will you marry me, Calliope?" My throat felt tight.

"Yes. I'd love to."

I kissed her, rolling her to her back, reaching over her to pull open the nightstand drawer. I'd kept the ring close, waiting for this moment.

I shifted to my knees, opening the velvet box. I slid the ring on her finger. "There. Now it's official."

She held her hand up, admiring the way the light reflected

off the facets of the diamond. "It was official long before this ring or our baby."

"Yes. Now you're getting it." I laid down, pulling her back to her side. She couldn't rest on her back for long.

I rested my hand on her hip. "Thank you for falling for me."

"You made it so easy." Her smile was light and easy, her skin glowing from the pregnancy, the engagement, or both.

My throat tightened. "You helped me be the man I was supposed to be."

Her expression turned serious. "You did that on your own."

I'd never get enough of her support or her love. I leaned down, kissing her lips lightly. I'd never get enough of her touch, her support, her essence.

I never thought I deserved a future filled with hope and happiness. Callie showed me I deserved everything, and I'd spend the rest of my life proving it to her.

BONUS EPILOGUE

CALLIE

I held our baby in my arms while a photographer hovered at the edge of the room, documenting the bridal party getting ready. I never thought I'd be holding a baby in my wedding dress. Things had turned out differently and more amazing than I could have ever imagined. I'd been alone for so long, never expecting anything or anyone to be permanent. Now everything had changed. I had friends, Jonah, and a family.

"I love her name," Jonah's mom said, touching a blonde curl on Everly's head.

"She's our happily ever after." Everly's lips widened.

"She's smiling," Dylan said over my shoulder where she'd been fiddling with the train of my dress.

I could imagine what the photographer was seeing, a woman holding her four-month-old baby, her bridesmaids making last-minute touches to my veil and dress, my mother-in-law gazing at her first grandchild with love. I wanted time to stop, to relish in each touch, each sensation.

No one knew, but we got married at the courthouse a few days after he proposed. He wanted me to carry his name before Everly was born, but more than that, we wanted to be each other's as soon as possible.

Today was a bonus wedding with our friends and family. A
nursing aide brought Grandpa from his home. If he was able,
he'd walk me down the aisle.

I thought my life had ended when my parents died, that
there wasn't anything to live for. I had no idea that Jonah and
Everly were my future. The joy that spread through my limbs
made me feel light, almost effervescent, like I could do
anything. I was happy and content.

A soft knock sounded on the door.

Everly wrapped my finger tightly in hers. This girl had
wrapped around my heart long before she was born.

"Callie," Avery prompted.

I lifted my head. "Jonah wants to see you. He has a
present for you."

"Let him in."

"Are you sure? Most brides don't want to see their grooms
before the ceremony," Tasha said, moving toward the door.

So far, we hadn't done anything the traditional way. We'd
had one date then one summer until we promised each other
forever. We'd gotten pregnant, then eloped, and now we were
having an elaborate ceremony for them.

"I want to see him." Everly was still smiling. I wanted
Jonah to see her smiling for the first time.

The room slowly cleared out. I heard Tasha murmuring
something softly to Jonah before he entered the room, closing
the door softly behind her.

Jonah fell to his knees in front of us. "Is she smiling?"

The awe in his voice tugged at my heartstrings more
than the appearance of him in a tux and me in my wedding
dress.

"Isn't she beautiful?" My eyes filled with tears.

He glanced from Everly to me. "You're not supposed to
cry on your wedding day. You're supposed to be happy."

"All brides cry on their wedding day, and this is so much
more than a typical wedding. I have you, Everly, your family,

my grandfather. I have everything." The emotion overwhelmed me.

Jonah's large hand cradled Everly's tiny head.

My heart twinged at this strong man brought to his knees
by his little girl. "I can't imagine life before her."

"You'll never have to."

"It's us forever, and however many more beautiful babies
we create."

"Today's the ceremony, a renewing of our vows, our
promises to cherish each other forever. It doesn't change what
we've already built—a life, a family, love." Jonah cradled my
cheek with his free hand, linking the three of us together.

"I love what we've created. I love us." My eyes stung with
unshed tears.

"Me too." He swallowed hard, making me think he was
overcome with emotion too. "I brought your wedding
present."

"I don't need anything." Our wedding bands were nestled
together in a velvet box Reid was holding on to for the
ceremony.

Jonah sat back on his haunches, pulling a red velvet box
from his suit pocket. His expression was hesitant. "Frank gave
me your mother's jewelry. I had her engagement diamond
made into a necklace."

He pulled a chain out of the box, holding the diamond
setting in his hand for me to see. Tears leaked from my eyes.

"It's beautiful." Jonah moved to stand behind me, clasping
the necklace on my neck.

I touched the cool diamond to my chest. "Thank you,
Jonah. It's beautiful."

I had no idea he'd asked my grandfather for my mother's
jewelry or that he'd have it made into something new. "I love
that my mother is here on my wedding day."

"Your father is too. Believe that." His tone was confident.

Jonah carefully took Everly from my lap, cradling her in

his arm, tugging me to stand next to him. He wrapped an arm around me as we gazed at the most beautiful person in our lives. I felt my parents' presence more acutely than I had since they'd died. Instead of feeling sad that they'd missed this moment, I felt happy because they were here.

"Are you ready to get hitched? Again?" Jonah's face relaxed into an easygoing smile. All seriousness was gone.

"There's nothing I'd rather do today than make you mine again."

Jonah kissed me. Of all the moments, I knew I'd remember this one—the one we claimed for ourselves. The rest of the day would be for our family and friends.

I hope you loved Jonah and Callie's story!

Ava's story is next in *Waiting for You*. Ava Breslin never thought her childhood crush and best friend's older brother would return home after medical school. Suddenly he's everywhere—living in her bed and breakfast, working at a local hospital, and playing his electric cello for his patients. He's all grown up, and impossible to resist.

BOOKS BY LEA COLL

All I Want Series

Choose Me

Be with Me

Burn for Me

Trust in Me

Stay with Me

Take a Chance on Me

Annapolis Harbor Series

Hooked on You (previously titled Easy Moves)

Only with You

Lost without You

Perfect for You

Crazy for You

Falling for You

Waiting for You

Mountain Haven Series

Infamous Love

Adventurous Love

Impulsive Love

Quick Snap Novellas

Lucky Catch

Trick Play

Download two free novellas, *Swept Away* and *Worth the Risk*, when you sign up for her newsletter.

To learn more about her books, please visit her website.

Made in the USA
Middletown, DE
12 August 2022

71242148R00165